WHISLING ISLAND CHRISTMAS

A WHISLING ISLAND NOVEL

JULIA CLEMENS

PICKLED PLUM PUBLISHING

For Alissa - the woman who somehow juggles it all. May all of my characters be as strong and resilient as you are.

CHAPTER ONE

"YOU DIDN'T HAVE to wait here for me," Ellis said with a smirk that showed off his dimple and instantly rewarded Julia for waiting for her boyfriend.

It was the end of a long evening and Julia would have liked to have already been in bed in the deluxe tour bus Ellis had outfitted for her as soon as she'd told him she would join him on tour, but she wanted to see the star of the show and the man of her dreams before she headed off to lala land for the night.

"It's your last show before the break. I thought I'd surprise you," Julia said, setting her kindle on the coffee table. Moments before she'd been wrapped up in one of her favorite novels, *His to Save*, but despite that preoccupation, she was only too glad to turn her focus to her real-life romantic lead as he joined her on the couch.

His scent—a combination of his musky cologne and a bit of woodsiness from the stage, as well as a tiny bit of sweat—was comforting to Julia. It was what she'd come to know as Ellis' smell in the last month on tour.

"*Break.* Two weeks of no shows. Sounds absolutely blissful. Now, whatever will we do with ourselves?" Ellis murmured as he pulled Julia closer and nuzzled her neck with his day-old scruff.

Julia squealed, loving every minute of it.

"It really means the world to me that you're here. Not just here in my dressing room, but here on tour. I can't tell you . . . " Ellis' words trailed off and Julia kissed his cheek because she was pretty sure she did know how much it meant to him. He'd showed her just how much he delighted to have her along—not only had Ellis gotten Julia her very own tour bus so she would be as comfortable as possible on the road, but he'd outfitted it with Julia's favorite mattress and the exact brand of sheets she'd been using for the last ten years. He and Daniel had scoured Julia's home on Whisling so that she had the same glassware, type of dining chairs—even the same toilet paper that Julia used at home. Best of all, he'd sent the drivers from his personal bus, the people he trusted the most, to Julia's bus and hired new people for his own. All while planning for a worldwide tour. The man was a saint. And she knew he loved her deeply. She wasn't sure how she'd gotten so lucky.

Julia put her arms around Ellis' neck and his smirk turned into a predatory grin as he began to lower his mouth toward hers. Julia felt her own lips upturn in anticipation when a sharp and very unwelcome knock sounded at the door.

"Go away!" Ellis called out, his eyes never straying from Julia's.

Whoever it was took that as an invitation to enter, and the squeak of the dressing room door warned Julia and Ellis that they had undesired company.

Julia edged back to put a decent amount of distance between herself and her boyfriend. She knew it was kind of silly, especially when they weren't out in public, but she'd never been one for PDA and Ellis understood that. It also made him really hate interruptions like this one.

"Good show," said Oliver, Ellis' brother and one of his tour managers, as he closed the door behind him without the slightest trace of guilt.

"Ollie, did you miss what I said before you opened the door?" Ellis asked, his tone giving away his frustration.

"Didn't miss it. Just chose not to hear it," Ollie shrugged, pulling a seat from the vanity and sitting across from Ellis. He winked one of those cyan blue eyes that reminded her so much of Ellis' in Julia's direction and she couldn't help but smile. The guy had become the annoying little brother she'd never had. She already loved him, although judging from the look on Ellis' face at the moment, he was feeling no such brotherly love.

"I talked to security and they apologized for the incident tonight," Ollie began, running his fingers through his hair that was a few shades lighter than Ellis' brown. Julia had marveled at how similar the brothers' appearances were even as their personalities were worlds apart. Oliver was as organized as a church secretary whereas Ellis liked to go with the flow.

Julia wasn't surprised security had felt the need to apologize. It wasn't like them to allow such a slip. Typically they did an incredible job but tonight a woman carrying a "Marry me, Ellis Rider" sign had managed to slip past them and somehow gotten onto stage with Ellis before she'd been escorted away. She hadn't actually gotten close to him but it was still disconcerting for Julia to watch. The woman seemed a bit unhinged and even so, Julia had to admit she was actually a little jealous. If anyone was going to propose to Ellis it would be Julia.

"I guess the venue security had promised to watch the part of the stage where the woman was standing, but there had been some kind of miscommunication," Ollie explained as he leaned forward, his forearms resting on his knees.

Julia could understand that. Ellis had a fairly large security team but they couldn't cover an entire arena. They had to work with venue security at each concert. If one team had thought the other team was covering an area . . .

"But they promised it won't happen again. They won't just take the venue people at their word. Next time they'll check and double check everything."

Ellis nodded. He'd taken the whole thing in stride. While Julia had gasped and most of the audience had seemed shocked, Ellis had cracked a joke about being worth jail time and the arena had filled with laughter. The man had a gift. Julia was able to command a movie set but there was something special about standing on a stage, live, and having the audience of tens of thousands eating out of the palm of your hand. It took a special person. And Ellis was most definitely special.

"That's good to hear, but can you have Daniel look into it too?" Ellis asked, referring to his assistant. "This is something we should also check and double check on our side."

Ollie nodded as he made a note on his phone.

"And now for our next piece of business," Ollie said as he met Ellis' gaze.

"No," Ellis groaned as he rested his head back on the couch.

"She's our mother. You can only put her off for so long," Ollie said with a shrug.

"I'm not putting her off, per se, but does it have to be at Christmas?" Ellis asked.

Julia's eyes ping-ponged back and forth between the brothers, feeling that she'd missed part of the conversation.

"Does what have to be at Christmas?" she finally asked when the brothers continued to stare at each other in eloquent silence.

"Mom and Dad's first visit to Whisling," Ollie replied.

"Mom, Dad, Rusty, Krista, and Ollie's first visit to Whisling," Ellis corrected. "If I'm hosting all of them, you'd better be getting your behind to the island for the holidays as well." He gave his brother a sharp look.

Ollie frowned. "I'd kind of been hoping for a more tropical locale for my break."

Ellis shook his head. "Keep hoping, bro. Because this year you'll be spending each holly, jolly moment with your family."

Ollie groaned but Julia had witnessed enough interactions between the brothers to know that Ellis had won this round.

"Isn't this good news?" Julia asked. She'd been hoping to meet the Riders for a while now but things had always been so busy for all of them. A family trip bringing them all together sounded incredible.

Ellis frowned but then nodded. "It is. Or it would be if they were coming at any other time. I just had hoped for some down-time with you this Christmas, since things have been so hectic on the road. I love my family, but having them come will add crazy to what I had hoped to be our relaxing break."

"You mean Krista will add some crazy," Ollie muttered.

Ellis didn't deny it.

Julia cringed. She'd heard stories about Krista but had hoped they were exaggerated. That hope was fast dwindling.

"So what day should I tell the fam to book their tickets to Whisling?" Ollie asked, pulling out his phone.

Julia and Ellis had been planning on taking a flight early the next morning back to Seattle and then the ferry to Whisling. They'd be back in their own beds by the following night and would then enjoy a blissful fourteen nights at home. Even though tour had been so much better than Julia could have ever anticipated—seeing her boyfriend command that stage and sing in his deep, melodic tone each evening had been incredible—she still missed home. A lot. There was nowhere like Whisling Island.

"Fourth of never?" Ellis asked hopefully, his lips hitched in a half smile.

"Very mature of you, big bro," Ollie deadpanned. He waved the phone to show he was still waiting for a true answer.

"When will *you* be on Whisling?" Ellis asked, knowing he was needling his brother.

"I'm booking my ticket now. I'll be there in two days," Ollie said, his voice lacking any type of enthusiasm.

"Then they can join us in two days," Ellis said resolutely.

Ollie nodded as he began texting.

"It'll be delightful." Julia tried to sound as upbeat as she could, rubbing her hands up and down Ellis' arms.

"Delightful isn't a word I've ever heard used to describe time with Krista," Ollie replied as his fingers tapped away.

"Discouraging, disappointing, disturbing," Ellis offered as replacement words.

"Demanding, difficult, or dissatisfying," Ollie added.

The guys sounded like they were joking so Julia let it go, even if she did feel a little bad that they were ganging up on Krista. But she understood what it was like to need to voice frustrations about family. The words were typically more dramatic than the true feelings, but it was therapeutic to just say them and not worry about repercussions.

"Krista's wondering if you'll send down a private jet." Ollie looked up from his texting.

Private jet? Wow. Even Julia's family wasn't quite that demanding. But Julia was determined not to judge. It seemed like she might need to play the role of peacemaker, something Ellis had done for her on more than one occasion. She was ready to step up and return the favor.

"She knows I don't own one anymore, right?" Ellis asked, arching an eyebrow even though he didn't really look surprised.

He'd bought one years before when he'd been traveling

much more, but now that he'd settled on Whisling and wasn't globetrotting quite so much, he'd sold his plane. He still rented one for international legs of his tour but that was pretty much the only time he needed one.

Ollie texted and grunted when he read the response. "Krista says it isn't her fault you decided to give up certain luxuries. Are you really going to withhold the finest things in life from your own family?"

Julia bit her lip. Oh dear.

Ellis sighed, glancing at his own phone. "It really would be nice for Mom and Dad if they could travel privately," he muttered as if he were thinking aloud. "I'll make sure a plane is there on Wednesday. I'll send them the time when I have it."

Ollie nodded, fingers flying over his phone screen.

"But tell Krista that if she can't be ready at that time she can fly commercial. On her own dime," Ellis added.

Ollie grinned.

Julia had a feeling this was going to be one of her more interesting Christmases.

"OH MY GOODNESS, Aunt Julia. I'm so glad you picked up," Wendy exclaimed as Julia answered her phone the next morning. They were just about to board their flight from Atlanta to Seattle and Julia was just putting her phone on airplane mode when it started ringing.

Typically she wouldn't have answered a call at this point. She wasn't exactly an anxious flyer but she didn't love it, and she liked some down time before her flights took off. But when she saw the call was from her niece who lived on Whisling, all thoughts of relaxing flew out the window. Wendy was a text-only type of girl, so an actual call must mean something was up, and Julia had answered immediately.

"Is everything okay?" Julia asked, the speed of her question conveying her concern.

Wendy was the reason Julia had hesitated about going on tour. She missed her friends and neighbors on Whisling, but she knew they didn't need her. Her niece, on the other hand, might.

Julia had had an estranged relationship from much of her family for most of her life, so when Wendy had decided to move to Whisling to be near Julia, the last thing she wanted to do was desert her. But Wendy had assured Julia she would be fine, that she'd use this time apart to spread her wings, so Julia had felt free to leave. And she knew that between Wendy's boyfriend and new friends on the island, her niece had a strong support system. But now, hearing the urgency in Wendy's voice, Julia wondered if she'd been wrong to leave. Thankfully she was on her way home, even if just for two weeks.

"That depends on your definition of okay," Wendy responded.

Julia's heartbeat increased. That sounded ominous.

"Mom just called."

Julia swallowed. She was glad that Wendy's issues didn't appear to stem from Julia leaving her behind, but hearing that Lacey had just called? Julia had to admit a pit opened in her belly. Julia loved her sister, she really did. Julia loved her sister, her mother, her brother, her dad, her whole family. But to say their relationship was complicated was putting it mildly. As soon as she'd graduated from high school, Julia had left home to pursue her career in Hollywood, and her mom and sister had never forgiven her for leaving the life they saw as perfect and right for all of them. But now, decades later, Julia and her family had worked through things and were trying their best. Of course, things were still a little tense at times, even though their relationship was currently much, much better than it had ever been. And at this moment, Wendy's voice had Julia feeling more anxious than a flight could ever make her.

"They're coming to visit," Wendy said.

"They?" Julia asked immediately.

"Mom, Dad, the boys, and Grandma. Uncle Jack and his crew are staying behind with Grandpa because Grandma said she'd rather eat her left arm than have to spend the holidays with Grandpa."

That sounded . . . lovely.

Julia's breathing became rapid. Her mom and her sister were quite the combo but adding more to the mix? And Julia already knew they'd be staying with her because Wendy didn't have the space, not that Julia would have wanted anything else.

Julia rubbed her forehead, trying to take deep, even breaths.

"When?" Julia asked.

"Um," Wendy paused and Julia could tell she wasn't comfortable with what she was about to say.

"Spill it, Wendy," Julia said, knowing that her niece was holding back but she'd have to get off the phone soon. Better to get all of the bad news now.

"Mom said as soon as you buy their tickets? I'm so sorry, Aunt Julia. They shouldn't expect this of you . . . " Wendy's voice trailed off.

"No apology necessary, sweet girl. Not your fault. In fact it's probably my fault since I did tell them they could visit whenever they'd like."

"I promise I'll spend all of my time off at your house," Wendy pledged, and Julia wished she could hug her niece. How had such a selfless young woman come from Julia's sister?

That wasn't fair. Lacey could be kind when she wanted to be. Her kindness was just hardly ever directed toward Julia.

"It'll be fine. In fact, it'll be fun," Julia said, forcing a bit of cheer into her voice even if she had a hard time believing her own words. But then again, she really should be grateful. This time last year she couldn't have even hoped for her family to join her on Whisling for the holiday. Now they were coming of their own accord. Sure, Julia would have to pay for it, but it was progress. That was all she could ask for.

"Really?" Wendy's voice was dubious.

"Really," Julia replied. "But I'd better go because my flight is about to take off. Let your mom know I'll make reservations and send her the flight info when I can."

"You're the best, Aunt Julia."

Julia could hear the relief in Wendy's voice. Although her niece's relationship with Lacey was complicated as well, Julia knew Wendy was grateful to be able to spend the holiday with her family. As she should be. And if Julia could keep Wendy from ever experiencing the loneliness Julia had, it would be more than worth it.

"Oh, and my stupid brothers made sure to make me add that they'd love to fly first class too."

Julia chuckled. She didn't know why it was adorable that her nephews requested first class, yet when her sister asked for free flights it was frustrating. But that was life.

"Noted," Julia said as she hung up with her niece.

Ellis raised an eyebrow. "Looks like we'll both be hosting Christmas?"

Oh heavens. How had Julia forgotten? She'd been so wrapped up in Wendy's call that she hadn't even remembered the plans she already had for the holidays.

"I'm so sorry. I hope you don't mind," Julia blurted, feeling terrible that she'd forgotten Ellis' dilemma.

"Didn't sound like you had much of a choice. And even if you had, I'm glad they'll be there. Maybe your family will help mine to look a little less crazy and vice versa. By the end of the trip we might be thinking both of our families are normal."

Julia laughed. "Let's not go that far. But really? Are you okay with this?"

"It'll be fine. Fun even," Ellis echoed Julia's words, causing her to laugh again. He slid to the far edge of his seat and patted the spot next to him in invitation.

"As long as we don't lose our minds?" Julia asked as she squeezed into the seat with him.

"Oh, we'll lose 'em. Let's just hope they don't stray so far we never find 'em again."

Julia chuckled as she nuzzled into Ellis' side and began to research flights from Travers to Seattle. They were going to be insanely expensive this last minute but Julia knew that was the cost of family. Or at least her family.

"I've already got Daniel on it," Ellis said as he gently took Julia's phone from her hands and switched it to airplane mode. "You take those few minutes you need to relax before a flight."

Ellis kissed Julia's head and she turned to meet his lips. This man was too much.

"I'll pay you back as soon as we land," Julia said.

"You'll do no such thing," Ellis said, lifting his arm so Julia could scoot even closer.

"Yes, I will. My family, my bill," Julia said.

"Compared to the private plane I have to spring for, this is chump change," Ellis joked.

Julia could feel the rumble of his laughter through his body and loved every minute of it.

"So let me pay it."

"Consider it an early Christmas gift," Ellis replied with a grin.

Julia shook her head. It was too extravagant a gift.

"Then consider it repayment. Ticket sales went through the

roof when people saw you were on tour with me. You've made me some major money, girl. It's only right that I pay for this."

Julia rolled her eyes. Ellis' shows had been sold out long before Julia ever joined the tour but she knew arguing would be pointless. She'd just have to find a way to pay him back. She typically hated being in someone's debt but she found that with Ellis she didn't mind it—she actually relished it. She loved the idea that she'd get to do a kindness for him in return.

But Ellis was right. She should take some time to practice her breathing before they took off or she could find herself facing down a panic attack at ten thousand feet.

She stood and returned to her own seat as she slowly inhaled and exhaled, eyes closed. Ellis took her hand, rubbing gentle circles on the back as she continued to breathe. Julia felt her heart rate calming even with all that she'd have to face as soon as they got back to Whisling.

Because even if her family and his family drove them nuts, she was going home with the man she loved by her side. She really couldn't complain.

CHAPTER TWO

"ALEXIS!" Trish shouted as Alexis entered the dance studio at the gym. Due to her cooking schedule, Alexis didn't often teach classes in the morning anymore, but whenever she could find the time and the gym needed her she jumped at the chance.

She was grateful that this was one of those mornings.

"Trish!" Alexis shouted right back as she hugged the woman who had been handling her classes ever since Alexis had taken over for Lou at Bess's food truck. She smiled over Trish's shoulder as she saw several other women who'd been there through some of her very lowest times.

She passed out hugs like candy before setting down her water bottle and sweat towel. She wasn't in quite as good shape as she had been when she'd been teaching the class three times a week so the towel was a necessity. She sweated like crazy anytime she taught or even took a class these days.

"And how's the good doctor?" Trish asked with a knowing grin.

Alexis couldn't help her blush. She still pinched herself at the thought that she was dating Jared Tuttle, her high school crush. Even at thirty-eight, Alexis became a giddy fifteen-year-old on the inside when her thoughts turned toward him. Which was often.

"Amazing. How are Ray and the kids?" Alexis asked about Trish's family.

"Boring. Not exciting like your love life," Trish shot right back and Alexis laughed. She loved Trish's straight shooter attitude.

"Life has actually settled down quite a bit for us. And I'm not gonna lie, I would take boring over the kind of excitement we used to have any day," Alexis said honestly.

The ups and downs of her relationship with Jared had been worth it but she was glad those days were in the past. Or at least some of them were. She expected a bumpy road ahead—co-parenting with Jared's ex Marsha would never be a breeze—but she and Jared were on strong footing. She knew he wouldn't dump her if she made a mistake and he knew she wanted to be in it for the long haul, whatever the cost.

The clock ticked to nine and Alexis smiled at Trish before walking over to the stereo system and starting the music for the class.

"Today is going to be a bunch of oldies but goodies because we all know I haven't come to class in way too long," Alexis called out over the peppy notes that were filling the room.

Those attending the class smiled at her. Alexis saw mostly familiar faces but even the ones she didn't know didn't seem to mind that she was taking over for the day.

"Are we ready for this one?" Alexis yelled as the intro to her favorite warm-up song came on.

She received whistles and cheers in response as she began to take them through the dance steps.

It took a minute, but Alexis soon fell back into the familiar rhythm. Thankfully, teaching three times a week for over a year had ingrained the movements in her mind and she was moving into the next portion of the choreography when the studio door opened for the last person Alexis would have ever expected to walk into her class.

What was Marsha doing here?

It took everything in Alexis not to stumble at the sight of her boyfriend's ex. Once upon a time Marsha had hated Alexis—so much so that she'd sabotaged Alexis' relationship with Jared by lying to her own children. A near-death accident had caused Marsha to re-evaluate life and feel badly about what she'd done to her kids, Brittany and Peter, but she'd told Alexis that even so, she would never like her. And Alexis was fine with that. She wouldn't ever like Marsha either. They maintained a cool cordiality for the sake of those they loved, but coming to Alexis' class?

Alexis did the same choreo for one count too long but luckily Trish noticed and seamlessly led the class even from her spot in line. Alexis needed to concentrate. She'd find out why Marsha was there sooner or later.

Class typically flew by for Alexis—she loved dancing more than any other form of exercise—but today her thoughts were distracted, swirling as she wondered what Marsha could possibly want from her. Her worry kept her from enjoying the dance moves as much as she normally would have.

Finally, the playlist came to an end and Alexis cheered with the rest of the class at the conclusion of their workout.

She smiled and said goodbye at the right times but if you asked her who she'd spoken to, poor Alexis couldn't have told you. Even as she talked to her departing class attendees one eye was fixed on Marsha, who'd found a spot at the back of the class.

Alexis wasn't surprised that Marsha had kept up with the choreography. She'd been a cheerleader back in the day and had kept herself in shape throughout the years. Where Marsha was all long limbs and grace, Alexis was curvy and cutesy.

"Need me to hang around?" Trish whispered when the only ones left with her and Alexis were Marsha and some woman Alexis didn't recognize, who was talking to Marsha.

"Thanks for the offer. But I think I'll be fine?" Alexis whispered back, hoping it sounded like she was joking. She may have been scared of Marsha in the past but she now knew how to stand up for herself. Whatever Marsha was about to sling, Alexis could take it.

"I'll text Dr. Tuttle, just in case," Trish said loyally.

Alexis grinned at her friend. "Thanks, but I really think I'm good. See you at the food truck?" she asked.

She knew it was ironic that she taught exercise classes and then cooked on one of the most decadent food trucks on the island, but hey, balance in all things, right?

"You know it. The pork special is on for this Friday, isn't it?" Trish asked.

Alexis straightened her shoulders proudly. Most of the truck's recipes were creations of her friend and boss, Bess, but the Kalua pig special was Alexis's baby. She was part Hawaiian and loved to show that off in her cooking.

"It is," she confirmed.

"Then I'll be there. Ray and I haven't missed a pork special in months, and we won't start now," Trish said with a grin. Waving, she backed out of the studio, showing that she had Alexis' back as she kept an eye on Marsha.

Marsha's friend followed Trish out the door so now there were two.

Alexis was glad for it. At that point she really did just want to know why Marsha was there.

"I'm surprised to see you here," Alexis said as she met Marsha in the middle of the studio.

"At my dad's gym?" Marsha responded, raising an eyebrow

as if needing to establish that she had more of a right to be here than Alexis did.

And maybe she did. Although Marsha's dad was now married to Alexis' mom. Yeah, their lives were twisted together way more than either of them would have liked. But Marsha didn't frequent the gym, opting to workout at the country club even though her dad would have loved her to support his business.

"I meant in a class I was teaching," Alexis opted to say instead of taking the bait, keeping her voice even. If she'd voiced her brain's automatic reply of, *But you never come to the gym your father owns because you'd rather show your face at the country club*, implying that Marsha typically chose her image over her family, that would not have gone over well. No matter how true it might be.

"I saw the switch in the schedule when I came to talk to Dad about something last night and . . . well, I hoped to have a minute alone with you and saw this as my chance," Marsha said, sounding much more meek than she had even a few moments before.

"Okay," Alexis said. Maybe not the most welcoming response, but she didn't want to outright lie and say that it was good to see Marsha.

They both knew if they could avoid the other forever they would. But they couldn't. Because for better or worse they were stepsisters and Alexis was dating Marsha's ex and would hopefully one day be stepmom to Marsha's kids. Alexis also happened to be best friends with Marsha's sister Lou. See, complicated.

Marsha twisted the straps of her gym bag before pushing a swath of blonde hair behind her ear and meeting Alexis' eyes.

"Because you aren't chomping at the bit for more info, I take it you didn't hear the news?" Marsha asked.

Chomping at the bit? What news? Alexis had been about to take offense at Marsha's assumption that she would push for information on something that wasn't her business but decided to let it go. She and Marsha were kind of getting along. Might as well make it last as long as possible.

"I didn't," Alexis acknowledged before taking a giant swig of her water. She had to admit her throat was getting dry from having all of Marsha's attention.

"I'm dating Chad," Marsha said cautiously, and Alexis felt her eyes widen. With a huge exertion of willpower she kept her mouth from dangling open.

Chad? *Her Chad?* Well, he wasn't exactly Alexis' Chad anymore. They hadn't been especially close in the last ten years since he'd married a controlling woman who objected to his friendship with Alexis and moved to Seattle, but they'd been good friends before that. Alexis had heard Chad had moved back to the island after his divorce and she'd actually tried to reach out a few months back but when he hadn't responded to her texts she figured he needed more time to lick his wounds. She understood that after a particularly tough breakup sometimes you needed time before facing the world.

But now Chad was dating? And dating Marsha, of all people?

Alexis wasn't sure why that stung. She figured he would have reached out to his friends before he started dating again, but then again he had been distant for all of his marriage. Maybe he was ashamed that he'd chosen his wife over his friends? Maybe he felt badly that he hadn't texted Alexis back?

Or maybe he had a new number? Alexis hadn't even considered that until now. Maybe Chad didn't even know that Alexis had reached out.

But that wasn't important right now. What was important was that Marsha was dating Chad.

And Alexis had no idea how to feel about it. Marsha of yore had been horrific, even worse than Chad's ex, and part of Alexis wanted to protect Chad from that. But were they even friends anymore? She doubted Chad would appreciate her butting in after all these years. But why, out of all the single men on Whisling, did Marsha have to choose Chad? The island was small, but not that small.

Granted, for Brittany and Peter's sakes Alexis was thrilled. There would be no better man for Marsha to choose than Chad —at least the Chad she'd known. But she couldn't help feeling that he deserved better than Marsha. Then again, who was Alexis to decide that for Chad? He'd known Marsha as long as she had. Maybe he hadn't seen her cruel side as often as Alexis, but he knew enough to choose better, if he wanted to.

And Marsha had changed a lot.

Alexis realized she'd been quiet for a long time.

"Are you wondering why we have to keep doing this? I almost didn't go on that first date with him because I knew you guys used to be close. But I decided to give him a chance and most of me is glad that I did. I just hate that this makes our paths intertwine once more," Marsha said with a frown.

Alexis was right there with her.

"Don't get me wrong. I'm not here to ask for your permission. I'm going to date Chad and he wants to date me. You don't matter that much to him."

Thank goodness Marsha had made that clear. Heaven forbid Alexis think that Chad, a friend she'd had for decades, cared about her. Alexis fought the urge to roll her eyes.

"But it will just be easier with the kids and Jared . . . I know you can vouch for Chad to Jared. That way maybe he won't give him such a hard time like he has to guys I've dated in the past."

Alexis refrained from voicing her first thought: Jared hadn't wanted his kids to hang out with Marsha's last boyfriend because he'd been married to someone else while dating Marsha. Jared was simply being a good dad protecting his children from that mess.

She also didn't say her second thought: was this the same woman who'd made life hell for Alexis when she'd tried to build a relationship with Marsha's kids . . . and now this woman was asking her help to pave an easier path for Chad?

Alexis could feel a frown take over her face. She thought about hiding it but decided against it. She'd already bitten back her two first thoughts. Marsha would have to live with a frown.

"So you want me to tell Jared that Chad's a good guy?" Alexis asked, propping a hand on her hip as she considered what Marsha was asking of her. Typically she wouldn't hesitate to vouch for Chad—she'd always liked him. But this was a little different than a job interview or even a friendship. If Alexis told Jared that Chad was a good guy, Jared wouldn't hesitate to let this man into the lives of his children, the people who meant the most to him in the whole world. And she hadn't actually interacted with Chad in the last ten years other than one ignored text.

Marsha nodded.

"I would love to," Alexis began as she crossed her arms over her chest. She'd sweated during class but now that she hadn't been moving for a few minutes the air conditioning blasting through the studio was making her a bit chilly.

Marsha grinned and took a step backwards before Alexis finished.

"But I'd need to hang out with him a few times first. I haven't actually spent time with the guy in years. Of course I hope that he's still the same guy, but . . . "

Marsha's grin fell away as she gritted her teeth. "I should have known you would make this difficult."

"I'm not trying to make this difficult, Marsha. But this is

about Jared and your kids," Alexis said. She hoped the message got through to Marsha but even if it didn't, she was going to stick to her guns.

Marsha closed her eyes and shook her head.

"Can't you just trust me on this?" she asked as she opened her eyes and tilted her head.

Alexis barked out a laugh. "Oh wait," she said when she saw Marsha didn't even crack a smile. "You were serious?" Alexis had been sure it was a joke. Maybe not a ha ha funny joke but a . . . well, Alexis didn't know, but she and Marsha weren't the kind of acquaintances that trusted one another. They were barely the kind that tolerated each other.

"Marsha," Alexis began calmly when she saw that Marsha was well on her way to fuming. "Jared is a lot more likely to trust you than I am. Why don't you just tell Jared that Chad is a good guy? Why use me as a middleman?"

"Because Jared doesn't trust my judgment in men at the moment and I thought . . . never mind. It was stupid for me to come to you," Marsha spat out the last word and Alexis worried they'd lost about ten steps of their progress.

"I shouldn't have laughed. I'm sorry," Alexis apologized. "And I do think Chad is a good guy. I just . . . maybe we could all hang out? Bill, Mom, Jared, Lou, the kids, you, Chad, me," Alexis offered before she could think it through.

"The whole family?" Marsha sounded as skeptical as Alexis felt.

"I wouldn't need to spend hours alone with the guy. I think I'd have a pretty good idea if he was the same after an evening. I get to spend time with my friend again and then I'll vouch for Chad to Jared," Alexis said.

Even as she spoke the words, she knew this was a terrible idea. So bad Alexis realized she was trembling, and not from the cold. She was fully aware that their whole family avoided get-togethers like the one she'd proposed because they knew it was a bad idea to have Alexis and Marsha in the same room for an extended amount of time, but it was too late to back out now. Hopefully Marsha would be smart enough to . . .

"Let's do it," Marsha said with an eyebrow lifted in challenge. She'd probably felt Alexis' hesitation after the fact and was now daring Alexis to back out.

But that wasn't going to happen. Suddenly the idea didn't seem so bad. If Marsha could deal with it, so could she.

"Next weekend?" Alexis asked, doubling down.

"Friday?" Marsha returned without batting an eye.

"Sounds like a plan," Alexis replied with a wide grin they both knew was fake. But it matched Marsha's so it was fine.

Marsha lifted a shoulder and then turned on her heel, leaving a baffled Alexis.

What in heaven's name had she done? She really did like Chad but no one was worth an entire evening with Marsha. Then again, she reminded herself, she wasn't doing this for Marsha. This was just for Brittany and Peter. If Chad was the person Alexis remembered, he really would be a great role model for them. So that was why she was doing this, planning a big family get-together with her arch-nemesis and her boyfriend who was said nemesis's ex-husband.

Good. Great.

But now onto the biggest issue—how in the heck was she going to tell Jared about their plans for this weekend?

CHAPTER THREE

NORA WATCHED as Amber sat quietly against the wall, away from the action. Elise stood in the center of the room, directing the conversation like she was the conductor as the others in the meeting clamored for their voices to be heard.

But not Amber.

Nora's heart ached once more. Had it ever stopped aching since they all learned the truth about Amber's ex-fiancé Raul?

"What do you think, Amber?" Elise looked in their direction, her eyes full of hope.

Nora understood that hope. It was the same she awoke with each morning. Maybe today would be the day Amber would feel some of the heaviness subside?

"About what? I'm sorry, I must have been wool gathering over here," Amber said with a smile that didn't reach her eyes. It barely curved her lips.

"We were discussing the song selection for the reception." Elise pointed to the screen where Ariana, the DJ Genevieve had hired for her wedding and reception, was meeting with them over video call.

"Won't Genevieve pick those songs?" Amber asked, cocking

her head in confusion.

Typically the Hollywood diva who had chosen Amber and Elise's new inn for her wedding had her hand in every part of the wedding planning. Nora could see why Amber would be confused.

Except that everyone at the meeting had just been discussing that since it was coming down to crunch time Genevieve was feeling overwhelmed and had asked vendors to make decisions on the things she didn't care about as much. Like the playlist for the reception.

"She asked us to come up with a preliminary list," Elise said slowly, probably hoping her words would jog Amber's memory from mere moments before. Even Nora had been listening to the conversation and she was just the artist, nowhere near as involved as Amber should be.

"Genevieve did?" Amber scrunched her forehead as if she were trying to scan through her memory bank.

"Yeah. She figures we know her taste well enough by now. We're supposed to . . . " Elise let her words trail off when she noticed Celine, the wedding planner Genevieve had hired for the big day, watching them intently.

The girls had an interesting relationship with Celine. Well, not that interesting. Celine didn't approve of how much Genevieve trusted the girls but the girls didn't care because the only thing that mattered to them was keeping their bride happy. Celine felt she was the only one Genevieve should speak to about wedding plans and she especially hated that Elise and Amber had held the wedding shower on Whisling instead of back in LA. Celine was an LA girl through and through and couldn't understand Genevieve's "obsession," as she called it, with Whisling. In Celine's perfect world the wedding would be in one of the many glamorous venues LA offered. Since Genevieve didn't want that, the next best thing was for Amber and Elise, the insignificant inn owners, to be seen and not heard. But Genevieve wanted nothing more than the girls' opinion . . . on everything.

Because that made Celine feel insecure during every trip she begrudgingly made to the island for wedding plans, she tried to establish her dominance, showing and sometimes outright telling the girls that her position was more important than theirs, making those few days she was there kind of a living hell.

And for this trip she was staying at the inn for four days, double her usual tenure. Elise had confided to Nora that she worried Celine was sticking around for so long because she'd noticed how out of it Amber had been. Celine would love an opportunity to point out Amber's inadequacies to Genevieve. So now Elise was working hard to protect Amber even if Amber was too preoccupied with her personal life to care.

"We'll get back to you on the playlist by tomorrow." Elise turned her attention away from Amber and back to Ariana. "I've got a ton of ideas and I'm sure Amber is full of them as well."

Ariana's eyes went expectantly to Amber.

Amber gave a single nod and with a strong tap Elise ended the video call.

Elise opened her mouth to speak once more but was cut off by Celine.

"So what are some of those song suggestions, Amber?" Celine pounced.

All eyes in the room turned to Amber at Celine's question.

And Nora officially put Celine on her IKOAPOP list. Nora had created the not-so-mature *is kind of a piece of poo* list back in college and hadn't had occasion to add anyone to it in at least twenty years. But Celine was proving to be special, in the worst kind of way.

Nora knew Celine had seen the way Amber had shied away from the limelight. She might not know why, but she'd clearly observed that Amber was hurting and wanted to exploit that weakness.

After only a split second most turned away from Amber. It was almost as if the room had collectively forgotten what was going on with her until they took one look at her, but after that, most had the decency to ignore Celine.

Thank goodness.

But Nora wasn't about to let her off so easily. Celine was messing with Nora's baby girl, kicking her when she was down.

Nora sat up and smiled at Celine, her smile as fake as Amber's had been. "I think the real question is, will you be helping with this list?" Nora asked as she met Celine's eyes.

Celine blinked once as if she hadn't even realized Nora was there before narrowing her dark blue eyes. "Of course I'll be helping. My hand is in every part of this wedding," Celine said as she squared her tiny shoulders. Nora marveled that Celine's blonde hair didn't budge in the slightest with the movement.

"Except for the wedding shower," Nora murmured, as if talking to herself.

Elise bit down on her lip and even Amber seemed to be fighting a smile. Good. The girls had dealt with enough abuse from this woman who thought she owned the world, or at least Genevieve's wedding.

"Excuse me?" Celine asked, those blue eyes going wide.

"So what would be your top pick?" Nora asked sweetly, moving right along in topics.

"Top pick?" Celine was struggling to keep up.

"For a wedding song. That's part of the list. Genevieve has asked the girls and Ariana to pick a song that perfectly describes the love that she has with Dan. As someone who has a hand in every part of this wedding, you must have something in mind?" Nora challenged with a raised eyebrow. She stopped short of baring her teeth.

"Of course I do. But why would I share that now? Then no one else would take the time to think of their own options." Celine shrugged one shoulder and turned as if she were cutting off the conversation with Nora.

Oh no, she wasn't getting away that easily.

"That would be a waste of time though. If you already have a perfect song? Why even have others come up with options?" Nora said, her voice practically dripping sticky-sweet syrup.

Celine's back was now to Nora and she saw the way Celine's shoulders tightened. She was unhappy.

That was fine by Nora. You couldn't go around pushing the buttons of someone who was already hurting and not expect any type of repercussions.

"Because it isn't my job," Celine snapped.

"But I thought you had a hand in every part of the wedding? Doesn't that make everything your job?" Elise asked, her voice going high as if she was asking a question she really couldn't understand.

Celine spun on her heel to face Elise, Amber, and Nora once more. Nora noticed that they were gathering more attention from the vendors. They were tuning into the verbal exchange like it was a boxing match, their smiles growing as each jab was delivered to Celine. Nora would bet all of the money Genevieve was paying her to paint the wedding centerpieces that Celine had bullied most, if not every single person, in that room.

"Fine," Celine spat and then she named the song that must have been the first dance at every one of her weddings, it was so incredibly cliché.

Nikki, the florist and the vendor who had probably received the most of Celine's bullying because she owned a small island establishment, snorted.

Celine spun to glare at Nikki.

"Genevieve doesn't want anything written in the last fifty years to be played at her wedding," Elise said as she crossed her arms over her chest.

"That was just off the top of my head. Surely you can't do better," Celine challenged as she crossed her own arms.

Amber immediately rattled off ten love songs that had been popular when Nora was a young child, perfect options for Genevieve's first dance. "But that's just off the top of my head," she said with a genuine smile.

Hallelujah, Nora's daughter was back.

Her eyes stung with unshed tears. Celine might have been a bully in four-inch heels but she'd also made Nora's little girl smile—however unintentionally—so she was officially off of the IKOAPOP list.

Celine stomped out of the room, but she was so tiny her progress hardly made a sound on the plush carpet of the inn's meeting room. She then tried to slam the door behind her but the girls had installed soft-close doors throughout the inn during the remodel process, so her exit must have been incredibly unsatisfying.

As soon as the door shut behind Celine, the room burst into laughter, and Nora swore she heard someone humming about the witch being dead. Celine really had been a burr under all of their saddles and hopefully she would think before she was unkind again.

"And I think that's it for today," Elise said as she gathered her papers, tapping them against the table to adjust them into a neat stack.

"I typically don't relish seeing anyone embarrassed but I almost lost this job because of her," Nikki said as she stood to leave.

"Me too," came echoes from around the room.

"She lied about me to Genevieve, telling her I'd pressed

forward with flower designs even though it had been Celine who signed off on it. She then said that my arrangements would of course be terrible because I'm from some backwoods island. Doesn't she realize that doesn't even make sense? Thankfully Genevieve gave me a second chance, speaking directly to me about what she wanted," Nikki said with a frustrated shake of her head.

"She told Genevieve that I refused to look at the menu she sent me when it was really Celine who had forgotten to send it and then blamed it on me," added Grace, the chef who would be heading up all of the catering.

Others told their stories and the eggshells that had filled the room seemed to dissipate. Nora had wondered at the earlier tension she had felt earlier but now she understood. They all felt they were one mistake—or what Celine said was a mistake— away from losing the biggest event of all of their careers.

"Well," Elise spoke up. "If it ever happens again, come to us. I know Celine is the wedding planner but Genevieve will listen to us if we fight for you. And we will. Each of you has been a pleasure to work with."

Smiles spread across the room as each person got up to leave.

"I'd say that was incredibly productive," Nora commented after thanking the final exiting vendor, and the door having swung shut.

"Right? I had no idea everyone was having such a hard time with Celine. I thought she was only awful to us because she was jealous that Gen likes us more than her," Elise said with a grin, her blonde hair bouncing on her shoulders as hair should. Nora still wasn't quite sure how Celine's hair didn't move at all.

"I kind of feel sorry for her," Amber said quietly as she pulled her knees up to her chest, her arms wrapped around her legs. "She seems lonely to me."

Of course Amber would see that. Nora had a lot to learn from her sweet girl.

"She does. But you have to wonder chicken or the egg, you know? Is she so unkind because she's lonely or is she so lonely because she's unkind, pushing away everyone who's tried to love her?" Elise asked.

Valid question.

"True. But I don't know what kind of person I'd be without you guys. Especially when you save me like Mama Nora did today. Thank you." Amber turned her gaze to Nora, her eyes glistening.

"It was nothing. Just my mama bear unleashing itself," Nora joked.

The girls laughed and Nora felt a sense of peace she'd been missing for too long. She hated the hurtful experience Amber was going through but she also saw that in its own way it was helping Amber. She'd one day come out of this stronger.

The door to the meeting room was flung open and Jenny, one of their front desk managers, lurched to a stop where tile met carpet at the doorway edge.

Entering, she threw the door shut behind her and the only thing stopping it from slamming was the soft-close mechanism. Nora was pretty sure that investment had already paid for itself.

"Guess—" Jenny leaned over as she panted and then put up a finger.

Elise handed her an unopened water bottle, left from the meeting, and Jenny took it, gulping a swig before locking eyes on Elise.

"Guess who just reserved the penthouse suite for ten days at the end of this month?" Jenny asked, her eyes bright with excitement. Her hands bunched in her skirt by her thighs as if that was the only thing keeping her from jumping up and down.

Elise shrugged her shoulders, but judging by Jenny's excitement and the fact that she wasn't taking her eyes off of Elise, Nora had a guess.

And she was nearly as thrilled as Jenny was. Nora moved to the edge of her seat in anticipation. Even Amber let go of her legs and seemed to sit a little taller.

"The penthouse wasn't already reserved for that week?" Elise asked, her lips turned down in dissatisfaction.

"That's beside the point but yes, it was. But it was cancelled last week, last minute, and I didn't say anything yet because I didn't want to freak you out. But now I have to say that it was serendipitous." Jenny squealed the last word and allowed herself a single giddy jump.

Nora didn't blame her. She bit her lip in anticipation of Jenny's announcement.

"So are you going to guess?" Jenny demanded in a way that was very unlike her usual sweet demeanor. Apparently even calm Jenny had her breaking point.

"I have no idea. I'm guessing someone deep in the pockets, judging by your reaction," Elise said with a tilt of her head.

"Ye-e-es..." Jenny waved an impatient hand for Elise to continue with her line of reasoning.

"That wasn't the beginning of a guess. It was the end of what I could figure out," Elise replied. "And why am I the only one guessing?" Elise turned to Nora and Amber.

"Because we've already figured it out," Amber said with a wink.

Oh, she was coming alive once more. Nora could see Amber trying hard to break from the shell she'd been living in for weeks —her beautiful daughter had been trapped in this misery for over a month now.

"You have too?" Elise turned to Nora.

She nodded.

Elise moved her attention back to Jenny.

"Dan and Gen?" Elise asked about the couple who would soon be getting married at the inn. But they weren't expected until the third week of January.

Jenny shook her head and then blew out an exasperated sigh. "Do you really not know? Has he not texted you that he's coming?"

Elise went stark still as the others watched realization crash over her. There was only one man who was deep in the pockets, who would have Jenny this excited, and would also be possibly texting Elise.

Her face went pale as she bit her lip before admitting, "He texted me a couple weeks ago but I didn't respond." She blinked a few times before coughing. Amber handed her a water bottle.

"You haven't texted him back?" Jenny squeaked, her eyes going wide.

Amber glanced from pale Elise to stupefied Jenny before declaring, "This conversation doesn't leave this room." Even while she was still not quite herself, she had her sister's back.

"Of course," Jenny said. She took a careful step back as if she was hoping to now go unnoticed and wouldn't be directed to leave before she got the full story.

And since Amber turned her focus back to Elise without another word to Jenny, her plan seemed to be working. "Why haven't you texted him back?" she accused, fixing Elise with a stern look.

Elise bit the inside of her cheek and shifted her gaze to the window, clearly thinking over her next words.

"It just didn't seem worth it. It's not like anything can happen," Elise finally said as she pointed out the window to the view of the Pacific Ocean just beyond their inn. "He's out there. I'm right here."

"Except he'll be right here in just about two weeks." Nora stated the obvious. But it seemed like it needed to be said.

Elise closed her eyes.

"He was supposed to get it. That we couldn't work. That I wouldn't make the effort for long distance," Elise spoke quietly.

The room went still, giving Amber a chance to look around and notice Jenny once more. "I'm guessing you need to get back to the front desk?" Amber said.

Jenny frowned but nodded. "I was asked to convey one last message."

"Message?" Elise cocked her head. Most reservations were made on their website.

"He called in his reservation. He wanted to make sure to speak to one of us," Jenny said.

Nora smiled. The guy was good. The fact that a Hollywood star the size of Aiden Christensen was personally making his own reservation instead of having an assistant do it for him was impressive. And then to call instead of using the online reservation system? Just another step to prove he'd make time for things and people who were important to him. And obviously Elise was important to him.

"He called?" Amber asked, trying to suppress a grin as Elise's eyes turned to her.

"He said he doesn't expect anything, but he would really appreciate if one of our owners would be willing to carve out some time for him while he's here," Jenny said, beaming. At least until she saw Elise's expression.

"What?" Elise jumped to her feet and began pacing, looking anything but delighted.

"Thank you, Jenny," Amber said quickly before joining Elise in her pacing.

Jenny understood that it really was now time for her to leave and shuffled out of the room as slowly as she dared, casting one more backward glance before letting the door fall shut.

"We might be going home for the holiday, right?" Elise asked Amber hopefully. "Mom and Dad miss us so much."

"Less than a month before Genevieve's wedding and when the inn is at capacity? Unlikely," Amber said briskly, sounding so much like her old self now that Nora had yet another reason to love Aiden Christensen.

Elise stopped her pacing suddenly and leaned her back against the windows that overlooked the ocean.

"But we could be?" Elise asked. Her hope was diminishing but she clung to it.

"Why would you want to go home? When this guy is showing up for you—he's showing he really cares, Elise. This is huge. Do you not like him?" Amber asked. She was pressing more than Nora had expected, but she should have known Amber would forget all about herself when a problem arose for Elise. That's the way these sisters were. They almost always put the other first.

"Maybe?" Elise said with a shrug before starting her pacing again.

Amber fell into a seat on the opposite side of the room, her eyes trained on Elise. "I think it's more than maybe if you're this freaked out," she said knowingly.

Nora crossed one leg over the other as she waited for Elise to speak.

"He's supposed to be filming a movie in Vancouver," Elise said, throwing her hands up in frustration. Or could it be excitement?

"Maybe filming wrapped up early?" Amber suggested.

Elise kept pacing.

"You would know if you'd texted him back," Amber pointed out.

"And just blithely text some guy I maybe kind of like while my sister's heart was shattered? Um, no way," Elise said, her eyes on the window ahead of her.

"You didn't text him back because of me?" Amber stood and joined Elise once more.

"Not just because of you." Elise slowed her steps, to Nora's relief. She was actually getting dizzy trying to keep up with the girls' pacing.

"Because of me and because you're scared?" Amber asked bluntly.

The quick drop of Elise's eyes told the others that Amber had been spot on.

Amber took Elise's hands and sank into the nearest seat, pulling Elise down beside her.

"You do know that nothing could keep me from being happy for you. Especially some idiot man that made me fall in love with him and then ran off with my heart," Amber said, her voice cracking over the last part of her sentence.

"Oh Amber," Elise said, squeezing her sister's hands.

"Nope. It's not about feeling sorry for me. This is about you now, Lissy." Amber used her childhood nickname for Elise that Nora rarely heard.

"But he lives so far away," Elise pointed out, her voice small and wistful.

"Fair. But he's coming to visit you."

"Until he leaves again."

"Isn't the time together worth it? Don't you at least want to try, to see if it's worth finding a way to make it work?" Amber pressed, leaning forward.

"He's a freaking movie star, Amber. He literally has women who would do anything for his attention. I just can't . . . "

Amber didn't say anything; she just held her sister's hands a little tighter.

"What if I fall for him?" Elise shared her fear uncertainly

and then her voice dropped even more as she whispered, "What if I already have?"

That's what this was about. Elise wasn't trying to keep from feeling for Aiden, she was trying to deny what she already felt. No wonder she was driving herself insane.

Elise closed her eyes and then opened them as she spoke once more, "He'll come here for this trip and it will be magical. I already know it. And then he'll promise to be back for the wedding in just three short weeks and then . . . he'll have no reason to come back, ever. And I become that woman he traveled to an island to visit, a great story to tell his friends. While he becomes that idiot man that makes me fall in love with him and then runs off with my heart."

Elise swiped under her eyes angrily, as if she couldn't believe her body had betrayed her by crying.

"Don't you dare compare Aiden to Raul," Amber said, her emotion matching Elise's. "They are nothing alike."

Nora had to agree with that one. Aiden had nothing to gain from pursuing Elise so hard other than Elise's heart. And although it was the greatest prize, worth far more than anything Raul had hoped to gain from Amber, it was the prize that love deserved to win. With Raul it had been about money, a green card, and maybe Amber's heart or just his own selfish enjoyment of her beauty somewhere in the mix of his other wants.

"And you're wrong. He'll have the greatest reason to come back. The only reason he's coming for Christmas," Amber said.

Elise began shaking her head.

"You can't deny it," Amber prodded.

"It's a game," Elise said.

"What makes you think that?"

"Because what else could it be? What could I possibly have to offer a man like Aiden Christensen?" Elise asked with such sincerity that Amber's mouth fell open.

Nora couldn't believe it either. Could Elise not see the woman that Nora and Amber plainly did?

When Amber seemed too stunned to speak, Nora knew it was her turn to step in.

"You are the most loyal person I've ever met, Elise. You stood by Amber's side as she met me, a woman who could have changed everything for you both, but instead of fearing what may come you encouraged your sister because you love her. You called me Mama Nora before anyone else in your family was quite ready to embrace me. You made me feel accepted and loved when I was scared and alone. You do the same for your mom, dad, other siblings, and even for Mack. Once you love, Elise, that person is locked in your embrace of loyalty forever. For that alone Aiden would be so lucky to get to date a woman like you."

Amber nodded vehemently. "You always tell the truth. Even when I hate to hear it," she chimed in as Nora sat back in her seat, happy to let Elise's sister take over. Elise couldn't help cracking a smile at that. "Your work ethic is beyond compare. I may have the brains," Amber said as she pretended to fluff her hair, "but you've got the brawn and the willpower."

"She has the brains too," Nora interjected even though she knew Amber was joking about that.

"Shh. Aiden won't want her if her head is too big to look pretty on her cute little frame," Amber joked once more.

Elise laughed but then went still. "This isn't a joke."

"When you say stupid things like what do you have to offer this guy? Yes, it is. He should be wondering if he's good enough for you, not the other way around. And only because he seems to recognize that do I think he's anywhere near the right man for you," Amber said sternly.

Elise sighed.

Amber waited.

"This guy may be a star, but he's human. And Elise, he is coming here after you ghosted him. If that doesn't show courage and a little bit of stupidity in just the right way, I don't know what does," Nora said as the sisters stared at one another.

"She's right," Amber confirmed as she maintained eye contact with Elise.

"I'm just . . ." Elise sighed and glanced down, conceding the staring contest.

"Scared," she continued softly to the ground. "I know you both are hoping for the best but I have to expect the worst. I can't . . . I'm not strong enough to handle it when he walks away."

"*If*, Elise. And it's a big if. When it's worth it, you have to take the risk for the chance for something incredible," Amber advised sagely.

Nora would tuck those words away to use later. She had a feeling Amber would need them directed back to her someday when she was ready to move on.

Elise paused at Amber's words but then shook her head once more, unconvinced even if she wanted to be. It was evident to Nora that she liked the guy almost too much.

But as Elise still examined the carpet, Amber and Nora shared a look. Even without words Nora could read Amber's thoughts. Elise might not be ready but they would be. When Aiden arrived they'd give Elise a gentle nudge, helping things along, and one day Elise would thank them for it.

Nora smiled back at her baby girl. She knew this would work out for Elise, that she would overcome her fears. But even more than that, Aiden's coming had helped Amber to break free from her stupor. She was Amber again. Nora knew Amber might take a few steps back or she might fall right on her butt once more, but today had proved that she was making progress. She would heal. And, for now, those two things were enough.

CHAPTER FOUR

A BALL NAILED Lou in the temple.

"If you throw that ball one more time . . . " Lou threatened her younger son Cash as she turned into the elementary school parking lot. Her older daughter Emma had joined the school choir that year and she and the rest of her children were happily coming to watch the Christmas concert—or that was at least the threat Lou had issued to her boys before they'd piled into her minivan.

"I didn't throw it. Hazel did," Cash accused his little sister.

"Don't lie, Cash," Lou warned as Hazel squealed, "I didn't throw it!"

Great. If they were already fighting like this in the car?

Lou pulled into a parking space and slammed on her brakes.

"We're done." Lou turned around to face her children, making pointed eye contact with each one. "Got it?"

Three heads nodded in acquiescence and Lou sighed. She knew some time in her future she'd miss these days, or at least that's what she was constantly told, but right now she was missing not being able to miss these days. That made no sense but Lou was going with it.

"Give me that ball," Lou directed Cash. The boy had been trying to slip it into his pocket but Lou was no rookie mom. She tucked the ball far under her seat after Cash reluctantly handed it to her.

"And you'll give these flowers to your sister after her performance." Lou handed her older son Aiden the bouquet she'd grabbed at the grocery store earlier that day. It was full of all kinds of color and she knew Emma would love them.

"Fine," Aiden groaned as he accepted the flowers.

Cash smirked at his brother, probably glad to be off the hook.

"Cash, since you don't have any flowers I expect you to give your sister a hug," Lou directed, squashing his smirk.

"Aw, man," the younger boy said but Lou knew he'd obey. Her boys might be rambunctious but they knew how to behave. Mostly.

"Can I give Emma a hug too?" Hazel asked, her cute brown ponytail bobbing with every word.

"Of course you can, Sweetie," Lou said as she put her bell necklace on over her very red and green sweater that read, Fa La La La La.

"Do you have to wear the bell too?" Aiden groaned again, sliding down in his seat. This time Lou didn't blame him. She was pretty embarrassing.

But she wasn't going to change who she was for anyone. Even anyones she loved as much as her children. She used to avoid wearing sweaters like this in public because it drove Harvey nuts. But one great thing about her divorce was that she could now wear exactly what she wanted and feel no guilt. Aiden could and would suck it up. He'd maybe even find it endearing one day.

"Mom's sweater is cool, Aiden," Hazel shot at her brother.

Aiden raised his eyebrows and looked ready to shoot something back at his sister.

"Inside," Lou commanded before he could.

Her kids piled out of her car and Lou followed, Hazel taking her hand as they all walked toward the school.

She noticed Cash and Aiden walked several paces ahead. She smiled, remembering doing the same when her mom had embarrassed her. It was fun to come full circle.

"Will they sing the bells song?" Hazel asked Lou hopefully, swinging her mom's hand.

"I'm sure they will," Lou replied, not wanting to correct her daughter. Hazel was at an age where she was learning so much but often getting things just a little wrong. Lou had noticed herself correcting Hazel each time and because of so many little mistakes Lou realized she was correcting more than anything else when it came to Hazel. So she'd correct some but she wanted to enjoy more. This was a time to just enjoy the cute words coming out of her daughter's mouth.

"And the angels one?" Hazel asked, eyes wide with expectation.

The girl was a fount of questions and although it was tiring for Lou to keep up, she also knew it was exactly what Hazel should be doing at her age. Cash had skipped much of this stage because Harvey and Lou had been going through the divorce when he was this age. At the time, neither she nor Harvey had had the bandwidth to interact with Cash the way she did now with Hazel, and of course Cash had picked up on that. So he just hadn't asked many questions. Once the divorce was final, and Lou had had a chance to look back, she had worried that the family trauma had hurt Cash developmentally—this stage was important, wasn't it? So she'd tried to get him to ask her about what was on his mind, what he wondered about. He'd asked a few questions but then had begun to get annoyed so Lou had let it go. She figured this was one of those things that would just work out. During the divorce she'd been assured frequently that kids are resilient, and she hoped all of those people weren't lying.

"That one too," Lou affirmed, even though she wasn't exactly sure what Emma and her choir would sing because all of Emma's practices had been private. She'd said she wanted the songs to be a surprise for her family.

"Where are Grandma Margie and Grandpa?" Hazel asked.

"They have a party with some of Grandma Margie's friends," Lou replied, reminding herself once more to film as much of the concert as she could. Margie had been heartbroken when she'd heard the concert was tonight because normally she wouldn't have missed it for the world, but this was the one night a year Margie met up with her high school friends back in Seattle. Each year at the party they set the date for the following year and they weren't allowed to cancel on one another for anything. Margie had told Lou that one of her friends had even asked her son to move his wedding date so she could attend this gathering. Even so, Lou might have still been hurt by their absence if Margie and her dad weren't the kind of parents and grandparents that went to literally everything. Lou knew they wanted to be there more than even Emma wanted them there. So Lou had promised Margie and her dad as well as Emma that she'd film the performance so they wouldn't miss anything.

"Is Aunt Alexis coming?" Hazel asked, mentioning Lou's best friend and stepsister.

"She can't. She has to work at the food truck and Uncle Jared is working late at the office," Lou replied. She'd be filming for them as well.

"And Aunt Marsha?" Hazel asked, her voice just a little quieter as she named Lou's sister.

"She's probably coming with Peter and Brittany but they might be a little late," Lou said, trying to sound upbeat.

Marsha was never on time for anything and she'd already texted saying they might be a bit late. In Marsha terms that meant they'd be lucky to make it for the last song.

Hazel pouted and Lou didn't blame her. The little girl was used to being surrounded by family at events like this. They rarely showed up alone.

"Dad!" Lou heard Cash shout.

The one person Hazel hadn't asked about was actually there. Not that Hazel should have asked for him. Out of everyone listed, he was the least likely to show up for them. But Lou had to give him credit. Ever since he'd started coming to Cash's soccer games last month he'd been better all around. But Lou was still surprised to see Harvey there—and early, no less. And of course with his lovely girlfriend on his arm.

Lou worked hard to loosen her clenched jaw. She might have to work with Harvey because of their kids but she doubted she would ever be pleased to see Felicia.

Cash ran to give his dad a hug as Aiden followed more cautiously.

Hazel gripped onto Lou's hand even tighter, showing just how differently her kids reacted when it came to their father.

"Did you see my goal at my last game?" Cash asked as Harvey swung him up into a hug.

"I did," Harvey said proudly. "I saw your science fair project as well, Aiden." Harvey spoke to his son who was still a few steps away.

"I know," Aiden muttered as he looked down, kicking the ground with the toe of his shoe.

Why hadn't Lou known this? She wasn't annoyed, per se, but she would have liked to have known that Harvey had gone to the kids' school. Granted, he was their father. And he wasn't her husband. She guessed it wasn't her job to keep tabs on the relationship her kids had with their father. And that was an awkward feeling.

"You did a great job," Harvey congratulated.

"I didn't win," Aiden replied.

"Second place is pretty dang awesome," Felicia said brightly.

Felicia knew that her son had placed second at the science fair? Lou's stomach turned. She didn't like this. But this was her new normal.

"So, should we get in there?" Lou offered as she joined the slightly merry group.

Things were still a little uncomfortable between Harvey and Aiden. They would be until Aiden forgave his dad and who knew how long that would be? Harvey had messed up. And Aiden was making him pay for it, maybe not consciously, but he wasn't ready to let his dad into his life the way Cash had. Lou hoped for Aiden's sake that he would be able to forgive soon. Holding onto anger could hurt, and Lou never wanted to see her children hurt.

Harvey took one look at Lou's get-up and grunted his annoyance. Lou shot her very brightest you-no-longer-get-a-say-in-what-I-wear smile and led the way toward the school's auditorium.

She'd noticed Felicia wore a very tasteful white sweater and a pair of forest green slacks, a much more subtle nod at holiday cheer. But Lou wasn't subtle. Nor would she ever be. If people didn't like that they could stub their big toe.

She was pretty sure that wasn't the saying, but it worked.

"Can you at least hold the necklace so that you stop jingle belling everywhere?" Harvey muttered from behind.

"Right?" Aiden miraculously agreed with his dad.

See, her necklace wasn't a mere decoration; it could help to mend broken relationships. Lou grinned as she ignored her ex's question. She may have put a little extra bounce in her step, causing the bell to jingle harder.

She marched up to the first door of the auditorium, opening it. As she started to step through she saw that Felicia had continued walking. There was another door down the hall that would let them enter from the other side of the seating.

Whatever. Lou didn't want to sit next to the woman anyway.

She was about to lead Hazel in, ushering Aiden and Cash behind her, when Felicia spoke up.

"I brought gummy bears."

Aiden's mouth dropped at the declaration. Gummy bears were his weakness.

"Mom, can I sit with Dad?" he asked as Felicia grinned widely, lording her win over Lou.

But this wasn't a game. This was about her kids. So Lou wouldn't play. Because the only people who had no chance of winning this game were her children. And they were her entire world. She needed to let Felicia know here and now that when it came to her kids, games were not allowed.

"How nice of you to bring Aiden's favorite candy, Felicia," Lou said as she closed the door, heading toward the other adults.

"Of course you can sit with your dad," Lou said as she continued her walk.

"Can I too?" Cash added.

"Yes, you can." Lou smiled at her younger son, closing the distance between herself and Felicia.

"I brought some Christmas sugar cookies too." Felicia added Hazel's favorite treat to the mix, taunting Lou as she drew even closer.

"Christmas cookies?" Lou heard Hazel whisper in awe before Lou came to a stop right next to Felicia's side.

"I see what you did," Lou whispered as her boys ran to Harvey. Only Hazel seemed to notice the conversation between the women so Lou kept her voice too low for her little girl to hear. "I am happy they want to spend time with their father. But if you pull a trick like that again, I will crush you. Don't play games with my kids, Felicia. I will make sure the only person to lose will be you. I might not be good at much but I am a woman of my word. Hurt them and I will make sure you hurt more than they ever do," Lou finished, a smile on her lips as Felicia's face went white.

Lou's actions might have been a bit extreme but this woman needed to know her place. Lou would put up with her, she would even invite her to events, but Felicia was not allowed to hurt her children. Not when she was in a position of trust in their world.

"Do you want to sit with your dad too?" Lou offered Hazel as she bent down so that she was level with her daughter. She wasn't against her children leaving her, but she was against them being manipulated to do so.

Hazel nodded but then shook her head.

"You can start with them and then come and sit with me later if you want," Lou offered and Hazel grinned before finally slipping her hand out of Lou's and going to her father.

"Why did we pass that door?" Harvey asked, not seeming to notice what his girlfriend was doing. He hadn't always been the sharpest crayon in the box.

"I wanted to sit on the other side of the auditorium. I heard the . . . " Felicia faltered as Lou stared her down, daring her to continue in her lie.

"Or we could sit in there." Felicia pointed to the door Lou had started to walk through.

In the end Lou sat a few rows in front of her kids and their dad and Felicia. It would have been too weird to sit closer but she also didn't want to put space between them just because of her issues. She wanted her kids to know they could have their mom and their dad. She wouldn't make them choose.

But somehow, even though she was still relatively close to them, Lou felt completely alone. It was a feeling she hadn't experienced since her divorce. Sure, she'd felt loneliness as a single mom, along with almost every other emotion, but with four young kids to fill the house she'd never really felt alone. And even when they weren't around she'd always had her dad or stepmom or Alexis or Marsha or Jared or . . . her heart thudded a bit harder as she thought about Jax.

But tonight it was just her. And she already regretted wishing she could say she missed these days.

She was fine. She was a big girl. Sure, there was an empty seat on either side of her, but down the row she spotted the family of Emma's friend Millie and behind her was one of Cash's teammates with his family. She was never really alone on Whisling.

It suddenly hit her why she felt so out of place. It was a Christmas concert. Everyone was here with family, whereas without her kids it was just her. Singular Lou. Single Lou.

She closed her eyes. It wouldn't be long. She'd have her kids back soon.

But then what?

She couldn't rely on them to be all she needed forever. And then of course her thoughts strayed back to Jax. The man she wanted to date. The man who wanted to date her. The man she couldn't date. Basically, Jax was her all-too-handsome guitar instructor who was off limits to Lou as long as she was his student. And Lou was stuck—she had to continue lessons because it was Emma's dream.

So she was in this weird state of limbo . . . would Jax have been at the concert with her if he could? Lou knew the answer was yes. She didn't even have to think about it. That was part of what made him so appealing. Unlike the typical handsome, charming bachelor, Jax seemed to adore the fact that Lou had children. Maybe because he was kind of a big kid himself. Lou smiled as she recalled the time she'd seen her kids swarming over him, using the man as their personal jungle gym.

The buzz of conversation in the auditorium hushed as the lights went low. The concert was about to start. And it had taken mere thoughts of Jax to help Lou feel a little less lonely. She wondered what actually having him there would have been like.

"Excuse me, excuse me." Two women pushed their way through people to get to the middle seats just in front of Lou.

Lou cringed. When you came in so late, wasn't it kind of rude to make your way into the middle?

Lou checked to make sure one of the offenders wasn't her sister and thankfully it wasn't. It did seem like something Marsha would do.

The women then proceeded to stand for a bit, blocking Lou's view as they took their time removing their coats and shifting their things around even as kids began to take the stage.

"Sit down!" someone behind Lou called and Lou turned to smile at whoever the knight with the loud voice was.

The women glanced behind them, seeming annoyed at the voice instead of embarrassed by their behavior but they did finally sit.

With their backward looks, Lou recognized them as moms of some of Emma's classmates. Both of them were divorced as well and although this wasn't the first time they'd annoyed Lou she did feel a slight sense of kinship with them.

"Can you believe how rude that guy was?" one of the moms whispered to the other. Lou thought their names might be Rachel and Satchie but she couldn't quite remember. It was one of those relationships where if Lou had had to speak to them she would have avoided calling them by name at all costs.

"Right?" Maybe Satchie replied with a huff. "This is why we're single."

Rachel nodded and although Lou was grateful for the guy who'd spoken up she was also all for women power. *Way to be proud of being single, girls,* she cheered in her mind but quickly forgot about the moms when Emma took the stage.

"Yeah Emma!" Lou cheered before whistling loudly and wildly jingling her bell necklace. She knew somewhere close by Harvey and Aiden were cringing and that thought made her shake her bell a little harder.

Emma beamed out at the darkness. Lou knew Emma couldn't see her but Lou would be sure to let her presence be known. Poor Emma had been sick with worry all morning over this concert and she needed to know that she had plenty of support.

Each of the kids took their place on the podium and the pianist began to play the intro to the first song. Lou started bobbing to the music and quickly forgot she was on her own. That was the joy of music for you.

"Oh shoot," she muttered when she suddenly remembered she was supposed to be filming. She pulled her phone out to capture the next song and was glad she'd remembered before the whole concert was over. And the delayed start was actually kind of a good thing since during song number one Emma had looked a little green, but by song two she was jamming out and totally in her element. Lou couldn't wait to share the footage with her, as well as the rest of the family.

A few more songs went by and Lou finally brought down her phone. Her arm was tired from filming and each song was starting to sound pretty much like the last one. The kids had played one of the songs on their own glockenspiels, which was a cool addition, but mostly it was cute faces singing familiar songs over and over.

"And now we'll have a brief intermission," the choir director announced, turning to face the audience.

Lou swore she heard Cash groan and hoped that Harvey had quickly put a stop to that. It was weird to be so near her kids and yet not with them. Maybe she should work harder to be friendly to Felicia? Then they could all sit together.

But as nice as that sounded, Lou wasn't even sure where to start. Felicia had done nothing to hide her distaste for Lou and Lou couldn't help but feel the same way about her. Maybe with time? Yeah, that was what Lou would tell herself. Because as things were, Lou wasn't in a place where she could extend a hand of friendship to Felicia. Maybe some other kind of olive branch? But even that . . . Lou worried that the offered branch would snap back in her face.

"I heard that too," said the woman Lou was going to call Maybe Rachel in her mind and Lou's ears perked up. Eavesdropping might be a bad habit, but one of the best things about living on a small island was the gossip. It was also one of the worst things when one was featured in said gossip, but because Lou had been flying under the radar since Harvey had moved Felicia in she figured she was safe to enjoy some juicy tidbits.

"I mean, she's beautiful, but catching the eye of a guy like Jax?" Maybe Satchie said and Lou felt her heart drop.

Jax was dating another woman? What did they mean by catching his eye? Lou's questions had to go unanswered because she shouldn't have heard the information. Her stomach turned but she figured this was what she deserved for participating in gossip even when she knew how harmful it could be.

Or maybe they were talking about another Jax. The island was small but not so small that people couldn't have the same name.

"That's true," Maybe Rachel acknowledged. "He has the talent, the accent, and those abs. I hear he's even got money. He's the full package and she's an eight at best . . ."

Maybe Rachel's voice trailed off and Lou vowed to never eavesdrop again. Her chest felt too tight as she recalled how Maybe Rachel had described Jax. It sounded exactly like the man Lou had been obsessing over. There couldn't be two Jaxes that fit that same description on the island, could there?

Lou bit down on her lip hard as she blinked against the tears trying to pool in her eyes. She was being silly. It wasn't like she'd expected Jax not to date, right? Just because he'd said he liked her and wanted to date her when she wasn't his student, what did that even mean? They'd go on a few dates one day after Lou quit lessons? Maybe just hook up? Lou's stomach turned once more because she wasn't that kind of woman. She liked steadiness and commitment in her relationships and she'd assumed Jax was the same, but you know what they said about assuming.

Lou sank back into her chair, wishing she didn't have another half concert to endure but she did. And her daughter needed her to not just endure but enjoy the time. Lou wasn't a heartbroken teen full of angst with time to nurse that pain; she was a mom with responsibilities and people to put before her own wants and needs.

So, good for Jax. He should be dating. He'd encouraged her to date, and why shouldn't he do the same? She hoped Jax and his eight would find much happiness together. She hoped . . .

And then Lou knew what the problem really was. Sure, she was sad about Jax, but tonight's circumstances had compounded her heartache. Being alone at this family event, seeing Harvey with Felicia—it wasn't that she'd ever want Harvey back, but he'd found his new person while Lou was just floundering through life the way she always did.

Usually she had her kids but tonight even they had chosen

to leave her behind. She didn't blame them that for that, it was just life. Yet it would have been nice to have someone to share her laughter about Aiden's embarrassment or Cash's inability to sit still or Hazel's cute questions. Instead she sat alone.

Time alone can be great, she tried to reason. Lou worked hard to buoy herself up but just wasn't feeling it.

She couldn't quite make her spirits lift until . . . a cute little girl squeezed past the people in Lou's row, whispering "scuse me" on repeat, and plopped down in the seat next to Lou, sliding her fingers into Lou's.

"Daddy told me I only get to ask fifteen questions. I already asked those so now I came to sit with you. And—" Hazel turned to whisper to Lou in a tone only a six-year-old could think was a whisper, "—Felicia's cookies were the kind you buy from the store. She didn't make them like you do, Mom."

Lou squeezed her little girl's hand tight, knowing that a better person wouldn't be exulting in the fact that Hazel preferred Lou's homemade cookies to Felicia's store-bought ones. Lou would never tell the sweet girl that she actually bought the can of cookies and all she did was cut them out before putting them in the oven. To Hazel they were home-made. And to Hazel that made her mom better than the woman her dad was dating. However petty that was, Lou had needed that acknowledgement that night. That pure, unadulterated, unconditional love that only a child could give.

So Lou lapped it up and got ready to enjoy the rest of her daughter's performance. Life might not be perfect and maybe a little lonely at times, but . . . she scooted a little closer to Hazel, who snuggled up against her. Life was good.

CHAPTER FIVE

"ARE you sure that's the answer you want to give?" Seren winked at the man seated beside her at what she called the round table in her office.

Piper's mouth fell open before she snapped it shut, and Seren fought against a grin. Most people would have taken the denial Seren had been given and walk away. She did realize that the words she'd voiced weren't what the CEO of a Fortune 500 company was used to hearing, but she'd found in her time working with these kind of men that they appreciated honesty and sometimes even bluntness. It didn't always pay off—Seren recalled the red, mottled face of one such man who had been less than impressed—but mostly they either appreciated her candor or laughed her behavior off as being so Seren.

While Piper had been shocked and Seren amused, the man that they were trying to cajole into dishing out a six-figure donation for Seren's latest baby, a teen hangout for cancer patients at Whisling Memorial, had been stewing over his thoughts. Just as Seren had hoped.

"What do you think I should say?" Bill Rogan, CEO of Rogan Industries, replied.

Seren put her forearms onto the table and leaned forward, pressing into Bill's space. She couldn't have asked for a better opening.

"I think you should say that this kind of opportunity doesn't come often. I know you're interested. A busy man doesn't choose a place like Whisling for his family vacation at this time of year unless he has an ulterior motive. How have you been enjoying the inn, by the way?" Seren asked. She'd discovered that inserting random questions in the middle of important conversations was a tactic that often worked well for her.

"It's lovely. The staff are excellent and we got to meet one of the proprietors yesterday. Elise. Lovely girl," Bill spoke even as his forehead creased in confusion at the unexpected topic.

Men like Bill saw it all. Seren loved the challenge of surprising the unflappable.

"She truly is. Her sister's mother is actually a volunteer in our program. Excellent woman," Seren said with a smile.

She saw Bill's forehead crease even more, doubtless wondering how Nora could be Elise's sister's mom and not Elise's. But that had been Seren's plan, to distract Bill with that conundrum and then have him come back to the matter at hand feeling less confident and more confused . . . and more willing to be directed.

"I know you came here because you are interested in the project. It's not the same flash and glam that too many charities have adopted. It will help you to appear to be the kind of man you really are: someone who gives to the truly needy, who knows what matters. Someone who doesn't care *who* is in charge of the charity project but rather that the charity is something of substance, something that will make a difference in children's lives. Piper's daughter . . . " Seren motioned to Piper, knowing she would seamlessly takeover. Piper had become as passionate about the cause in these last couple of weeks as Seren was.

"My daughter had a love-hate relationship with Whisling Memorial. It was the place where her body was cruelly battered by chemo treatments but it was also the only place where she could find people who truly understood her. That one room in the hospital with a few games was her safe haven. But I can't help but think she deserved more than that. Seren's plan gives the kids a place close to the safety of the hospital, but offsite in a fun cabin. That gives them a feeling of independence during a time of life that they should gaining more freedom but it's robbed from them because of this disease. And it also gives them a break from the hospital, the ability to get away from the place so associated with pain and suffering. I hate cancer with all that I am. But I love that Kristie found a group of people who cared for her, a boyfriend who'd been through the same, volunteers who were there to make a difference." Piper took a breath to collect herself as she was flooded with memories. "Seren's and my hope is that we take all of the goodness of the teen hangout and amp it to a thousand percent. For some of these kids, these years are all they will get . . . " Piper's voice broke and it was easy to see that her emotion was entirely genuine.

Seren felt tears prick her own eyes and noticed that Bill had blinked a few too many times during Piper's plea.

"Can you think of a better place to put your money?" Seren asked, turning her entire body to Bill. "So I'm going to ask you again, are you sure that's the answer you want to give?"

Seren locked eyes with Bill, holding his gaze steadily. She could feel Piper holding her breath. Bill was a tipping point. All three of them knew it. The fact that he had taken Seren up on the free trip she'd offered to see the sights of Whisling had been a huge win. Men like Bill received similar offers frequently and the last thing a man with his kind of dough needed was a freebie. His time was so much more important than any dollar amount. So when he'd come, he'd initially conveyed interest, but then said it wasn't quite the right fit. Until Seren took over the conversation. Now she could almost taste the victory. If Bill Rogan donated, so would the rest of the world.

After a moment's hesitation, Bill nodded and a smile took over his face. "You two are good. Maybe some of the best I've come up against, and I've seen almost everyone." He shook his head as if he couldn't believe what he was about to say. "I'll do it."

Seren felt her heart leap even as she once more fought against tears. She knew this work wouldn't bring her baby back —nothing could undo her loss—but each time she won a victory for kids like her Milo, she felt a little closer to him. It was a high she'd begun to crave.

"Thank you," she said, trying not to gush. She knew Bill wouldn't appreciate it.

Bill nodded as he offered his hand, and Seren shook it soundly before Piper took her turn. "You know you have a treasure in this one," Bill said, motioning to Piper.

Seren nodded. "I knew from the first moment I saw her. I call her my golden face."

Piper giggled nervously and Seren knew why. The woman couldn't seem to admit how gorgeous she was, but Seren's nickname for her was more than an acknowledgement of her beauty. If any person on earth wore a halo, it was Piper. Light just shone through her.

"Well, if you're ever looking for work . . . " Bill offered Piper.

Piper shook her head. "I don't think you can offer the kind of cause that Seren has."

Bill turned back to Seren. "You are right about that."

Seren took that as the highest kind of compliment.

"Well," Bill said as he stood, one of Seren's staff already at her office door to usher Mr. Rogan out. "I'd say it was a pleasure, but my bank account is crying. However, I will be sure to spread the news of this latest charitable cause I've deemed as worthy. Get ready to start your project. I'd be willing to bet you'll be fully funded before the holidays."

Seren beamed along with Piper. She was so grateful that she'd listened to her new friend. When Piper had come on board, Seren had been in the process of organizing a giant gala to raise the money for the teen hangout. It was the way things were done. But then Piper had looked at their plan of action and had asked if it was necessary. It cost so much and really, wasn't there a better way? Seren hadn't seen the possibilities until Piper had asked a single question: is there a kingpin? Seren had laughed at first; surely it couldn't be that simple. But then she'd thought of Bill. Bill Rogan was at the top of his world—everyone knew he made sound business as well as charitable decisions— and his sweet wife was known for her social connections. What the Rogans did, everyone followed. So Piper had pressed, why focus on all the possibilities instead of zeroing in on the one person who could singlehandedly help them bring their vision to life? It was a brilliant idea but also risky. But today that risk had paid off.

"Let Susan know I'm sorry we missed her," Seren said, gripping the table to keep herself from jumping with joy. Fully funded before the holidays? She couldn't have dreamed of a better scenario.

"I'm sure she's sorry to have missed seeing you as well. But you know how she is when the kids are around. She wants to do everything with them and this island has a lot to offer. I believe they're at an art gallery today," Bill said as he started toward the door.

"And you were worried Susan's soft heart would have your pocketbook out before you were ready to commit?" Seren asked cheekily.

Bill chuckled. "You hit that right on the nose. But it turns out Susan isn't the only Rogan with a soft heart. Just don't let that get around," Bill said even though they all knew the world already understood that. It was why he was constantly approached for help.

"Thank you again, Bill," Seren said before he nodded once more and left the room.

Piper looked about ready to burst but Seren put a hand up before she started counting down softly, "five, four, three, two . . ." At "one," the women burst into shouts of excitement. They'd done it!

"I can't believe you said that to him," Piper said with wide eyes, shaking her head in disbelief.

"I can't believe it either. But we were about to lose him, so I figured why the heck not?" Seren replied with a shrug as she fell into her seat, exhausted from her efforts.

"Only you, Seren. Only you," Piper said as she leaned down by her chair and then stood, throwing her purse over her shoulder.

Seren grinned, used to hearing those kinds of exclamations. She'd never done what people expected of her. She found life a lot more interesting this way.

"Thanks for coming today, Piper. I couldn't have done it without you," Seren said when she realized Piper was leaving.

"That's debatable. But I'm glad I came, even if it was just to see you in action. I'd heard rumors, Seren, but you are a force of nature."

Seren laughed at Piper's description and then shrugged. "I just do what I have to do." But she was done talking about herself so to throw a curveball into the conversation, she added, "Oh, and give that yummy Carter a giant kiss for me, will you?"

Piper grinned but she didn't laugh off the question the way Seren expected. Instead it was almost as if she'd anticipated

Seren, and immediately turned the question around on her: "And when are you going to find a yummy man for yourself?"

Seren swallowed hard. They were moving into uncomfortable territory. She knew that her marriage status was a topic of conversation on the island. A woman couldn't just move to a small town like Whisling and think she could keep all of her secrets. But Seren wasn't quite ready to reveal to her new island who she was—or rather, who she had been.

"Maybe I will," Seren said with a wink, as if that were the plan. But honestly she had no idea if she even wanted a yummy man. Who knew what Seren wanted? Certainly not her.

Knowing what she wanted took effort and right now all Seren felt was an intense exhaustion. There were days like today when miraculous things would happen and some of that constant, squeezing tension would ease, so she was grateful for today.

But that very act of easing would then spark guilt for escaping the exhaustion . . . it was a never-ending cycle. Because the exhaustion had started when he'd gotten sick. It was a strange thing to hold onto, but letting go of that exhaustion would feel like letting her Milo go, truly moving on from that phase of her life.

And though he might have been taken from her arms and from this life, Seren would never, ever let her little boy go.

"Are you okay, Seren?" Piper asked the question Seren hoped no one would. She'd escaped everyone close to her. Her parents, her sisters, even her ex. Anyone with the nerve to break past the upbeat demeanor Seren used as a shield. She should have known Piper would get too close and see behind her mask. Seren wasn't sure if she'd allowed Piper into her circle despite that or because of it.

"How couldn't I be? We just landed the donation that will

put us over the top," Seren said in her typical bright manner, flashing a brilliant smile.

"And I can tell you are thrilled about that, but it only goes so far . . . " Piper's voice trailed off.

Seren figured if anyone understood it would be Piper. They shared the unspeakable experience of losing a child. Seren swallowed. No one could understand that kind of pain unless they'd lived it. And although Piper would never know what it was like to lose Milo, she had experienced her own version of the same hell.

Piper's gentle questioning told Seren that she wasn't letting go without a bit more of an explanation. So because Piper had been there for her, Seren would give what she could.

"There are better days," Seren confided softly, trying her best to open up. As much as her life here was exactly what she wanted it to be, she'd never considered how isolating the loneliness of cutting herself off from all she'd known could be. Seren had never been on her own, ever. As one of six sisters she'd grown up in a house so loud she couldn't even dream and then had gone straight to the college dorms at Stanford before entering a life of glitz and glam on the arm of a Lamb.

"I understand," Piper said, taking a step back and showing that she truly did. Most would see this as a moment to push forward. But Piper saw that Seren had already given all she possibly could for today.

"Do you ever talk to him?" Piper suddenly asked.

Seren raised her eyebrows, clearly at a loss as to Piper's meaning.

"I know this sounds crazy." Piper paused as if second guessing what she wanted to say. "I talk to her. To my Kristie. Sometimes at home, sometimes while I'm driving, but mostly when I'm at the cemetery."

At Seren's continued silence Piper shook her head. "I

shouldn't have pried. I just . . . never mind what I thought. Congrats, Seren. You really are a marvel." Piper began to walk toward the door.

Piper spoke to Kristie? Did it help? It must if she was bringing it up. And Seren really wanted to connect with Milo even if it was just in her mind. Seren didn't know if it was curiosity or desperation but she couldn't let Piper go without more of an explanation.

"I don't talk to Milo," Seren said so suddenly that Piper stopped in her tracks. "I think I might want to—" Seren heard her voice break and had to stop. She took a deep breath before continuing.

"Are they really somewhere?" Seren asked the question that had been plaguing her ever since the moment she'd learned her son's life would be cut so very short. She'd grown up in a household with some elements of religion. Her mother liked the idea of it while her father had thought it was a farce. So they'd had statues of Buddha as well as crosses scattered around their home, though Seren had never been to an organized church meeting in her life. And she hadn't ever thought she needed one. Her mentality was: be a good person and good things will follow. For years that philosophy had seemed to work. But with the person she held dearest to her heart gone, she wanted to believe he wasn't gone forever. She didn't care how the afterlife went, only that there was one. But she just couldn't be sure.

"I believe they are," Piper said as she turned to face Seren with a sympathetic smile. "Sometimes closer than I could have dared to wish. Kristie came to me in a dream once. And I know. I get it. Dreams are dictated by our subconscious. Most would say that I dreamed what I wanted to believe. And maybe I did. But I really don't think so."

Piper crossed her arms over her chest, rubbing them absently to comfort herself during a conversation that couldn't be easy for her. Seren was grateful Piper was willing to talk about this for her sake.

"You think that it was actually her?" Seren ventured. "Her spirit or her soul?" She had no idea what the right wording would be.

"Something like that," Piper said with a shrug. "I'm not claiming to understand it."

"But you still believe it?" Seren asked, trying not to sound as hopeful as she felt.

"I do," Piper whispered.

Seren considered her options. She could go on as she had been. Some days she pretended like she'd never had a son even as the ache threatened to eat her whole, while on other days she'd allow that pain to consume her, not knowing if she could or even if she wanted to survive another day in this world. Her will for so much had left this world with Milo. The only thing she found any kind of comfort in was raising money for kids who were living the same hell her Milo had been through.

Or she could try talking to Milo. She didn't have to believe in any one thing to do so. She knew she wouldn't. She was fine with her state of nonreligion as long as she could still feel a connection and know her son was somewhere out there. That his entire soul hadn't been snuffed out by cancer.

Seren missed Milo with every part of her being. She didn't know how to not crave holding him one more time, how to stop hating the disease that had stolen him from her. She didn't want to move on. She didn't want to stop feeling that pain, her last link with Milo. But more than anything else she wanted to feel close to him once more. Had Piper just given her access to that? Could it really be that simple? It didn't seem possible.

Seren's emotions flooded to the surface as she brushed at a tear she hadn't realized had fallen down her cheek, more rushing to follow it.

"I'll see myself out," Piper said, her voice full of concern but knowing she'd said enough for one day.

Seren's mind understood her concern and somewhere deep down she knew she should do something to ease Piper's conscience—she'd only been trying to help—but the ice-cold wall of grief that had encircled her heart in the last few moments kept her from doing anything about it.

She kicked at the ground so that she spun around in her chair, the room blurring as she watched it move through a veil of tears. When the chair stopped she kicked again. She sat in that office chair for who knew how long as tears continued to fall. The gray day visible through her windows matched her mood and Seren just wanted it all to be done. She was so tired of trying so hard to feel something she'd never feel again. Talking to Milo couldn't change that, could it? Seren hated that she couldn't even allow herself to hope for things to get better, for eventually finding a closeness with her son once more. Because if she'd learned anything in the past few years, it was that reality always stole hope away.

CHAPTER SIX

"BESS, you do know what a normal dinner for four looks like, don't you?" Julia asked, shaking her head but smiling fondly as she took in the seven varied dishes that Bess had set out on platters in the middle of the dining table Dax had built for their first wedding anniversary.

"I've been testing a holiday menu for the truck . . . " Bess began.

"You already have a fantastic holiday menu at the truck. I tasted all you had to offer two nights ago," Ellis interrupted their friend.

Julia nodded. Their first stop back on the island had been to Scratch Made by Bess because they'd both missed their friend's cooking like crazy. Ellis had an incredibly talented chef that fed them while they were on tour, but nothing could quite match up to Bess and her homecooked meals.

"That's what I've been trying to tell her," Dax said with a nod in Ellis' direction.

"I just thought it could get boring since we've had the same specials for three weeks now. I wondered if we shouldn't change it up in the weeks leading up to Christmas," Bess said as a blush rose to her cheeks.

Julia put her arm around her friend's shoulders. "You, girl, work too hard. But as long as you keep feeding us your marvelous creations we'll be your biggest cheerleaders."

Bess slid her own arm around Julia's waist and squeezed. "Thank you."

Bess then looked to Dax, who raised his hands in the air. "I know better than to say anything. You are a master of your craft and I am your humble servant."

"And don't you forget it," Bess replied jokingly, tossing an affectionate look at her husband. He laughed in response, gazing at her with something akin to adoration.

"So now that the teasing Bess portion of the evening is complete, let's get to eating," Bess said with a good-natured grin. It took a lot to get Julia's friend down. Especially these days because she was just so danged happy to be with Dax.

Julia glanced between her friends, thrilled to spend time with them on their one island night before their families descended upon them. Julia had worried that their families being on the island would keep them from seeing any of their friends, but this dinner would ensure that didn't happen. Julia hoped to have another few nights with friends before they went back on the road.

When she noticed neither Bess nor Dax making a move to eat, Julia grabbed the platter nearest to her, which was full of succulent roast beef, realizing their hosts wouldn't start serving themselves until she and Ellis had. She passed her platter along and then took the green beans from Ellis, followed by a platter of rosemary and garlic mashed potatoes. She tried to take small helpings of each dish but after seven dishes even tiny portions piled up. Still, she was feeling proud of her conservative servings until she got to the homemade cornbread dressing . . . and Julia was done. She piled on two large spoonfuls, knowing her waistline would regret it later, but she couldn't bring herself to care. Bess made the most delicious cornbread on the planet. Putting that in dressing form? Sign Julia up for the rest of the platter later.

"So how was life on tour?" Bess asked Julia, who had just taken an enormous bite of dressing.

"Oh my gosh," Julia moaned, ignoring Bess' question. Nothing could be more important than that dressing.

"Buttery goodness." Dax nodded, seeming to completely understand Julia's reaction.

"Tour was good. Tiring but good," Ellis answered for Julia since he had yet to take a bit of the cornbread dressing. Julia knew that when he did he wouldn't be wasting his time with talking either.

"What he said," Julia said in the split second between swallowing and shoveling in another bite. This had to be what heaven tasted like. And if it was, she would be a saint for the rest of this life just to be sure to make it there.

"Is it really that—" Ellis tried a bite and groaned. "Holy crows on toast, Bess. You have found your calling."

Dax nodded as Bess laughed.

"Crows on toast?" Bess questioned before taking her own bite of the dressing. Julia noticed the sly smile on the woman's face. She knew she'd knocked it out of the park.

"As soon as Ellis is putting things on toast you know it's good," Julia managed, barely getting the words out before her next bite. She never wanted to stop eating. She knew she should try some of the other deliciousness as well but how could she when this delight was staring her in the face?

"Noted," Bess said as the table fell silent once more. No one wanted to interrupt their eating with anything as mundane as conversation.

"This is going to sell out every day," Ellis predicted minutes later as he twirled the lazy Susan in the middle of the table to scoop another heaping spoonful of dressing onto his plate.

"By noon," Julia predicted. She too was running low on dressing but even as she eyed Ellis' second portion longingly she couldn't do it. Her stomach was already pleading with her that it was time to slow down even as her tongue danced with pleasure.

Julia knew the time had come to try the other dishes on her plate. She dipped a bite of roast into the fluffy mashed potatoes. "Wait, how are they so creamy?" she asked as the potatoes melted against her tongue. The flavors were incredible, although she noticed her eyes straying again to the platter of cornbread dressing, tempting her from the center of the table.

Bess laughed as Dax answered, "Sticks and sticks of butter."

"My kind of dish," Julia answered as she sampled the cranberry, apple, and broccoli slaw as well as the green beans, candied buttered yams, and wild rice.

"We're thinking about doing a holiday combo plate. You can choose either the turkey we've already been serving on the truck or this roast beef as your main and then you can add any two sides," Bess said as she pointed to the options on the table.

"The dressing and mashed potatoes," Ellis said pleasantly.

"But this slaw . . . or the green beans . . . " Julia gestured helplessly at the impossibility of choosing only two sides.

"Or the yams and the rice," Dax said with a pointed look at his wife and Julia was right there with him. She was grateful to have some of every single dish on her plate. It would be sad when this meal was over and Julia would have to go to the food truck like everyone else to get her portion.

Bess laughed once more and Julia knew she delighted in feeding well those she loved. And she'd definitely done that for Julia. Julia sat back in her seat, her hand over her stomach. Even as she eyed the dressing she shook her head. She would burst if she tried to take even one more bite.

"How are your kids doing?" Julia finally managed to ask now that her mouth wasn't full of food.

"Wonderful. Stephen and Jana are going to make me a grandma," Bess said, beaming in delight, and Julia, despite her tight pants, jumped up and raced around the table to give Bess a hug.

"This should have been the first news out of your mouth!" she reprimanded but quickly forgave her friend.

"It's all so new I'm not sure what to make of it other than I'm so danged excited," Bess said, her ear-to-ear grin somehow growing.

"She's going to be the hottest grandma ever," Dax muttered under his breath as Julia and Ellis laughed and Bess blushed to high heaven.

"Do they know if they're having a boy or a girl?" Julia asked, trying to let Bess off of the hotseat.

Bess shot Julia a grateful smile, understanding what her friend had done. "Not yet. Jana's about ten weeks along. They'll tell more people in the next two weeks and then they want to do a gender reveal party at about eighteen weeks. Apparently they're all the rage on social media," Bess said with a shrug that told Julia she didn't understand it but she'd still support it fully.

"And Lindsey is being Lindsey. She's working her little tail off to get to the top of her company, leaving not much time for anything else. I thought she'd learned some balance after losing her job before, but she's as motivated as ever. Saving up like a squirrel for winter. I worry that she's missing out on great things because she's too focused on the good things."

Julia understood that. But she knew as well as Bess that Lindsey would be unlikely to change anything because of what her mom said. Julia remembered how important it had seemed to be to be completely independent in her twenties. Even though she could have learned so much had she heeded the advice of those older and wiser than she had been.

"And James is being James. Mostly sweet. Lots of dating but hardly ever a second date. I worry about the hearts he's out there breaking. He insists these girls feel nothing for him as well but . . . ."

"We've all dated our own versions of James," Julia said, meeting Bess' eyes.

"Haven't we, though? I never thought my sweet boy would be that guy." Bess shook her head, a crease of worry between her eyebrows.

"He's figuring himself out," Julia assured her.

"And then he'll get this," Dax added as he pointed between Bess and himself. "He'll find that one woman and realize he just has to take her on a second date. And then the fun will really begin." Dax laughed and Bess joined him. Julia could see this was a topic of conversation they'd covered often.

"And are you working much?" Ellis asked Dax.

"Not too much, though . . . " Dax let his words trail off as he looked at Julia. She noticed Bess wouldn't meet her eye.

"Ulterior motive for this invite?" Julia asked with a raised eyebrow. Dax had been her manager for long enough that she knew how he worked.

"We would have wanted you over regardless," Bess put in quickly.

"But yes. We do have an ulterior motive. I wouldn't bring this up typically, but hear me out," Dax said.

Julia crossed her arms over her chest. She hadn't worked with Dax in a while now. He'd helped to sell her manuscript. It had done relatively well, but nothing to shout from the rooftops about. She would probably write another one at some point but since no one was presently chomping at the bit for any more

Julia Price manuscripts she was enjoying retirement for the time being.

"Shiloh came to me about a role," Dax said, and Julia nodded as she recognized the name of one of his managers. He still owned his talent company but had people running it for him so that he was mostly retired. Dax still stepped in on the big decisions but he'd left the day to day with people he trusted, like Shiloh.

"I'm not interested in playing the grandma or the washed-up has been, Dax. I left my career in a good place," Julia said with a shake of her head.

Julia had saved enough over her career that she could never work a day in her life again and be just fine. In fact, she could be just fine for a few lifetimes over. Script writing was a fun pastime that had eased her transition into retirement but now that she was on tour with Ellis and had her family, Julia's plate was relatively full. It was kind of nice not to worry about work at all. Dax had to know that he was fighting an uphill battle if he wanted Julia on the big screen again.

"It's Heath Wagner. He wants you to play his lead," Dax said. He sat back in his chair and watched Julia carefully, knowing he'd thrown out two things that would surely entice her. Heath Wagner, the incredible director that almost every actor in LA was keen to work with, who also happened to be one of Julia's favorite people on the planet. And then a lead role. This wasn't a side role or a cameo where Julia would play on her past fame; she'd be the star of the show. A part Julia had and would always crave. It was just who she was.

Julia glanced at Ellis, who smiled his approval. That was all she needed.

"I'm listening," she said, leaning forward and pushing her plate back to rest her forearms on the table.

"*Coming Home* is the working title, but basically it's the

story of a woman who is reuniting with her estranged family after more than thirty years apart. They've got Frisco and Pete writing the movie."

Frisco and Pete were the writing duo who were known as having the Midas touch in Hollywood. And not only were their movies box office gold, but anything they wrote tended to sweep at the awards shows as well. Julia had always wished her last role had won her the coveted acting award but had accepted that the others she'd won in the past were enough. But to get one more? Right at her true retirement? It was incredibly tempting.

"They already have Lila, Ross, Sadie, Zac, Colton, and Maxon committed." Dax continued dropping names while watching Julia closely.

Those names were not only some of the biggest in Tinseltown, but they were people Julia admired and either enjoyed working with or had always wanted to work with. Dax knew exactly what he was doing to her. Then again, that was what made him the best agent on the planet.

"So?" Dax asked as she sat in silent contemplation.

Julia rubbed her hand over the back of her neck, overwhelmed. This was a lot. She had vowed that she was done with acting, but this sounded like the role of a lifetime working with people of a lifetime. It wasn't an opportunity she could simply ignore.

Julia looked to Ellis, who was still grinning broadly. He knew that this was something to jump at. But for the first time in Julia's life, she was scared to take a professional leap. Personal leaps, relationship leaps, even housing leaps she had balked at in the past but never a professional one.

This was the first time she had something in her life that she treasured far more than any role. If she took this part, she couldn't stay on tour with Ellis. She knew a project like this one probably already had a green light. She guessed they'd start filming shortly after the holidays and . . .

"Can I have some time to think about it?" Julia asked faintly. She knew her shock must be showing on her face.

Sure enough, one glance in the mirror on the dining wall opposite her showed exactly what she'd expected.

"Not much, I'm afraid. If you say no they need time to find someone big and bright," Dax said honestly. "Oh," he added. "Wagner knew this would be important to you so he promised to get the studio to write this into your contract, but you don't have to lose or gain any weight for the role. He insists he wants you just as you are."

That seemed too good to be true. Hollywood always wanted Julia to lose weight.

Julia scoffed. "Wagner hasn't seen me in years."

Not since Julia was in her prime at a red carpet premier.

"He knows. But doesn't care. He told me he understands that your looks sold movies in the past and though that wasn't fair, it was the way things were. Especially back then. But you've proven your worth. You don't need your face or your body to sell anything. Your acting prowess is more than enough to carry his entire movie."

Julia knew that was a compliment of the highest order, especially from Heath. But could she do this? Carry a movie? She hadn't acted in years. Granted, this role sounded a lot like playing herself.

"How long do I have?" she asked Dax, her mind whirling.

"Until tomorrow at noon. They need an answer or they have to go elsewhere. Filming starts in late January. They have everything else in place, so they're just waiting for you," Dax said.

Julia suddenly understood why they were so desperate, why everything seemed to be in place.

"Who told them no?" Julia asked curiously. Did she really want to go back for a second or even third hand role that some other actor had rejected?

"No one, I swear. It just took Wagner this long to work up the nerve to ask for you. That's why the studio put him on this deadline."

"So the studio doesn't want me?" Julia asked.

"The studio wants what's best for their bottom line. They aren't sure it's you. Wagner wants what is best for the movie. He knows that's you."

Julia nodded. She understood Dax's point. What the studio wanted didn't matter much when they had a guy like Heath Wagner on their payroll. They paid him to know what was best.

"I'll call you tomorrow by eleven," Julia promised as she stood. Ellis followed suit, edging close in silent support.

"Julia," Dax said. She knew he didn't want her to leave without giving him an answer, but she shook her head.

"I need this time, Dax," she warned.

He nodded once in understanding.

"Are you sure you don't want some dessert?" Bess offered.

Julia turned to her friend. "Thank you, Bess. But I couldn't eat another bite after that delicious meal. I'm fine, I really am," she said when she saw the concern on Bess' face. "It's just a lot. And I need to talk it over with Ellis."

"Of course. We understand. Don't we, Dax?" Bess said in a way that had Dax nodding. The man was smart and knew what was good for him.

"Eleven, Julia. Wagner will be hounding me but I'll ignore his calls until noon. Then I'm telling him to move on," Dax said, his professionalism blunt but effective. It was why Julia had hired him.

"I understand," Julia said as she turned to give Bess a hug and then walked away from the table, her mind in the clouds.

Playing the lead in a Heath Wagner movie was nothing to sneeze at. Julia of yore would have jumped at the chance.

"Where are they filming?" Julia asked Dax, suddenly realizing she was already at the front door and the rest of the dinner party had followed her.

"Toronto," Dax replied.

Ugh. Toronto in winter would be brutal. But perfect for a movie called *Coming Home*.

"Thanks for dinner, Bess. You'll be hearing from us soon, Dax," Ellis said as he led Julia out the door and into the car. He then rounded the vehicle and got into the driver's side.

"You okay?" he asked as he turned on the ignition and Julia wrapped her coat more tightly around her body.

Wait, how had she gotten her coat on? She really was out of it.

"Yeah. I think," Julia said as Ellis reversed the car and pulled onto the street.

"You're not worrying about me in all of this, are you?" Ellis asked.

Julia turned to look at her boyfriend. "Of course I am. I told you I'd go on tour with you."

"And I would never expect you to give up something like this to go on the road with me. Perks of dating another person in this kind of career, Jules—I get it. This is the role of a lifetime. You'll have the awards stacking up. But I also get it if you don't care anymore. You've walked away and you are a legend. That's why they're clamoring to get you back. Either way you do what you want, Julia. But do not let me get in the way. I'm with you, on either road. Your biggest supporter," Ellis promised and Julia leaned over to kiss him on the cheek.

She'd give him a better one when he wasn't traversing icy roads.

Julia fell back into her seat as her thoughts ran wild. Why

should she take this role? The reasons were endless. The cast would be a dream, she'd be acting out a script by the greatest on the planet, she'd be directed by a friend and man she admired. There was no way a movie like this one would flop. Heath would never let it. She trusted him to direct her to greatness. So what were her reasons to decline? She was comfortable right where she was at. Going on tour with Ellis. And she would miss him like crazy.

So there was only one question left: which option would she regret not taking? The answer was easy.

Because as much as she would hate missing Ellis while she was filming, it was something she could endure if she were busy enough. And heaven knew there was nothing busier than filming a movie. She wouldn't have to worry about Ellis because he'd be crazy busy doing what he loved as well. If they couldn't be together, this would be the next best thing.

Julia knew her answer. She was pretty sure she always had.

"Call him," Ellis said as he turned into Julia's driveway.

"What?" Julia blinked at him. She hadn't said a word.

"You've made up your mind and I'm proud of you, Jules. And you'd better believe you'll have the most handsome date on your arm at your premier," Ellis joked, bringing a laugh to Julia's lips.

She would miss him something fierce, but they'd be together again. Ellis wasn't a man who was going to disappear from her life. Julia had forever with him.

Julia was still chuckling as she picked up her phone and dialed Dax's number.

"Oh thank goodness," was how Dax answered the call and Julia laughed once more.

It looked like her time in the limelight hadn't quite come to an end. Julia Price was headed for the silver screen once more.

CHAPTER SEVEN

───────────────

ALEXIS TOOK a deep breath as she pulled into the parking lot of Marsha's condo complex with Jared in her passenger's seat and Brittany and Peter in the backseat. She knew her mom and Bill as well as Lou and her brood would be joining them soon. A big family dinner would hopefully keep Alexis from having too much one-on-one time with Marsha and Chad.

Marsha had called Alexis once more, trying to convince her to give Chad her mark of approval before this dinner, but Alexis just couldn't do it. Not when Jared and his kids were the ones who would suffer if she acted too hastily. Marsha had pouted and moped but Alexis hadn't really cared. She'd see him tonight and decide what she wanted to do from there. If she felt good about voicing her approval after one evening together then she would. If she felt she needed more time, she'd tell Marsha that. Alexis wasn't about to rush anything. Even if it would give her some peace of mind to not have Marsha hounding her.

Lou must have pulled into the parking lot at the same time because her kids were piling out of her car as Alexis, Jared, Brittany, and Peter were walking toward the condo entrance. Brittany broke away from the group to catch up to Emma while Peter lagged behind, eyes glued to his phone.

"Be ready to put that away," Jared warned Peter as they walked into the condo complex and waited for the closest elevator along with Lou and her kids. The younger ones were chattering excitedly while Brittany and Emma spoke in hushed tones about something Alexis was glad wasn't her business. She saw Lou eyeing them and knew she was on the case.

"Why?" Peter asked, stubbornly indignant as only a true teenager could be.

"Because this is supposed to be a nice family dinner," Jared said, clearly frustrated that he had to spell this out for Peter.

Alexis felt his grip tighten on her fingers as if he were calling for help. She sent him a grin that told him she was right there with him before he turned back to his son.

"But I'm on my phone at family dinners all the time. If Mom wants to bring her boyfriend to this one, that's her problem. I'm not ignoring my friends," Peter shot back.

Alexis could feel Jared tense beside her and the attention of all of the kids were now on them.

"Elevator," Lou called out in a way-too-cheery voice as one opened and she ushered all of the kids into it.

Alexis could see this wasn't how Peter and Jared should enter Marsha's. They needed time to resolve this situation before the dinner began.

"How about we wait down here for the next one?" Alexis offered and Jared nodded.

Peter was about to join his aunt and cousins but Jared laid a hand on his arm.

"What's up, Peter?" Jared asked as the elevator doors closed and Alexis pushed the up button once more.

"Nothing. I just don't see why we have to change because you and Mom date new people. You divorced. Whatever. You started dating Alexis. Whatever. Now mom's dating Chad. Whatever. Your lives. Why does mine have to change because yours did?"

Peter had a valid point but Alexis didn't say that out loud. At least not yet.

"Because we're family," Jared replied.

Jared's point was just as valid.

"And so what? That doesn't mean much from where I stand. Mom hates Alexis. You aren't sure about this Chad guy. Most families love one another. Ours can barely stand each other."

Alexis' heart hurt for the boy who was experiencing such upheaval. Brittany had acted out or voiced her opinions loudly. It was evident Peter had just as many. He'd just been silently holding them in.

Alexis squeezed Jared's fingers and looked up at him, silently asking permission. He gave a slight nod of approval.

"You know, families are weird. Sometimes they do hate each other," Alexis began, not sure this was the right route, but she was on it so here she went.

Peter sent her a skeptical eyebrow lift.

She didn't blame him.

"My Aunt Val hates my Uncle Simi. Like she kind of tried to kill him."

Tried to kill him? Jared mouthed to Alexis.

Yeah. She probably shouldn't have said that.

"Anyway, long story but Aunt Val is my aunt and I love her and Uncle Simi is my uncle and I love him. Their relationship doesn't dictate my relationship with either of them. It's separate. Even though we're all family."

Alexis hoped that she made sense. Thinking back, her reasoning wasn't bad, though it wasn't great either.

"Can I meet your aunt?" Peter asked, obviously intrigued. Of course that would be his takeaway.

"I'm sure one day you can, but today?" Alexis pointed at the phone.

"You want me to give Chad a chance because I love Mom and she likes him," Peter interpreted. He pressed his lips into a thin line and looked down at his phone. "But my friends are going through something right now. Can I just . . ."

Alexis looked to Jared as another elevator opened and the three of them got on. The elevators at Marsha's place were pretty danged slow.

Jared nodded once, telling Alexis he understood she was passing the parenting baton back to him. "Go ahead. Deal with that and then come in once you're done—and be ready to give Chad a chance."

"Thanks, Dad," Peter said with a grin before looking down at his phone, fingers flying.

The elevator finally dropped them off on Marsha's floor and they walked the short distance to Marsha's apartment as Peter lingered behind.

"Oh, and Alexis?" Peter said as Jared opened Marsha's door. "Mom is the only one who hates you. Me and Britt think you're pretty cool. Since according to you and Dad family can be weird, I guess you're a part of ours."

Alexis clenched her teeth to keep back a squeal of joy. Peter would hate it if she were overly exuberant.

"I guess I am," she said, hoping she sounded cool as Jared had to drag her into Marsha's because she couldn't move on her own.

Peter had just called her pretty cool and a member of his family. Did life get any better?

"Did you hear what he said?" Alexis whispered giddily as they entered Marsha's living room. She knew she should be greeting people and trying to help Chad assimilate into their weird family, but she couldn't bring herself to care about any of that for the moment. She was still back in that hall, floating on cloud nine.

"I did," Jared affirmed with a grin that was nearly as wide as Alexis'. He knew how much it meant to her to get his kids' acceptance. Heck, it meant the world to him as well.

"We have such a weird family," Alexis said in her best teenaged impersonation, causing Jared to laugh and Alexis to feel lighter than air.

Brittany and Emma glanced over at the pair, rolling their eyes, before going back to whatever they were talking about.

Alexis did a survey of the room, deciding it was time to descend from her cloud and join the party.

She noticed that Chad was in the middle of what looked to be a good conversation with her mom and Bill, the kids had gone straight to a snack table that Marsha had put out just for them, and Marsha . . . well, Marsha was marching their direction and judging by her frown, they were in trouble.

Oh, dear. What had they done wrong now?

As Marsha's eyes zeroed in on Alexis, she quickly realized it wasn't what *they* had done wrong. It was what Alexis had done.

"Where is Peter?" Marsha whispered urgently as she pasted on a thin smile and darted a look in Chad's direction. When she noticed he wasn't looking, the poor attempt at a smile slid off her face as she focused on Alexis.

"In the hall," Jared replied, bodily moving so that he was partially blocking Alexis from Marsha, putting himself between Alexis and whatever angry tirade Marsha wanted to direct toward her. Alexis loved that man. "One of his friends is having a problem and I told him to deal with it out there so that when he comes in he can focus one hundred percent on this family dinner."

Marsha's glare became a little less pronounced with Jared's

words but she still didn't look pleased. Alexis had a feeling the evening's fun had just begun.

"What's up, party people?" Lou asked as she joined them all, her body perpendicular to the standoff Marsha was trying to have with Alexis.

"Stop it with the pep, Lou. This is already a disaster." Marsha threw her hands in the air and then pasted that smile back on before turning on her heel to stand by Chad.

"What's with her?" Lou asked as she popped a pig in a blanket into her mouth.

Oh, were those at the snack table? Marsha might have a plethora of faults but she knew how to appetize a party and Alexis wanted to get over to that table ASAP. If she was going to endure Marsha's ups and downs she wanted to do it on a full stomach.

"Who knows?" Jared muttered. "I'm going to grab a drink. You two want anything?" he offered.

Alexis shook her head. What she wanted was at the snack table, not the bar.

"Maybe a bottle of water?" Lou asked.

"One bottle of water coming up," Jared promised before escaping.

Alexis didn't blame him. They all needed some downtime, because with the way Marsha was whipping things up there would be a storm coming soon and they needed to be prepared.

"I think she's just nervous." Alexis offered the only explanation she could. "She's worked all of this up in her head and wants it to be perfect. Peter not coming in yet isn't perfect so her illusion is already falling apart."

"Nice analysis," Lou admired. "I think my sister's sometimes neurotic behavior has pulled out a talent I didn't know you had. Pretty sure you have a future in psychology, girl." She winked.

Alexis balked. "Yeah, no thanks. I'll stick to cooking, thank you very much. Speaking of which." She angled her head toward the snack table. "Anything good out?"

"The pigs in blankets are amazing but they're going fast. The kids aren't touching the brie with cranberries but it's good too. Haven't had a chance to try anything else," Lou said as Alexis began walking toward the snack table. She knew Lou would follow.

"Alexis," Hazel squealed as she hugged Alexis' legs.

"Hey, Haze," Alexis said as she tried to lean down to give the girl a hug but it was a little awkward thanks to Hazel's height and the way she was wrapped around Alexis' legs.

"Cash, Aiden," Alexis added as the boys came running up, excitedly waving a tablet. She ruffled their hair and each pulled away as quickly as he could.

"Aunt Marsha said we could watch a show on the tablet. Can we, please Mom?" Aiden asked as Cash bobbed his head.

Hazel let go of Alexis' legs and rushed to her brothers' sides.

"I want to watch too," Hazel said with a giant smile.

Lou glanced from child to child before responding, "Fine. But you have to all agree on a show."

"*Fighting Ninjas!*" the boys cheered in unison as Hazel pouted.

"I hate *Fighting Ninjas*," the little girl declared.

Lou cocked her head as she looked down at them. "What did I say?"

"How about we watch *Pretty Ponies* for ten minutes and then *Fighting Ninjas* until dinner?" Aiden offered his sister.

"*Pretty Ponies?*" Cash groaned.

"We have to compromise, Cash," Aiden said, causing Alexis to bite down on her smile. He sounded so adorable and grown up at the same time.

"Fine," Cash muttered with a frown but at least he'd agreed.

Hazel beamed. "Okay, Aiden. I compromise," she proudly repeated the big word she'd just heard her brother say.

Aiden glanced up at Lou, who nodded, and the three scurried into one of the bedrooms. Alexis was sure it was the same place Brittany and Emma had escaped to.

"Compromise. Nice," Alexis said as she popped a cracker with brie and cranberries on it into her mouth.

Yum. Lou had been right. They were delicious.

"Yeah. It's been our lesson for the month. They were driving me nuts demanding their own way and I saw that I was yelling way more than I wanted to be. But then when I thought about it, I realized wanting our own way is totally human nature and the way we deal with it in the real world is . . . compromise," Lou said as she tried the bacon-wrapped green beans.

"Oh, these are good too."

Alexis took her advice and wasn't disappointed.

"Your sister sure can cook," Alexis said around her full mouth before adding, "you really are the best mom, Lou."

Lou shook her head. "Barely keeping my head above water but sometimes something I try to implement works."

Alexis wished Lou could see what she saw. Sure, Lou had to be making mistakes but most of the time? Her kids were happy and healthy. They mostly got along and they were gracious people. Heaven knew Harvey had little to do with that and Lou really was incredible.

"Just take the compliment, Lou. And maybe you'll finally see what the rest of us do," Alexis said as she nudged her shoulder into her friend's.

Lou smiled. "I guess I can try."

The women laughed but their mirth was cut off when Marsha seemed to materialize out of nowhere. "Are you two going to hide out here all evening?" she demanded in an urgent whisper.

"Of course," she said in a louder voice, followed by a trilling laugh as she latched her hands onto Alexis' arm and then Lou's in a death grip.

Of course what?

Alexis figured she'd never know because thanks to Marsha's yanking they were soon joining Chad, Bill, and Margie, whether they wanted to or not.

"Lou was just saying she needed a reintroduction. She said you two probably haven't spoken in years?" Marsha said to Chad in an overly sweet voice that sounded nothing like the woman who had been speaking to Alexis moments before.

Alexis tried to smile but she had a feeling she just looked like she had indigestion. Being this close to Marsha was doing all kinds of messy things in her stomach.

"Exactly what I was just saying," Lou lied through her teeth with a sickly half smile. Anyone who knew her would see right through her. Lou winced and Alexis would wager almost anything that Marsha had pinched her sister's underarm.

Chad seemed oblivious to the whole exchange and smiled as he held a hand out to Lou.

Lou gladly escaped her sister's grip to take Chad's hand and shake it.

"Good to see you again, Lou," Chad said before turning his attention to Alexis. "Alexis," he added with a slight nod of his head, his greeting rather cold for how close they'd once been.

"Why are we all standing around? This is a fun, informal family gathering. We should be relaxing," Marsha said as she waved her hands around to the couches just beside them, finally releasing Alexis.

Alexis wasn't sure about anyone else, but this was the least relaxed she'd been in months. Still, she wasn't about to turn down the opportunity to escape from Marsha and sit.

Marsha's couches were set up across from one another with

large armchairs on either side, making her living room seating one big square. Alexis took a seat as far from where they were standing as she could, hoping that would leave her on the fringes of the conversation, but when Lou sat next to her and Margie took the armchair closest to her, Alexis knew she was out of luck.

Sure enough, Bill perched on the armrest of Margie's chair, so Marsha placed herself just across from Lou and then Chad ended up in the seat directly facing Alexis.

Great, one awkward family gathering coming up.

Alexis glanced over and saw that Peter had come in. Jared was speaking to him in hushed tones by the door and Alexis had wished they could have been around when everyone was first getting seated. Anything so she wasn't so painfully aware that Chad wouldn't meet her eyes.

What had she done to the guy? She honestly had no idea but he evidently no longer considered them friends. But then again, hadn't he been the one to tell Marsha they'd once been close? Why do that and then act like this? It made no sense.

"So Chad, you're in finance?" Bill broke the silence and Alexis felt a rush of gratitude as he fell into easy conversation with Chad about his job and then the gym.

"I'm out of the daily operations for the most part now. Lou's taken over," Bill said with pride as he looked over at his younger daughter.

"And me," Marsha squeaked.

All eyes turned to Marsha, Chad the only one unsurprised by Marsha's exclamation. Marsha rarely went to the gym to work out, much less to actually work.

"I went in the other day and the front desk guy was chatting. I told him to get to work," Marsha said to the questioning eyes in the room.

Margie nodded as if that were explanation enough, but Lou

and Bill shared a look that didn't seem like it would end well for Marsha.

"I would appreciate it if you wouldn't reprimand my employees," Bill said, his voice light but his intent clear.

"*Your* employees?" It was obvious to Alexis that Marsha was embarrassed to be caught in whatever web she'd woven, but she really should let it go before she got further entangled. She was clearly trying to impress Chad, but pushing things now would only make her look worse. "Would you say that to Lou?" Marsha asked, her pitch just barely low enough for humans to discern.

"Lou works at the gym," Bill said matter-of-factly, as if he wasn't sure why they were still having this conversation.

Alexis saw her mom take hold of Bill's arm, a warning to let things go.

"So does Marsha," Chad interjected, standing up for his girlfriend.

Alexis cringed. What kinds of lies was Marsha telling now? Alexis slid back as far as she could, hoping she'd never have to enter this conversation.

"At my gym?" Bill asked with a chuckle before looking to Lou. "Have you seen your sister work there a day in your life?"

Margie's tugging on Bill's arm became more insistent as Lou's conflict showed in her face.

"Marsha is a very hard worker," Lou tried to answer diplomatically.

Margie nodded at that and Alexis hoped this would be the end of it.

"She really does care about the gym," Chad added.

Oh heavens, just shut your mouth, Alexis tried to telepathically tell Chad but he was still doing everything he could to avoid her eyes.

"Does she?" Bill couldn't help but ask.

"Of course. She knows she needs to put the work in if she wants to see her inheritance succeed," Chad said, his focus on Marsha. Almost as if he were repeating something he'd heard her say.

Alexis felt her eyes go wide. First, what the heck? Even if what Chad said was true, he really shouldn't be talking about inheritances, considering two people in the room would have to die before Marsha could gain that inheritance. Second . . . oh Marsha, stop with the lies.

"Her inheritance?" Bill's response was immediate.

"Daddy, can I—" Marsha began as she half rose from her seat but sat back down when it was evident Bill was going nowhere.

"The gym is Lou's. She has not only put sweat equity into it, but she's added her own capital so that she already co-owns the place. Marsha will have an inheritance but it definitely won't be the gym," Bill stated clearly, directing his words mostly at his eldest rather than Chad. He seemed to realize that this misunderstanding must stem from Marsha.

"Wait, you put money into the gym?" Marsha turned to Lou, her eyes narrowed.

"With Dad in semi-retirement, I'm taking over little by little. I felt it was important that I invest in the place so that it's fair that I get it one day. It only made sense," Lou replied as she too sank into the couch, probably sharing Alexis' wish that it could teleport her elsewhere.

"You don't even want the gym. You've never shown any interest in the place. All you've said about it to me is that anyone worth their salt wouldn't work out there. I thought it was an embarrassment to you," Bill said, appearing as lost as the rest of us, but still pressing forward with the conversation. Margie seemed to realize all of her tugging at Bill was for naught and released his arm with a resigned expression.

"So wait, if you don't work at the gym, where do you work?" Chad had joined the ranks of the confused.

That was why Marsha had lied. She didn't want Chad to know she did nothing all day and that Jared still supported her.

"Mom doesn't work," Peter interjected from his spot by the door, at exactly the wrong moment.

Marsha's face turned beet red as Chad focused on Peter.

"You must be Peter," he said because the two hadn't been introduced.

Peter nodded and then looked to his mom. "Mom stayed at home with us and since the divorce she didn't see why anything had to change." His gaze moved to his dad. "Right?" he asked Jared to clarify.

Chad's gaze bounced from Jared to Peter to Marsha.

Now that Jared and Peter were involved Alexis had to do something.

"Britt!" Alexis called out, startling the whole group but causing all eyes to move to her. "I just thought it might be nice to have Brittany out here too since Peter has joined us."

Alexis was trying to pretend that the conversation they were having wasn't as awkward as heck and that it would be pleasant to ask Brittany to join them.

"Yeah," Brittany came out of her room, Emma trailing behind her.

"Why don't you come hang out with us?" Alexis asked, pleading with her eyes.

Brittany shrugged before taking a seat in the chair on the other side of Marsha, Emma squeezing in beside her.

Jared moved across the room to sit next to Lou and Peter took the last armchair. Peter had definitely been right. One big, weird, awkward family.

"I'm going to get us some drinks," Marsha declared, jumping

up as soon as Peter sat. Probably hoping everyone would forget the last conversation by the time she got back.

Doubtful. Alexis had a feeling there would be many private discussions in the future. Chad with Marsha. Bill with Marsha. Maybe even Lou with Marsha.

But for now she believed everyone got the message that it was best to lay that topic of conversation to rest.

"Do you want anything?" Marsha asked Chad.

He nodded and Marsha left without asking what Chad wanted.

Alexis guessed Marsha already knew Chad's typical drink order. But it was still strange. Then again, what about this evening wasn't?

"So middle school, huh?" Chad said to Brittany after a moment of uncomfortable silence.

"Yup," Brittany said in her typical way.

"And I'm in high school," Peter added as if he was amused by the terrible approach Chad had taken with his sister. The last thing Brittany liked talking about was school.

"Brittany sings in the middle school choir," Alexis tried to add helpfully. Brittany might hate school but she loved choir.

"Nice," Chad said to Brittany before finally looking at Alexis for the first time that evening. "Alexis and I joined the choir back in high school."

"Oh gosh. I'd forgotten you were the one who talked me into that. You were so bad," Alexis recalled, taken right back to that year. It had been near torture to hear Chad sing but fun because she hadn't had to endure Mrs. Morowski on her own.

"So were you," Chad pointed out and they both began chuckling at the memories of their off-key attempt at vocals. "Remember when Mrs. Morowski asked you just to mouth the words?" Chad asked.

Alexis' mouth dropped open. Not because it wasn't true but

it was rude to tell others about it. But she was snickering soon after. "Remember when Allen Rutgers asked to be moved because he swore you made his eardrums bleed?" she shot right back.

Chad was now laughing as hard as Alexis and although others hadn't joined in the laughter the mood of the room had lightened.

"Mrs. Morowski was so mean," Lou added her two cents. Even though Lou hadn't been in choir, the teacher's strict demeanor had been legendary.

"Right?" Alexis replied. "She was especially hard on me."

"Because you couldn't hold a note in a handbasket," Chad teased.

"Hey!" Alexis replied, stepping forward to give him a friendly shove.

She noticed that everyone was enjoying the conversation but Brittany seemed particularly enthralled, her head shifting back and forth between the speakers.

"So you guys were friends when you were our age?" Brittany asked Chad and then turned to Alexis too.

"Yeah," Alexis said fondly. Chad's teasing had taken her back all those years to a time when he had been someone near and dear to her.

"Chad used to come to our house for dinner at least three times a week," Margie added.

How had Alexis forgotten that? She wondered if she'd been so hurt by Chad's sudden disappearance from her life that she'd pushed all of those memories to the back of her mind.

"You always made the best spaghetti," Chad said to Margie.

"And Alexis made the best everything else. She was always a good cook," Margie spoke glowingly of her only daughter.

"It was why I fell in love with her," Chad said quietly.

Everyone froze and his mouth fell open as he realized what he'd let spill.

Brittany gasped and Peter snickered. The adults all seemed unable to speak or move for a long moment.

"I mean, I had a huge crush on her back then, but she only had eyes for one guy so it didn't matter," Chad said as he looked to Jared, who seemed to be the first to unfreeze.

Alexis glanced at her boyfriend, grateful to see that he was now smiling, accepting the news easily. But that didn't surprise her. Jared was always telling her that every guy was in love with her but he was the only one lucky enough to have her. Thankfully he never got jealous because he knew how much Alexis loved him and only him.

"Wait, you liked Alexis in high school but Alexis liked Dad? I thought Dad went to high school with Mom?" Brittany asked as Marsha re-entered the room with two drinks.

"What did I miss?" Marsha asked, the smile on her face confirming that she hadn't overheard what Chad had said. And Alexis was going to do everything in her power to keep it that way.

"Not much," Alexis and Lou said in unison as Chad silently took the drink Marsha offered.

Marsha needed to be kept in the dark.

But before they could relay that message, Brittany said, "Did you know Chad had a huge crush on Alexis in high school?"

Marsha's smile immediately fell but she hastily tried to resurrect it. "Really?" she managed to grind out.

"But Alexis already loved Dad. Even back then," Brittany continued as if she were relaying an episode of her favorite TV show instead of news that really shouldn't have ever left Chad's brain.

"But Dad loved you in high school, right?" Brittany asked Marsha, who immediately nodded.

"Of course he did."

"That's not quite true," Jared countered, turning to Brittany though his eyes drifted to Alexis. "I did love your mom eventually but not way back then. I actually had a bit of a crush on Alexis too. I just didn't say anything because I was so focused on school. I didn't date anyone until your mom during college but if I had dated anyone in high school it would have been Alexis," Jared revealed.

Alexis' heart leaped with joy to hear Jared's affirmation. Then she glanced around at the ring of faces. Right, they had an audience. One that wouldn't appreciate that Jared had always kind of loved Alexis even if Alexis thought it was charming.

"So you would have rather married Alexis than Mom?" Brittany asked, one eyebrow raised in confusion.

Peter, who had used the tense conversation to pull out his phone, looked up as well.

"Nooo," Jared dragged on the word longer than he needed to, shifting from foot to foot. "Saying I would have rather done something makes it sound like I regret marrying your mom. And I can't ever regret that, because marrying your mom brought me you two," Jared said as he turned from one child to the other.

Marsha practically had steam coming from her ears and when she opened her mouth, Alexis held her breath.

"That's so *nice*. All of you were in love with Alexis but you stuck it out with me because of our kids," Marsha spat at Jared and then glared at Chad before storming out of the room.

Alexis blinked, trying to figure out how to salvage the situation. Judging by the stupefied expression on Chad's face he was considering the same thing.

Alexis turned to Jared and saw him glancing uneasily between his kids.

Yeah, things were a mess.

Lou suddenly stood. "I think we'd better head home. It's late and a school night," she said, even though it was barely past six o'clock and they had yet to eat dinner.

"Kids!" Lou yelled and for once all three appeared without question. Even Emma stood to follow. Alexis wondered if the tenseness in the room had spread throughout the house, considering the speed at which even the kids were ready to get out of there.

"I should probably . . . " Chad pointed toward where Marsha had gone.

Both Jared and Bill nodded, Jared because he was glad he didn't have to be the one to comfort Marsha this time and Bill because he wanted to see if Chad could manage the handful that was his eldest daughter.

"Say bye to Grandpa and Grandma Margie," Lou directed and the kids gave their hugs before waving at the rest of them and scurrying out the door.

"But I'm hungry," Alexis heard Cash whine.

"We'll get burgers and fries on the way home," Lou promised as she shut the door behind her.

Jared noticed the downward gazes of both of his children and stood, pulling Peter up from his chair so they could all sit on the couch Brittany was now solely occupying.

"You know you two are my world, right?" Jared asked.

Brittany pushed some of her dark hair behind her ear before nodding. Peter joined his sister.

"And as much as I love Alexis, I am so grateful to be right here, right now. I wouldn't trade a single minute of my life— the ones that brought me Alexis and especially the ones that brought me you," Jared said, pulling one child under each arm.

Brittany nuzzled into her father's side and Peter didn't pull away for once, and Alexis warmed at their affectionate response to their dad.

"But you hate Mom?" Peter asked in a low voice.

"Nope. Not at all. Sometimes I really don't like some of the things she does, but we all have times we really don't like people we actually love. But I do love your mom as the mother of my kids. And I have a deep respect for her. Though I'm not *in* love with her anymore. That's reserved for Alexis," Jared tried to explain a very adult concept.

"I think I get it," Brittany said and Peter nodded, pulling away and then looking toward the kitchen.

"I'm starving," Peter added, telling them all that he was just fine.

"Me too," Brittany said, following her brother's gaze. No way would this girl be talking about food if she was still upset, so Alexis counted both claims of hunger as a win.

"Should we try to serve what your mom made?" Margie offered as she stood from her seat.

The hallway door to the living room suddenly opened, Chad came through, and then he slammed it closed, causing everyone in the room to immobilize as they watched him hurry past them, coming to a halt before opening the front door.

"It was nice to meet you folks," he managed in a strained voice, but all could see that keeping a civil tone was difficult for him in that moment.

"Nice to meet you," came a bunch of murmured replies before Chad bolted, this time refraining from slamming the door.

Alexis looked at each face in the room, all a different variation of stunned, as Marsha emerged.

"This is all your fault!" Marsha screamed, stabbing a finger in Alexis' direction.

"Get them out of here." Jared glanced at his kids and then

Bill and Margie. Without a word, Margie grabbed a hand of either teen and led them to the door but Bill didn't move, looking like he planned to stay and referee whatever was about to go down.

"I've got her. Please go," Jared promised his ex-father-in-law and Bill nodded once before following Margie and the others out the door so that Jared and Alexis could turn their full attention onto the raging Marsha.

"Why do you have to ruin everything?" Marsha yelled and Alexis hoped the elevator was faster this time than it had been earlier. She really didn't want the kids hearing all of this.

"From what I've seen, Alexis has bent over backwards to accommodate you. She wanted to be able to sign her approval on the guy you've been seeing so she came to this dinner, knowing it was going to be awkward for her," Jared spoke calmly.

"It's only awkward because evidently she's been pining for both my ex and my boyfriend at the same time!" Marsha's voice only seemed to grow.

Alexis wasn't sure where she got that but it was time to speak up for herself. "I have feelings for one man and one man only," she stated clearly. She could have added *unlike the other woman in the room*, considering Marsha had cheated on Jared, but she was aiming for the higher road.

"Jared is all I've ever dreamed of and until tonight I hadn't seen Chad in years," Alexis said.

"That's what you'd like us to all believe, right? Pious, wonderful Alexis would never hurt a fly. Chad told me how you led him on for years and then when he finally got up the nerve to ask you out, you said no," Marsha spat.

Wait, what? Chad had asked her out? Alexis searched her mind but came up blank until . . . wait. Hadn't that been a joke? Chad had said it would be fun to go out, just the two of them, a few months before he'd started dating the woman who was now his ex-wife. She'd laughed and he'd joined her. The idea of dating Chad had been ridiculous. He'd been like a brother to her.

Or so she'd thought until today, with his admission of his crush on her and what Marsha was now saying. But had she led him on? She hoped not.

Wait, was that why he'd fallen out of her life? She'd never put two and two together.

"He told me you were the reason he took things so fast with his ex. He blames his entire marriage and divorce on you!"

Okay. Ouch. But maybe Alexis deserved it.

"Then why did he tell you he was friends with Alexis?" Jared spoke up.

Thank goodness Jared had. Alexis' mind was all one big jumble.

"Because he liked me so much and when I told him I was worried about how you'd react to him," Marsha said, directing her glare to Jared, "he told me about his past friendship with Alexis so she could vouch for him. He figured she owed him that much. And yet she couldn't even do that. I've never met anyone more selfish."

Alexis fought the urge to roll her eyes. That was rich, coming from Marsha.

"And now that I've met him I'm glad she didn't. That guy isn't ready for a relationship with our kids," Jared explained.

"How dare you?! And she is?" Marsha took swift, angry steps forward and jabbed her finger into Alexis' chest.

Alexis swatted at Marsha's finger as Jared took it and firmly pushed it back toward Marsha.

"Do not put your hands on her," Jared growled fiercely.

Marsha took a step back.

"None of this is her fault. And if you can't see that then you are blind. She worked hard to be kind to that man while he was saying all kinds of crap behind her back. Blaming his failed marriage on Alexis? Even I don't blame the entirety of our failed marriage on you and you cheated on me. Alexis just said no to a date," Jared spoke.

Alexis thought about adding that she hadn't even realized it was a true invitation but decided that wasn't important at the moment.

"I understand that you're upset. And I'm sorry that you're hurt. But this isn't Alexis' fault. You need to speak to Chad. You two need to work through your issues and then we'll see if he is ready to take on the responsibility of knowing our children. You might not like Alexis but you know she wants what is best for our kids. When I can say the same of Chad, I won't hold it against him if I don't like him. I just need to see that he cares for our kids."

Jared's rational way seemed to be getting through to Marsha because she nodded once.

"And you will never speak to Alexis in such a manner again. Until you are ready to apologize to her this is the last time I will speak to you about anything other than our children. I will pay you nothing above the alimony I owe you. You have disrespected the woman I love and I will not tolerate that."

Jared pushed Alexis behind him just in case Marsha reacted once more. But she merely folded her arms and gave him a contemptuous stare.

"Really? This is how you want to do this, Jared?" she asked.

"No. Not at all. But you've made your decisions so I have to make mine. What I would like to do is have a civil relationship with you. I want to know that you will respect the woman I love. But because you've chosen not to, now I've made my choice."

Marsha's eyes darted from Jared and she made a lunge at Alexis but Jared had anticipated her move and fully positioned himself between them. Alexis could only make out what Marsha was doing when she leaned far to the left but a moment later Jared shifted so Marsha was blocked once more.

"I need that extra money, Jared," Marsha nearly pleaded.

Alexis knew that without Jared's generosity Marsha would have to move out of the amazing condo she lived in.

"Then you have a choice," Jared replied simply.

"There's absolutely no way I will ever apologize to that—" Marsha began.

"Choose your words wisely," Jared warned.

Marsha seethed but ceased speaking.

"I can get the kids. Full custody," Marsha spoke quickly.

"You've tried and failed, Marsha. Do you really want to spend all of that money that you don't have to fail once more?" Jared asked, reminding Marsha that the judge had sided with Jared last time. With how unstable Marsha appeared on paper he'd probably side with Jared again.

Marsha closed her eyes as Alexis clutched the back of Jared's shirt. She just wanted to escape. Marsha had never liked her, but to go back to this?

Jared seemed to sense Alexis' tension and turned carefully, keeping Alexis in front of him as they walked toward the door.

"When will the money stop?" Marsha asked and Alexis knew she'd be getting an insincere apology before that time. But honestly Alexis didn't care about that. As long as Marsha didn't mess with the relationship she had with Jared and his kids, she could say whatever she wanted to about Alexis.

"Next month," Jared said before ushering Alexis out the door.

When the door closed, Alexis collapsed into Jared's arms, her tears kept at bay only because Marsha was still so close. But she couldn't continue forward without one good hug.

"I can't believe we're back here," Alexis whispered.

She was so tired of fighting Marsha.

"We're not back anywhere," Jared said into Alexis' hair.

"What if she turns the kids against me again?" Alexis asked, voicing her deepest fear. She'd been so thrilled just a short time ago when Peter had called her family.

"I'll make sure she doesn't. Marsha knows what will happen if she lies to them again. I have enough on her to get any judge to grant me full custody. I only let the kids see her for their sake. But as soon as it isn't good for them? She won't be seeing them or any of my money again. She knows that," Jared promised.

Alexis knew it was true but her fear had overwhelmed her common sense for a moment.

"I'm sorry. I wish I could give you a different life," Jared spoke once more.

Alexis shook her head vehemently. "What you said to your kids—it's the same for me. I have you and them now and I wouldn't change a moment of your past because of the present that I have. Even if it means dealing with Marsha's vitriol."

"You deserve better," Jared murmured against Alexis' ear.

"So do you," Alexis said.

Jared might not get the brunt of Marsha's wrath but he constantly put himself in her path in order to protect Alexis.

"I love you," Jared said, dipping his head to kiss the hollow of Alexis' neck.

"I love you," Alexis echoed just before Jared captured her lips, his kiss starting with an apology before growing to something more.

Alexis finally pulled back, her head feeling like it could float away.

And this was why every moment with Marsha was worth it. She would take a hundred Marshas if it meant she got to spend forever with Jared.

Jared took her hand and led her to the elevator.

"Can you believe Marsha told Chad she works?" Jared said as the elevator doors opened.

Alexis laughed and the last of the heaviness after Marsha's lies and Chad's accusations fled.

Life might get hard and wild but she knew with Jared by her side, Alexis would always wind up kissing, laughing, and enjoying even during the worst of times.

CHAPTER EIGHT

"NOW?" Jax asked as he looked up at the clock to see that the time Lou paid for was done. But they hadn't fit their lesson into that first half hour for months now. "I thought Cash didn't have a game today," he added, citing the one reason Lou was typically in a hurry to finish lessons.

"He doesn't. But Margie has the kids and she's had them so much recently. I just think it would be better to end lessons at this time," Lou said, looking anywhere but at Jax.

She didn't want him to see right through her lie. To know that she'd heard he was dating someone and that she was so petty that she couldn't spend extra time with him. But then again, she wasn't really being petty. It was more about self-preservation. Spending time with Jax like this made her hope for things that would never happen. She'd been a fool to ever hope for them in the first place. Men like Jax didn't end up with women like Lou.

"Hey Em, let's head out," Lou said, pressing the button that turned on the mic in the room Lou was in so that Emma, who was practicing in the recording booth, could hear her.

The only way she did this guilt-free was because Emma had

already finished her portion of the lesson. It was just Lou's one-on-one time with Jax that had been cut short. And right now Lou found that a necessity. Hopefully it wouldn't take her too long to get her head screwed on straight and accept reality, but until that time, Lou needed some space.

"Are you sure everything is okay?" Jax asked as they watched Emma gather her things through the window that looked into the recording booth. Well, Lou watched. She could feel Jax's eyes on her.

"Super. Fine and dandy. Wonderful." Lou was back to giving Jax three answers when she really just needed to supply one.

She exhaled in relief when Emma entered the side of the recording studio where Lou and Jax had been waiting. She needed to get out of there ASAP.

"Thanks for the lesson, Jax," she said as she ushered Emma toward the door.

"Why are we leaving so early, Mom?" Emma asked the question Lou had hoped would wait until they got to the car. She should have given Emma a heads up but she'd been so preoccupied with trying not to lose her lunch on the way here that she hadn't really thought things through.

"Grandma Margie shouldn't be left with your siblings for so long," Lou replied quickly, surreptitiously nudging Emma to move faster. A few more feet and they'd be out of there but it almost seemed as if Emma was walking backwards and the door was an elusive goal Lou couldn't quite reach.

"Grandma Margie just said she never has enough time with us," Emma said, her face scrunched in a way that Lou typically found adorable, but in that moment she couldn't quite enjoy it because from the corner of her eye she'd seen the way Jax had tensed. Lou had been caught in her lie.

"Em, can I have a minute with your mom?" Jax asked.

Lou ducked around Emma and rushed ahead; it was every woman for herself now. If Emma didn't want to leave with Lou, that was fine. But Lou couldn't just stand back and wait to have a minute with Jax. What would that do to her poor heart? The little sanity she had left?

"Lou." Jax's tone was filled with warning. He was daring her to leave, knowing he wanted to talk to her.

"Sure," Emma said as she looked from her mom to Jax. "Maybe you can figure out why she's been acting so weird."

Lou narrowed her eyes at her tween daughter. *Really, Em?*

Besides, Lou hadn't been acting *so* weird, other than trying to convince her daughter that she was too sick to go to lessons that day even though Emma had never been healthier. When that hadn't worked, Lou had attempted to convince Emma that Lou was too sick to go. She really needed to work on her fake cough.

Oh, and there was that day last week that Lou had driven two blocks out of her way when she'd seen Jax's car parked on Elliot Drive, but to be fair it had been parked by a swanky restaurant and Lou couldn't bear to see Jax with his date. It would have gutted her. Besides, Emma was the only one of her children who'd even noticed the detour. Lou had told her it was because the street she'd driven down instead was where the last of the autumn leaves were falling. Emma hadn't bought Lou's act but Lou had stuck with it. Lou's strongest point when it came to acting? She never gave up on a part. Ever.

"So weird, huh?" Jax asked as Emma grabbed Lou's keys from her hand and ran right out the door. *Now* the girl knew how to skedaddle.

Lou kept her gaze on the door even as she felt Jax's eyes boring into her back. He wanted answers. They were friends. And she wasn't acting much like a friend that day. But they'd always been friends with the idea that they were one day moving to something more—or at least that was what Lou had thought. And Lou wasn't sure how to make the transition to just friends. Not when she'd allowed her heart to get invested. Of course it was easy for Jax to move on; he was leaving just Lou behind, along with all her baggage. But Lou had to forfeit hope for a future relationship with Jax. Kind, funny, humble, sweet, and ridiculously handsome. Not to mention that accent she could listen to all day long. Smart, hard-working Jax.

It wasn't a wonder only one of them was having a hard time with this transition.

"Lou?" Jax's tone was soft this time. The question clear.

Lou bit her lip. She knew what she should say. What she'd overheard. But then she'd have to tell Jax all was well, she was happy for him and those were lies she wasn't ready to commit to yet. So she went with a version of the truth. Because by Jax's tone Lou could tell she'd hurt the man and the last thing she wanted was to hurt Jax. He'd been so good to her and her family.

"I'm just going through some things and need some space," Lou said, looking down at her feet and focusing on the fact that her shoes were far too scuffed considering she'd just gotten them two weeks before instead of on the man she was speaking to. Being alone with Jax in this place made her feel things she knew she shouldn't. Not if she wanted to walk away from this with any of her heart intact.

"From me?" Jax asked the question Lou should have been anticipating. But honestly she hadn't foreseen any of this. She'd just assumed Jax would be grateful for a way out. That Lou hadn't turned into one of those clingy women who couldn't let their crushes go.

"Not exactly," Lou said, feeling the words weren't quite a lie. If Jax weren't dating someone new she definitely wouldn't need space from him. But he was. So she did need space from him. Okay, her words had been a total lie.

"Is Harvey messing with you again?" Jax asked, his tone now more brusque, as if he wanted to get his hands on Harvey for Lou's sake.

"Always," Lou tried to joke. She made the mistake of glancing up at Jax and saw fire in his eyes. "I was joking. Badly, apparently. Things with Harvey are fine."

"You mean super, fine and dandy, wonderful?" Jax asked.

So he had caught that Lou had lost a few screws. Lou should have been embarrassed but the man had seen too many of her ridiculous moments for her to care . . . much. Her cheeks were a little warm.

"Not exactly," Lou proceeded. "He showed up at Emma's concert. It was wonderful for Emma. But his new girlfriend . . . "

"Felicia," Jax supplied, showing Lou the man paid attention. Why did he have to be so danged perfect?

"Felicia," Lou repeated, "she brought the kids' favorite snacks and bribed them to sit by her. My parents couldn't come so it was just me and I felt like I was getting a glimpse into my future."

Why was she unloading all of this onto Jax? Her cheeks had surpassed warm and were now flaming.

He just made her feel so danged comfortable.

"I'm sorry, Lou," Jax said as he reached out a hand.

She could not let him touch her. Lou stepped back out of Jax's reach and she saw the immediate hurt in his eyes.

She needed to get out of there. Jax was too kind of a friend and if she stayed she'd wind up hurting him or attaching herself. She couldn't allow either occurrence.

"Me too. I shouldn't have unleashed my inner dialogue on you," Lou said lightly as she kept taking small steps backwards. She should be bumping the door any moment.

"I didn't mind—" Jax began.

"I'm just weird right now. Like Em said. I just need . . . " Lou fumbled for the doorknob and turned, opening it and walking outside. She tried to close the door behind her. It felt like a good exit point but as she did, the door held firm.

Jax had moved with her and was holding the door open above her head.

"What do you need, Lou?" Jax asked the question with such sincerity Lou felt her knees buckle.

"I need to go," Lou managed to whisper before she turned and fled to her car.

She knew she was taking the coward's way out but she just couldn't do this anymore. It was too much. Jax was too much.

She craved him. Not just physically, but she wanted parts of him that he couldn't offer her. He could give friendship, but Lou craved a partner. Something she couldn't ask of a man she'd known for such a short period of time. So she'd run.

She'd have to face him at next week's lesson, but that was a problem for next week. For now she was doing all she could to maintain her dignity and sanity.

The question was how long she could do so. Because she had a feeling these growing feelings she had toward Jax wouldn't just disappear . . . and then what?

LOU SMILED as she breathed in the brisk evening air mixed with pinecones and the scent of fried foods. That smell could only mean one thing on Whisling. It was the night of the elementary school's Winter Carnival.

She had been on the board of the PTA in past years but had taken a break when she'd had to go back to work fulltime. However, the current board knew of Lou's willingness to help so when big events like this happened, she often found herself signed up for multiple shifts.

First she'd worked the funnel cake booth and she had the burn on her arm to prove it. Then she'd moved on to the dunk-a-teacher booth. It was a chilly one even though the booth was inside the school cafeteria. But that particular station made the school tons of money so the teachers were willing to suffer the cold. Lou loved teachers.

After that shift she'd had an hour off and had met up with her parents and Alexis, who were on babysitting duty for Lou's kids. And honestly, after an hour with her own kids Lou figured she'd gotten off easy with all of the shifts at the booths. Especially this last shift because she'd be at the decorate-your-own-winter-scene booth, an activity known for being less attended as the evening went on. The little kids did seem to love it, but by eight pm when Lou had been assigned her shift, those little kids were either going home or tucked into strollers for the rest of the evening. Plus, the tent was outside and when the sun was still out, especially with the space heaters they'd placed here and there, the temperature wasn't bad, but now that night had set in, even with the space heaters, things had taken a turn for the nippy. Lou had a feeling she'd be doing a whole bunch of nothing. But after participating in the cake walk with Hazel six times until she'd finally won a cake, a bunch of nothing sounded right up Lou's alley.

"We haven't seen a single kid in thirty minutes," said Jan, the mom who had the shift before Lou, as she handed off the reins. Which just meant pointing out to Lou the two winter scenes the kids could choose from as well as where the extra boxes of crayons and cannisters of glitter were kept just in case a huge influx of kids came in and the four dozen crayons and two cannisters of glitter on the table weren't enough. "I sent Doug over to Santa's Village. I figured they needed the help," Jan said about the man who'd been assigned to the booth with her. "He's supposed to be with you for this shift as well but I told him you'd probably be fine on your own. You can just text if you need him."

Lou nodded as she took in the completely empty tent. Yeah, she had a feeling she wouldn't be texting Doug.

Now that darkness had set in, the twinkle lights on the tent made the place appear cozy, but Lou was already chilly and doubted anyone would be foolish enough to send their kid out here to color. It was debated every year where the winter scene should be but with so many booths that needed to be inside of the school the coloring booth often got booted; it just didn't take priority. Besides, the glitter the kids seemed to get everywhere drove the custodians nuts. It was better to keep this sort of mess outside. So Lou would stick it out here with the space heaters and the fried food booths. The other messy booths. But at least in the food booths the fryers kept the attendants warm.

Any feelings of envy vanished, though, when Lou glanced at the gigantic lines for the corndog and funnel cake stations. She'd take the cold but empty booth any day.

"I'm off to the corndog booth," Jan said with a groan. "Do you think we could convince H&H to *not* donate their generator next year?" She and Lou shared a smirk. The only reason the PTA was able to have the fried food booths was thanks to the kind donation of the local company.

"Don't wish for that, Jan. Because you know who will be on the committee to find a new generator if you do," Lou joked.

Jan laughed as she nodded. "Touché. Helen would never allow a winter carnival sans fried food," Jan said about their PTA president.

"The kids *love* it." Lou parroted the line Helen was notorious for saying anytime she wanted to go above and beyond what the rest of the PTA wanted to do.

Jan continued to chuckle as she walked away, leaving Lou alone.

Well, not really alone. The funnel cake and corndog booths really weren't that far away but it did seem like she was off in this corner of the field all on her own.

Lou dragged one of the chairs as close as possible to the largest of the space heaters. It was also right next to the tarp that had been hung in the direction of the food booths since that was where the strongest wind came from. She dug through her bag to look for the blanket she'd packed—she'd prepared for this shift—and after Lou wrapped that around her shoulders, between the tarp, space heater, blanket, her jacket and gloves, she really was actually quite comfortable. With the sound of Christmas music coming through the speakers that had been set up outside as well as the chatter of families it was quite cozy and Lou was taking note to sign up for this booth every winter carnival during this shift.

"So how does this work?"

Lou's eyes sprang open. She hadn't even realized she'd let them shut.

At first she'd wondered if she was dreaming. That voice haunted her dreams often enough. But then she remembered where she was and the fact that she wasn't really asleep . . . Lou jumped out of her seat, her blanket falling to the ground.

Her first thought was to run. She was supposed to have a good three days before she had to see the man again. She still hadn't come up with a game plan on how to keep her heart while not being completely aloof.

Right now she had nothing.

But she couldn't run. She was in charge of this empty tent. Maybe no one was here now, but Helen would surely be around at some point and if she saw that Lou had abandoned her post?

So she had to stay here. Woman up. What had Jax asked? Right, how this worked.

"Um," Lou looked at the table she'd been assigned, glancing from the broken crayons to the red and green glitter everywhere as she carefully kept her eyes from meeting Jax's.

"You can pick a scene." Lou pointed at the two options.

But Jax wasn't actually here to color a picture, was he?

Lou finally worked up the nerve to peek at the man in question and immediately wished she hadn't. His dark hair had been swept under a hunter green beanie, the same color as his beautiful eyes. A shirt of the same color peeked out from under his black jacket and his cheeks were slightly flushed as if he'd been out in the cold for a while.

Why did he have to be so gorgeous? And why did he have to be here?

"I didn't really come to create a—" Jax scrutinized the banner that had been hung on the tarp next to Lou. "—winter wonderland scene."

Lou had guessed as much. But pretending that was better than blurting out her question, asking why he was there.

"Really? Because once you finish one you can hang it up in the hall until Christmas break. Just imagine, your art gracing the halls of Whisling Elementary," Lou grinned, joking because that was the way she dealt with everything hard in her life. Pretending she didn't have deep, growing feelings for Jax was hard. Really hard.

"Lou," Jax said, shaking his head as if he couldn't understand why she was joking. He obviously realized it was a way for her to keep her distance, and what else should she be doing? He was dating another woman. And she was trying to make peace with it. What more could he want from her?

"Why are you here?" Lou finally asked the question she'd

been trying to politely sidestep before she could lose her ever-loving mind.

"You mean besides trying to find time with you alone?" Jax asked, causing Lou's heart to flip.

No! Lou ordered her heart. *No flipping for this man. You will only break.*

"Cash texted me about the carnival last week. I promised him I'd come so here I am," Jax said.

"Cash texted you?"

Cash didn't have a phone. None of her kids besides Emma did.

"From Margie's phone," Jax explained.

"My kids invite you to things?" Lou asked, trying to wrap her mind around what was happening.

Jax nodded. "Not all the time. Just to things they think will be fun for me."

Lou chuckled. Of course Cash thought an elementary school carnival would be fun for Jax. But still . . . Margie knew about this and hadn't told Lou?

Granted, Lou had been so weird about Jax since the concert that Margie was probably trying to avoid an awkward situation. She could see Cash begging to text Jax and Margie allowing it, but then not knowing how to tell Lou. But speaking to her would have been better than just having Jax show up. The way he had.

Unless Margie had doubted Jax would come. Because what grown man in his right mind came to an elementary school carnival—unless there were people here he wanted to spend time with?

Did Jax want to spend time with Lou?

Her heart began to lift.

Nope. He was here for her kids. He'd come because Cash

had asked. He was simply a nice man, taking compassion on some kids whose dad wasn't here.

But if he was here for the kids, why was he here, alone, talking to Lou?

Her poor mind was playing a game of ping pong and losing big time.

Lou decided it was time to be straight. Beating around the bush hadn't worked. Giving herself time hadn't worked. And she really was being selfish. Her kids loved Jax. If she pushed him out of their lives because she couldn't have what she wanted with him, what kind of mom did that make her?

Not one Lou wanted to be.

So it was time to put on her big girl pants. Tell Jax the truth. Get over it. And move onto being just friends. Because Lou knew she wouldn't be able to act normal until she got everything off of her chest.

"Well, I'm glad you came," Lou said, meeting his eyes as she gave up the pretense, finally choosing full honesty. She *was* glad that Jax had come. It had reminded her of the things that mattered, things she'd ignored because of her foolish crush. She wasn't a young girl who could follow her own whims. She was a woman with responsibilities and children who needed her. If Lou acted weird that could mess things up with Emma's lessons. Cash loved that Jax came to his games. Aiden often asked when Jax could start teaching him guitar. Hazel wanted to know if Jax could come over to play playground (a game in which Jax was the swing, slide, and monkey bars all in one). For her kids, she was glad. For herself she was a little embarrassed but she'd get over it.

"Are you? What's going on, Lou?" Jax asked, concern etched on his face.

Lou dropped her eyes. She couldn't look at that gorgeous face as she spoke. She'd trip up—or worse, lie again—so that she wouldn't feel so ridiculous. She turned her attention to the table, focusing on a green crayon that lay in three pieces as she spoke. "I was just being silly. I heard you're seeing a woman here on the island and I freaked out a bit. I took what you said at that soccer game a little too seriously and my heart . . . anyway, I'm realizing how absurd I've been. You are a friend. Who you date shouldn't change that," Lou said, feeling lighter after her last words. She should have been truthful from the beginning.

"What?" Jax asked and only then did Lou look at her friend.

His eyebrows puckered adorably under his beanie as a frown covered his face.

Lou pushed aside the thought that she'd love to kiss that frown away. They were friends.

"Lou, I—I don't even know where to start."

Lou felt her cheeks flame once more. He hadn't realized he'd caused her to fall for him. He'd probably meant little by what he said at that soccer game. Oh dear, did he even remember what he'd said? Every word was etched into Lou's brain forever, so she hadn't even considered that he could forget.

"It's not like I was in love with you. It was a crush. Kind of a big one, but have you seen yourself? Of course I would have a crush on you after you've been so nice to me and so wonderful to my children. Really this is all your fault." Lou sputtered to a stop. She hadn't just said all of that out loud, had she?

Mortified, she sank back into her seat, lifted the blanket off the ground, and pulled it over her head. Where were those giant meteors threatening Earth when you needed them?

"Lou," Jax said as she felt a tug on the blanket.

No, she couldn't face him. Not tonight. Couldn't he just walk away? Then they could pretend this whole thing never happened when she saw him next—because she'd have to see him if she wanted to be the kind of mom her kids deserved.

But tonight . . . couldn't he let her die of humiliation just for this one night?

"Lou." The tugging became more insistent.

Jax clearly wasn't going anywhere so Lou pulled the blanket down, her hair now covering her face.

Mortified didn't begin to cover what Lou was feeling. And she'd just covered herself with a blanket. Like a five-year-old terrified of monsters. Even Hazel knew blankets couldn't actually protect you from anything.

Lou felt Jax's hand gently brush her hair away. First he tucked it behind one ear, then the other, his fingertips brushing the tops of her ears and sending shivers down her spine.

"I know you don't know me well, but I don't go around making declarations of liking to all of the women on the island."

Lou knew Jax was attempting a joke to help Lou feel a little less humiliated and she loved him even more for it.

"Stop being so perfect," Lou pouted.

Jax laughed.

"I mean it. I'm trying to keep my heart locked away in this chest that I put it in after Harvey and each time I see you it threatens to burst out. It isn't fair."

"I think it's perfectly fair. Considering you're doing the same thing to my heart."

Lou's eyes shot up to Jax's, searching for any signs of humor but she didn't see any. But he couldn't be serious.

"Lou, I'm not dating any other woman. First, I told you that I liked you, that I want to date you as soon as you stop taking lessons from me. I take that as a commitment to you."

"But I was dating other guys."

Other guy was more like it and it had been horrible, but still, Lou had gone on a date.

"And I hated every minute of it. But I understood that. I

didn't want you to put your life on hold for me and my standards. You're getting over a terrible divorce."

"Over it," Lou interrupted. "The second I met you I was so over it."

Jax laughed once more.

Lou bit her lip. She loved making Jax laugh even if it was at her expense.

"Well, good. You're over your divorce."

Lou nodded.

"And second, I can't imagine even wanting to date another woman after meeting you. You said you have a big crush but what I feel for you is already so much more than that," Jax said. He was crouched so that he was eye level with Lou as she sat on her chair. "I guess I didn't make it clear before but I'm waiting for you, Lou. However long it takes, I want you and only you."

Lou's heart tripped as her eyes went wide. She'd never been pursued in such a way. And by such a man.

Jax met her eyes and held them until Lou had to look away; the feelings growing between them were more than she could handle.

"I might have been a little less than honest when I said big crush." Lou directed her words toward the tarp. "But saying I was already falling for you while I thought you were dating someone else felt a bit stalkerish."

Jax chuckled.

"How could I do anything but fall for you, Lou? You're brave, funny, brilliant, you never let life get you down, you put everyone before yourself and . . . I'm going to stop there to keep from appearing a bit stalkerish myself," Jax said.

This time Lou laughed.

"This is why you were acting so weird? Who told you I was dating someone?" Jax asked as he stood and brought Lou up with him. His arms wound their way around her waist, bringing her closer to him than she should be, considering they weren't supposed to date.

"I overheard it at Emma's concert," Lou said, glancing down because looking into Jax's eyes when they stood like this would overwhelm her.

"So that was why the concert felt so lonely," Jax said, his voice full of sweet understanding even as his chest puffed out with pride. "Don't get me wrong, I hate that you were feeling alone, but I'm thrilled to know that all you needed was me to make things better."

Had Lou thought he was humble? She was taking that one back.

"Well, I was mostly lonely because I didn't have my kids sitting with me." Lou shared a semi-truth. But she needed to keep Jax's head from swelling too big.

"But your kids were back with you by the end of the concert, right? The person you were really missing was me," Jax said with a cocky shrug that pulled Lou in closer.

He wasn't wrong. And even arrogant Jax was super-hot. With them this close Lou couldn't help thinking that if she just tipped her head back the smallest degree . . .

If she thought she'd craved Jax before, she'd had no idea. Now that she stood within his embrace, every part of her wanted Jax even closer.

She shook her head, trying to free herself from her Jax-induced fog, and somehow found the willpower to step away.

Jax groaned.

Lou chuckled. "I feel the exact same way, but I want our first real kiss to mean the beginning of us. I want to show you that I'm supporting your standards."

"Standards, smandards," Jax joked, showing Lou she wasn't the only one who could be juvenile. And she loved it.

But as she gazed at Jax, so ruggedly appealing in a way that had Lou's entire body heating, she reconsidered everything. One kiss wouldn't be a big deal. They could pretend they'd found some mistletoe, even though Lou knew for a fact the PTA didn't put up the stuff—it had caused too many issues in past years.

You're at the elementary school. The thought pierced Lou's mind and she wanted to push it away but her subconscious was right. Anyone could see them if they gave into temptation right then, and wasn't she staying away from him for Emma's sake?

And it was only with that mother's strength that Lou took one final step away, her breathing quick as she watched Jax's chest match pace with hers.

"So we're back where we started?" he asked.

"Not exactly. I probably won't be so weird again. At least until I hear another rumor about some other woman you're dating," Lou joked.

But Jax was completely serious as he shook his head. "Doesn't work for me. I don't ever want you to doubt what I feel for you. Even if I can't show it yet."

Lou understood that. She didn't want Jax to doubt what she felt for him either.

"Maybe if we talked to one another more than we do. I mean, I hate to admit this but I was kind of jealous that Cash texted you when I don't even really do that," Lou said, knowing that communication was key in any relationship. Conversing more, even if just by text, could only help her and Jax, right?

Jax smirked.

"What?" Lou asked.

"I made you jealous twice in one night. Got to say that's good for the ego."

Lou smacked his shoulder.

"But how about this? I promise to text you twice as much I text your kids, combined," Jax said as he laughed.

Lou sighed, but she was ready with a comeback. "I guess I could agree to that. But that means I'll have to up the amount of texts to the other guys I'm dating. It's only fair."

Jax mouth dropped open before he dragged his fingers across Lou's side, causing her to yelp and then laugh.

"No tickling!" she demanded, swiping at him but missing as he easily dodged her.

"No texting other men," Jax raised his eyebrows.

"Really?" Lou asked. This was a huge step for them. They weren't actually dating but they were promising themselves to one another at a future point when they could. "Isn't this the same thing as dating?"

Jax shook his head. "When we're dating, you'll know it."

Lou's stomach took a leap at those words.

"This is a commitment to be friends who are there for one another but don't date other people," Jax replied.

"Sounds like dating to me," Lou said with a shrug.

"That's because you haven't dated me. Yet."

Her danged stomach took another tumble.

"Does that work for you?" Jax asked, his smoldering eyes looking as if he were mere moments from throwing his no-dating-students rule right out the window.

Lou nodded her agreement, Jax's intense gaze making her feel a bit smug and a little like a temptress. "But I think that maybe we should seal our agreement with a kiss."

"What happened to standards?" Jax teased with the kind of smirk that begged to be kissed away.

"Mom! You found Jax!" Cash's happy voice called out to them and Lou looked over her shoulder to see her entire family coming out of the elementary school's doors.

Thank goodness she hadn't actually kissed Jax. If they'd been caught in the act by her kids? She wasn't ready to answer the kinds of questions that would have brought up.

When she turned back to Jax she saw relief evident on his face as well but then he leaned in close one last time.

"I guess you'll have to tempt me again another night." Jax's words and entire demeanor promised more nights like this to come. Because with the interesting commitment they'd just made to one another, they had more time. Lots of it.

Lou grinned. She couldn't wait.

CHAPTER NINE

NORA JUST HAPPENED to be painting on the afternoon that Aiden Christensen was set to arrive. She also just happened to tell Jenny, who was manning guest check-in, that Nora needed to be told the moment Aiden pulled onto the property.

"He's here!" an out of breath bellboy said as he sprinted back the way he'd come before Nora could follow.

Aiden Christensen was here. Nora had been alerted. But now came the hard part: somehow getting Elise to the lobby so that she could be there to greet Aiden. Nora knew Elise had resolved to spend most of the next ten days avoiding the heartthrob so she wouldn't fall even harder. But that didn't work for Amber and Nora. Not when they saw the possibility of something promising between the sister they loved and a really great guy. She and Amber had worked hard to formulate a plan to get Elise to show up for Aiden as he arrived, but with Elise knowing exactly when Aiden was due to check in, they were sure she'd see through any excuse. So here they were—Aiden was checking in and they were no closer to getting Elise to deconstructing her wall.

But sitting here, thinking about all the ways they'd failed, would help nothing. So Nora jumped up and flew down the hall that led to the check-in desk, nearly colliding with Amber in her haste.

"He's here," Amber said breathlessly.

Nora grinned at her daughter, who was sounding and looking more like herself every day. Aiden's plans had put a new pep in Amber's step and Nora would forever be thankful to the man for that, whether or not anything happened between him and Elise.

"Where's Elise?" Nora asked.

"Hiding," Amber said as she glared toward the ballroom. "She's insisting that she has to go over Genevieve's plan for seating during the ceremony right now."

"But Genevieve doesn't need that to be done for a few days?" Nora guessed.

"On the nose. Poor girl has been so stressed about Aiden coming that she's worked twice as hard and now she has nothing to keep her occupied so that she can avoid him. She really didn't think things through," Amber replied with a grin.

Nora grinned right back.

"Well then, I guess it's up to us to convince Elise that she really shouldn't be wasting her time doing something that could be done later when an important guest has just arrived," Nora decided.

"You read my mind," Amber said as the two fell into step beside one another and entered the ballroom.

"If we put twelve people there it won't be symmetrical with the other side," Elise said as Nora and Amber came close. Almost as if she were making up something to say just so that she sounded busy.

"I wasn't suggesting twelve. I said ten," replied Hillary, one of the new employees the inn had hired just for the wedding, her head tilted in confusion.

"Right, ten. Ten would work," Elise replied as she made a show of marking something off on her clipboard.

"Can I see that?" Amber asked, pointing at Elise's clipboard as they approached.

Amber and Nora both knew that if Amber could get Elise's clipboard they'd be able to easily point out that Elise really had nothing urgent to do and she'd have no real reason to avoid welcoming Aiden to the inn.

"This? Oh no." Elise clasped her clipboard protectively against her chest.

The women all looked up at the sound of footsteps entering the room and Nora brightened when she realized who had just joined them. She stepped back from the girls to greet Mack.

Elise and Amber went right back to their bickering.

"Why not?" Amber asked, trying to get a hand on the clipboard as Elise took a giant step away.

Mack sidled in beside Nora before giving her a sweet kiss. "He's here," he whispered in her ear.

Nora nodded. "We're trying to get her out there," she whispered back.

Mack grinned.

"How did you know just when to get here?" she asked Mack, keeping one ear on the girls' conversation as Elise explained, "It's the master checklist. Amber, this is my copy. Don't you have your own?"

"I asked Marv down at the ferry to let me know when Aiden got off," Mack said, as if it were obvious.

"You are ridiculous," Nora said, but secretly she was loving that Mack wanted to be here as well. He loved being involved with all of this stuff and Nora loved that he loved it.

"I'm doing this all for you," Mack whispered, his eyes wide

with mock innocence. Both of them knew the truth: he'd have major FOMO if he hadn't come up to the inn. "Because now we've got another set of ears and eyes. We won't miss a thing." Mack looked from Amber to Elise before sending his eyes in the direction of the lobby where Aiden was.

Nora nodded and shook her head fondly at his joking, squeezing his hand to show Mack she was thrilled he was there with her, but their conversation didn't continue as they both turned their attention to the girls.

"You're right. I do have my own list. And according to it, you are days ahead and we really don't have anything we need to be doing," Amber said.

"The seating arrangement," Elise protested in a scandalized voice, waving a hand over what she was doing right then.

"That isn't due to Genevieve for a week," Amber countered.

"But it doesn't hurt to be prepared," Elise said stubbornly, hugging her clipboard even closer to her chest.

"It does hurt if it means neglecting other parts of our job. Like greeting VIP guests." Amber nodded toward the lobby.

"But I'm busy here. Surely you can do that," Elise said as she looked down at her clipboard.

"Busy with stuff that can wait. And our VIP guest asked specifically for you. What does it say to him if you don't show?"

"That he can't command a woman to greet him when he comes to her place of business?" Elise countered with a sassy raised eyebrow.

"He didn't command anything. He asked nicely."

"Meaning he'll be fine if I'm not there."

"Elise!"

"Amber!"

The two women stared at one another until more footsteps sounded by the door of the ballroom.

Smart Hillary took that moment to slip out.

"Knock knock," Jenny said loudly, taking in the showdown between the sisters. "When I told Mr. Christensen that you two were hard at work preparing for his friend Genevieve's wedding, he insisted that he stop here first before going to his room."

Nora grinned approvingly at Aiden's bold move but bit down on her lip to hide it before glancing over at Elise. She would not be pleased that he'd thwarted her plans. But instead of glaring at Aiden like Nora had expected, she saw that Elise's gaze was pinging off nearly every part of the giant room before landing on her clipboard once more. Aiden's gaze, on the other hand, was steady. Right on Elise.

"So good to see you again, Aiden," Amber said as she walked forward to greet their guest.

Nora had also noticed that Aiden wasn't alone. With him was another man Nora knew on sight. Joshua Baker had graced both the big and little screen, a household name much like Aiden.

Aiden gave Amber a hug before turning to his friend. "Amber, this is Josh. Josh, Amber. When I told Josh about this place he wouldn't stop pestering me until I let him come along."

"More like Aiden couldn't stop talking about how amazing it was up here and I thought he'd lost his mind. It was either bring me with him or I'd have him committed," Josh teased right back.

Both men smiled and Nora had a feeling they'd be a delightful addition to the inn this holiday season.

At least as long as paparazzi didn't get a whiff that they were staying here. Two eligible Hollywood bachelors at the inn? Nora had a feeling if this got out they'd be dealing with a whole slew of single women.

"Nice to meet you, Josh," Amber said as she offered the actor her hand.

Josh's eyebrows rose slightly as he took in Nora's beautiful daughter. Nora didn't blame him. Mack seemed to notice Josh's interest as well since he took a step forward.

Nora put a gentle hand on her boyfriend's arm, reminding him to chill out.

Mack's shoulders eased a bit but he still seemed ready to protect Amber even if she didn't need it.

"And this is Nora, Mack, and Elise," Aiden introduced, gesturing to each person as he spoke their name.

Nora noticed the way Aiden lingered over Elise's name as well as the way Josh appraised her, the way any man would do if his friend was interested in a woman. Aiden was talking to his friends about Elise. Didn't that prove he was more invested than Elise tried to pretend?

Josh shook Nora's hand and Mack's—Nora noticed Mack's grip was firmer than it needed to be—and then Elise's.

"It's good to finally meet all of you. I've heard a lot about the proprietors of this lovely inn," Josh said as he looked at Elise.

Elise gave him her best professional smile. "We love it when word spreads about our inn."

"They've put a lot of work into it." Nora couldn't help bragging a bit about her girls.

"I can see that," Josh said as he stepped back and surveyed the ballroom. "The fact that Gen wants her wedding here speaks volumes. And from what I've seen of the place I can't blame her. It's absolutely stunning."

Nora was a fan of this guy.

"Maybe you could show us around?" Josh asked Elise innocently.

Aiden couldn't hide his smile.

"Um, well, I was in the middle—"

"Of something that can wait," Amber said decisively, linking her arm through Josh's and setting off.

Nora knew what her role was and she hurriedly took Mack's hand to follow Josh and Amber, leaving Aiden and Elise on their own.

Even if Elise was loathe to admit it, she really liked Aiden. She was just scared. The man was a Hollywood icon. The kind of man women went crazy for. Elise didn't trust that he really wanted to settle down, that he wouldn't move on as soon as he found something more interesting. And while neither Nora nor Amber could be sure, he'd made his intentions clear time and time again. They were convinced Elise should at least give him a chance.

"Should we join them? Or I could help you with your work?" Nora heard Aiden offer as she and Mack walked away.

Nora pretended to wipe at the side of her mouth to hide her giant smile. This guy was good.

She and Mack hurried ahead, catching up to Josh and Amber to give Aiden and Elise some alone time.

"But he's not a player?" Nora heard her daughter asking softly.

"How many names have you seen him connected to in the tabloids?" Josh asked, turning to Amber even as they continued walking.

Nora considered that question along with Amber.

"Lola Nolan," Amber finally said, naming the actress Aiden had dated years before.

"And no one since. Lola did a number on Aiden. He didn't really date after her for a while. But then he came back from Gen's wedding shower and I could tell he was changed. He'd really connected with someone. That's why I had to come up with him. I don't want another Lola. But your sister seems as far from Lola as a woman could get. Lola threw herself at Aiden till she wore him down. Your sister acts like she can't even see him."

The way Josh cocked his lips told Nora that he wasn't sure if Elise was better than Lola, or just different.

"She's scared," Amber defended Elise.

"She doesn't need to be. Aiden really likes her. And isn't his coming back here when she's done nothing but ignore him indication enough that he's invested? If he were dating her, trust me, nothing would get in the way. Distance, time—he'd find a way to make it work."

Amber was quiet as she mused on that.

Nora appreciated Josh's frankness.

"Do we trust the kid?" Mack whispered to Nora, tipping his head toward Josh.

Nora wasn't positive but she thought she did. Josh gave off a good vibe and everything he'd said felt true so far. Why would Aiden work so hard to get to know Elise if he was going to play her? There were much easier targets that wouldn't involve traveling to an island.

"If she does," Nora replied with a glance at Amber.

She realized all of this was really up to Amber and Elise. Whatever they decided, she'd go along with it. Unless she saw any major red flags. She'd learned from Raul when and when not to keep her mouth shut.

"How do I know Aiden didn't put you up to saying that?" Amber replied. "He knows how close I am to Elise."

Josh nodded. "He does." He then shrugged. "I guess you just have to trust him or me or both."

Amber pursed her lips. She didn't like that answer but she knew she had to accept it.

The four of them walked in silence, each deep in their own thoughts, before Josh came to a stop.

"Did you guys get that made just for Gen's wedding?" He pointed to a statue that was a miniature of the original in

Denmark—something Gen had indeed commissioned just for her big day.

"You know Gen well," Amber said, pausing to give Josh a once over. Nora knew she was still trying to decide if she should trust him.

"I've worked with her and she is definitely one to make her own opinions known." Josh chuckled.

"Why didn't you come to the shower?" Amber asked, almost as if she were testing him. Knowing how protective her daughter was of Elise, she probably was.

"I took the last possible flight to Seattle because I was filming and my plane got delayed. Gen would have killed me for missing the party if Aiden hadn't smoothed things over."

Nora remembered that just one of Genevieve's close friends had missed the event. Genevieve had not been happy but then she'd seemed to forget about it. Nora guessed Aiden was behind her change of heart.

"So you owe him?" Amber asked, her eyes zeroing in on Josh.

"If you think that's why I'm here, it's not. Look, you can think this is all a game. But I'm not wasting my time like that. Aiden really likes Elise and I'm here to make sure he doesn't get hurt."

"And I'm here to make sure Elise doesn't get hurt," Amber countered immediately.

"Cool. Looks like we're on the same team then," Josh said, stopping once more to look Amber in the eye.

Nora tugged on Mack and he took a few steps back with her. The other couple knew they were there but it still felt like they should give them some space for this part of their conversation.

"I just said I want to make sure Elise doesn't get hurt, not Aiden."

"But if Elise gets hurt, Aiden gets hurt," Josh said matter-of-factly.

Nora could see the way Amber's mouth tightened, her shock at Josh's statement evident.

"He really likes her that much?" Amber asked.

Josh nodded his head. "I wish he didn't, but yeah."

"I think she really likes him too," Amber revealed and then her fingers flew to her lips as though she hadn't meant to say that.

"She isn't playing him," Josh said softly, as if Amber's surprise admission was the only thing that would have made him believe that truth.

He surveyed Amber and then seemed to come to a decision.

"So they'll both be happy if they work out," Josh concluded.

Amber nodded.

Suddenly Josh grinned and Nora could see Amber lean forward. She probably didn't even realize what she was doing, but Nora could see that Amber was intrigued.

"You ready to make this happen?" Josh asked, still smiling at Amber.

Amber cocked her head as she waited for him to continue.

"We want them happy, right?" Josh asked.

Amber nodded.

"And don't you think they'll be happy together?"

Amber nodded once more, still not sure where Josh was going with this.

"But they're getting in their own way and they could use a little help. So we get them together. Like those cheesy Christmas movies my agent keeps trying to get me to star in. Maybe if I do this and it works out, I'll finally take one of those roles." Josh's grin grew until his dimples were on full display and Nora swore the whole room lit up.

Amber crossed her arms as she considered Josh's words.

Nora could see she was already almost there. They'd spent days trying to set Elise up to meet Aiden in the lobby. But she was just so danged hesitant. Maybe Aiden could get Elise to bring down her walls on her own, but it seemed a lot more likely to happen with a little push from their friends . . .

"I guess it is Christmas," Amber acknowledged. "But we can't let them know what we're doing. Elise would kill me."

"Aiden would love me, but yeah, we can keep it quiet."

Amber nodded before glancing back to where Elise stood at least ten feet ahead of Aiden, obviously trying to prod them closer to the group, as Aiden worked hard to keep Elise to himself.

"We'll have our work cut out for us," Amber warned.

"I don't mind getting my hands dirty."

Mack grunted.

Nora elbowed him in the side.

"Fine," Amber agreed.

"Fine," Josh replied with a lift of his eyebrows.

Nora beamed. Because while those two had been deciding to bring Elise and Aiden together, she had come up with a little matchmaking plan of her own. Who better to help Amber through her broken heart than a gorgeous star who had just committed to working with her on a very romantic project?

CHAPTER TEN

"YOU WANT me to video call with our dead son's grave?" Max asked incredulously, and Seren felt a frown overtake her face.

Her heart hitched at the words *dead son*. How could the man who'd lost Milo with her say those words so callously?

"My friend who also lost a child said that speaking to them can help with the healing process."

After Seren had cried her tears that day Piper had left her office, she'd decided she had nothing to lose. She didn't know what speaking to Milo would do, so she was trying to keep her expectations low. But if she could do it with the one person who loved Milo as much as she had . . . maybe it could work.

So she'd called Max from Milo's gravesite, nearly begging him to go on this journey with her.

"You do understand, Seren, that the body under all of that dirt isn't really the boy we knew. If he could communicate with us, he wouldn't be there," Max said in such a brusque manner that Seren couldn't help the tears that flooded her eyes.

She flipped the phone camera so that it was now focused on the beautiful view of the ocean from the cemetery instead of on her face. She didn't want Max to see her cry. Years of experience told her that her tears wouldn't move him.

"You've asked me what you can do to save our marriage. What you can do to prove to me that you're here with me. I've asked this of you. Just this one thing in months." Anger was now pushing away the sadness.

"Oh, stop playing the martyr, Seren. You may have only asked for this, but who pays all of your bills? Who helps support your little pet projects so you can feel closer to Milo? Who works his butt off so that you can stay on that island near our son's grave?" Max demanded, his tone growing steelier with each word.

"I didn't ask for any of that, Max. You bought this house without my permission. I wanted something small, sweet. You were the one to insist it be this ostentatious mansion. You were the one who said you wanted staff here with me since you couldn't be."

Seren shook her head. She should have known that Max's earlier words had just been tools to get his way. He'd been begging Seren not to divorce him, though she hadn't seen an alternative. They weren't good for one another. Max had begun to scare her. But then he'd been so supportive about her moving to the island, even buying a house for her, so Seren had put a pause on the divorce proceedings. She'd allowed them to live separated, but not completely severed, yielding to Max's pleading.

Seren felt the lump in her throat grow.

She needed to get off of this call. She'd hoped that calling him from this place would have brought out that softer side of Max, the man who had once been, but . . .

"You were the one who insisted on leaving me," Max hissed.

She heard a thud on the other side of the call and was pretty sure Max had punched something. Maybe his desk, maybe the wall. This was a big part of why Seren had left. Max hadn't always been like this. It was almost like Milo's death had carved out the man's heart.

"This was a bad idea. I'm sorry I bothered you during a workday," Seren apologized. She was always apologizing to Max. She'd never been able to stand up for herself when it came to him. Moving out of his home had been her biggest victory and yet she was still married to him. Because she couldn't pull the trigger on her divorce.

But after this call . . . she had to do it. Even if just the idea of fighting Max Lamb made her knees tremble. She knew Max would see divorce as war.

"All so that I could speak to our son's grave," Max muttered but Seren could feel his anger bleeding away.

Thank goodness.

She'd been hoping to do this with Max. If he could support her in this, maybe they could find a future together. Milo had been their link before and she'd harbored the hope that if they could keep that alive—no, she'd been silly. Grasping at straws after her conversation with Piper. Piper may have been able to reach out to her Kristie but Max, even if he had been blunt as well as just plain cruel about it, was right. Milo wouldn't reach out to them now just because Seren needed a sign from him. Just because it was the two-year anniversary of his death. None of that mattered to Milo where he was.

Max was sure Milo was just gone but Seren had to believe her little boy was somewhere else for the time being. She didn't know if it was heaven or somewhere like it but her angel boy deserved the best and only by believing that could she find some peace.

Seren thought about giving Max the heads up that she was finally going to start divorce proceedings even though she was sure his lawyers were already prepared in every way. It was how

Max worked. Even if he didn't want the divorce, Seren knew the man wouldn't allow himself to be blindsided. Seren had left enough clues that this was her next step.

But she didn't have the chance to say anything more because Max ended the call without a goodbye and Seren fell to her knees. A few rocks hidden in the lush grass beside Milo's grave poked through her jeans and dug into her skin, but Seren scarcely noticed the pain. It was miniscule compared to the ache in her heart.

She covered her face as tears fell, missing her little boy so fiercely. It had been a mistake to reach out to Max when she was already so fragile. This day . . .

A sob broke through Seren's thoughts and all she could do was cry.

Time was supposed to make this better. Time healed all wounds, right? So why, two years later, did it hurt just as badly as the day they'd laid Milo to rest? Maybe even worse, because in that moment Seren couldn't even quite remember what it was like to hold her baby boy. It had been so long that the memories of his touch and smell were fading and . . . Seren just couldn't do this.

She fell forward, her hands hitting the hard rock of his gravestone as she collapsed against it. Its rough surface tore at her flesh and still Seren didn't move, her body wracked with torment.

"Milo, are you there?" Seren whispered brokenly, each word punctuated with a sob.

When the world stayed quiet, Seren knew the truth. Piper had been lucky or delusional—then again, even if she had been delusional she'd been lucky—to hear Kristie speak to her. For Kristie to appear in her dreams.

It wouldn't be the same for Seren. Milo shouldn't be expected to comfort his grieving mother. In fact, she hoped wherever he was he couldn't see her. She should probably be grateful that he hadn't responded. No boy should see his mother fall apart.

Why couldn't she be stronger?

She wanted to be stronger.

Seren lifted her head and saw that her phone had fallen to the ground, so she picked it up and slid it into her back pocket. If nothing else came from this day, at least she'd finally resolved to leave Max once and for all.

The man had anger issues but he wouldn't hurt her. At least not physically. She knew he would do everything in his power to make sure she was left with nothing after their divorce—he'd promised as much when she'd moved out of his home. But she had to do it. The comfort of her lifestyle wasn't worth being tied to Max. Because he paid her bills, he felt he owned her. Maybe he would always feel that way. But the worst part was that Seren felt like Max owned her. And she couldn't live with that. Not anymore.

If she wanted to be that strong woman Milo, wherever he was, deserved, she would start with this.

Seren wiped her eyes although the pain was ever-present. But at least she'd gained a measure of control over her body again.

Even if she didn't want to admit it, that was an improvement from two years before. Maybe time had healed a little something.

Seren stood, feeling slightly better than earlier. Her stomach didn't feel as if it were going to turn in on itself, and her heart felt as if it could do its job once more.

"I love you, Milo," Seren whispered as she pressed a kiss to her two fingers and then slid them over the gravestone.

She didn't know where Milo was. She wasn't sure of much, but she did know this place helped her feel more connected to her son. And if that was the case, she wouldn't let anyone make her feel guilty about it, especially Max.

Seren turned and walked slowly back to her car, allowing plans of moving forward with her divorce to fill her mind instead of who she was leaving behind.

Max had his team of attorneys, but nearly a year before, Seren had met with an attorney in Seattle and the two of them had clicked. The woman had also lost a child, and that connection had drawn Seren to her. The attorney hadn't lost her relationship with her husband at the same time, the way Seren had, but she'd understood some of Max's behavior.

Max had never been the best of husbands. He'd worked too many hours, cared too much about his career, loved the praise the world gave him for being an intellectual. Yet he'd been Seren's. He'd always been faithful to her and he'd loved Milo with all of his heart. That Seren had never doubted. So when Milo was diagnosed with cancer, Max had thrown his entire effort into Milo's fight for his life. But in the end he had failed. They all had, but Max seemed to be unable to live with that failure. So he'd turned away from Seren, put everything into work once more, and had built a wall of anger and callousness around his heart.

Seren had wanted to give Max time, space, whatever he needed to process the death of their son. Heaven knew she had needed it. But time had passed, and they'd only drifted farther apart. Seren knew unless they put in some effort that wouldn't change. So Seren had gone to a dinner with Max a few weeks before, something he'd been requesting for months. It was a work thing that had bored Seren to death but Max had claimed to need her. Although he ignored her for the majority of the evening and she'd been left to speak with the wives of Max's colleagues, she'd done it. He'd said he was grateful.

Today it had been Seren's turn to ask Max to give something. And when she had . . . well, Max would give nothing. That much was apparent. And it was the last straw. Seren couldn't do this anymore. She'd always been the one to give, to sacrifice, when it came to Max and she was just done. Tired, morose, and wrung out. She'd cried every tear she could for their marriage and what could have been. Had Milo not died she was sure things would have been different.

But Milo's death had shone a spotlight on the unsavory parts of their marriage and now Seren couldn't unsee them. If she'd had hope of fixing things, she would have kept trying. But Max had proven time and time again that he didn't feel their marriage was worth it. That Seren was worth it. So today would be the last time.

Letting go was simultaneously a relief and the scariest thing Seren had ever done. She hadn't lived life without Max since her sophomore year at Stanford. Nearly half of her life had been with him. Not to mention that she couldn't just walk away—she already anticipated the rage he'd surely rain down over her—but she'd deal with that when the time came.

"Excuse me," a sweet voice called out, causing Seren to look up as she approached her car. A woman who looked to be at least thirty years her senior stood smiling at her.

She couldn't have been more than five feet tall and her silver hair was curled and arranged meticulously. She was decked out in a dress and beautiful silver earrings—a knockout to be sure.

"I'm here for a date with my husband," the woman explained after Seren's silent perusal. The woman pointed to a gravesite close to them and tears immediately sprang to Seren's eyes.

"Well, you look lovely," she managed. She didn't want to cry in front of this sweet old woman. The poor thing had lost someone she'd loved as well.

"This was always one of Tom's favorites." The woman

smoothed her skirt with a reminiscing smile. "Although he did hate the way other men stared at me when I wore it. But I never noticed a single one of them. The man should have known I would only ever have eyes for him."

Seren bit her lip, whether to keep from crying or laughing she wasn't sure.

This was what she wanted. If Max passed that very day, Seren wouldn't be able to say the same about the man she'd once loved.

Once loved. She hadn't even realized her love for her husband was a thing of the past until this moment.

So it was high time she do something. She'd allowed her grief to be an excuse for inaction too long.

"I'm sorry. You don't care what I'm doing here," the woman said. "My daughter Anna is always telling me I need to stop sharing my business with everyone."

Seren's watery eyes felt a little drier as the ghost of a smile played over her lips.

"I love that you told me," she admitted. It had helped to solidify her decision. And she was able to feel a little levity on a day like today.

"And thank you. Today is a hard day and you've made it a little brighter," Seren said, feeling the need to speak her gratitude to this stranger.

"I get hard days. Birthday, anniversaries, holidays—they just aren't quite what they used to be," the woman said, understanding shining in her eyes.

Seren nodded hard. It was a relief to talk to someone who got it, especially after the conversation she'd just had with Max.

"Well, I didn't stop you to tell you my life story, if you can believe it," the woman joked before asking. "I was just wondering the time."

Seren glanced down at her smart watch and gasped.

11:11.

She and Milo had become obsessed with angel numbers after his diagnosis. It was a way of connecting the here and now with the vast unknown and they'd both clung to it. Every angel number they noticed they'd point out to the other but 11:11 had been special. Milo's favorite of all the numbers.

"It's eleven eleven," Seren choked out before scurrying off to her car. She knew the woman would understand.

As soon as her car door closed behind her Seren burst into tears. She'd been asking for Milo to speak to her and even though she hadn't heard actual words she somehow knew this moment was from him. Getting to speak to the sweet woman about her husband, having someone with her who understood loss and how hard this day was. Milo had sent the woman to Seren. She knew this in her very soul.

Some could call it coincidence—Max undoubtedly would—but no one could feel the welling in her heart, the feeling that Milo was closer than he had been. No one could understand that. So she wouldn't ask them to.

But she did. It was almost like Milo was responding to the *I love you* Seren had left at his grave. His very own way of saying *I see you and I love you too*. And she'd forever hold this memory in her heart.

CHAPTER ELEVEN

"READY OR NOT," Ellis said as he joined Julia in the kitchen. They were opening the takeout Julia had ordered for their very first get-together with both of their families.

At first, Julia hadn't been sure she wanted to have this dinner. Her sister and mom had proven they could be prickly on their best days, but things had been so pleasant with her family since they'd arrived two days before that she thought it might actually work. Their families would have to get to know one another someday, since she knew Ellis was her forever, so better to move forward, right? Besides, knowing she'd be away from Ellis so soon when filming of her new movie began, she was anxious to bring them together any time she could.

Of course Ellis had been supportive. He loved the idea of mingling their families although he had been a bit hesitant because of the newest addition to his own family Christmas get together. His youngest brother and his wife had decided to join in the family festivities.

"Rusty is great," Ellis had explained. "Easygoing as a lazy river."

Julia had laughed at that while wondering how much

offense Rusty would take at that comment. But having met him the day before she now understood exactly what Ellis meant and knew that the man would have taken Ellis' comment as a compliment. His wife on the other hand . . .

"Krista loves a bit of drama," Ellis had warned and Julia had seen it immediately. She knew many women like Krista. Those who loved to stir the pot, who would do anything for a scrap of savory gossip.

But Krista was harmless, mostly, and Julia realized if she didn't get the two families together there would be little time for Julia to spend with Ellis' family at all. It wouldn't exactly go over well if she left her family to spend time with his.

So together they'd be, for better or worse. Hopefully for better.

"Can I help with anything, Julia dear?" Krista asked as she flounced into the kitchen in a dramatic red evening gown.

Minutes before, when the Rider clan had arrived, Lacey had taken one look at Krista's outfit and dashed upstairs to change.

Julia had cringed, fervently hoping her sister wouldn't spend the whole evening trying to one up Ellis' sister-in-law.

"I would have loved to host Christmas at our home but since Mama and Papa Rider decided to spend the holiday on the island here with you, the least I can do is help you host." Krista kept a smile on her face but Julia was pretty sure there had been a dig at her somewhere in those words.

Oh well. Julia wasn't going to allow herself to care. She was there to enjoy the evening and keep the peace.

"I mean, I've hosted every Christmas for the past twenty-five that Rusty and I have been married. I can help you avoid any of the mistakes you're bound to make, having so little experience," Krista added, her perfectly white teeth showcased as her grin widened to an extraordinary size.

Okay, that was definitely a dig. Julia felt her own smile

tighten. But she was determined not to let anything ruin her evening.

Ellis had warned that Krista might also be out of sorts because this was her first Christmas with both of her kids spending time with their spouses' families. Krista was a mama hen and didn't like it when her babies weren't close by her side. Never mind that her babies were twenty-two and twenty-four.

"If you'd like to start dishing these onto the platters here?" Julia motioned to the silver takeout container full of Pad Thai. She and Ellis had opted for Thai food that evening since it was something both of their families enjoyed.

"Oh, how nice. I wouldn't have ever considered not cooking if I was hosting a holiday dinner. But I guess as a movie star you all are given free passes when it comes to normal things like cooking and cleaning, right?" Krista asked with a wink. As if that could somehow soften the blow of her words.

"Julia is an excellent cook," Ellis spoke up when it was apparent all Julia would do was stand there and smile.

Julia put a hand over his to show that she didn't need it. She was fine. Krista was so much like her own family that it made her feel right at home.

"I'm sure she is," Krista said in a placating way that clearly stated she knew Ellis was lying for his girlfriend.

But Julia squeezed Ellis' hand and he thankfully let it go.

See, enjoying the evening.

Lacey swept into the kitchen moments later, her daughter Wendy trailing after her. Wendy had a hand discreetly over her mouth but as she met Julia's eye, Julia saw she was trying to contain her laughter. Clearly she'd wanted to see Julia's reaction to Lacey's costume change.

Costume was the right word for it. Lacey wore a gold gown that looked vaguely familiar. Wait . . . was that Lacey's pageant dress, the one she'd worn when she'd won Miss Indiana over thirty years before?

One, how the heck had Lacey fit into the dress, and two, why had she brought it to Whisling?

Thankfully those questions kept Julia from laughing along with Wendy. Really, Julia was too shocked to be amused. At least at first.

"You look beautiful," Ellis remarked smoothly, and Lacey's ensuing grin told Julia he had earned some major brownie points with her sister.

"This old thing?" Lacey said coyly as she actually twirled in a circle.

Oh good heavens.

"I didn't realize the dress code was quite so formal. But I love a good evening gown," Lacey said, her chin pointed in Krista's direction.

The truth of the matter was that both women were sorely overdressed. Julia wore a simple emerald green sweater dress with a pair of black tights. Wendy was slightly more dressed up in her silver crepe skirt and sleek black turtleneck but no one was close to evening wear. In fact, Julia was pretty sure Rusty was wearing the same shirt she'd seen him in the day before.

But neither seemed embarrassed at the way they were dressed. Nope, they were only concerned that they outshine the other.

"Ellis, did you know that your brother got me this dress for our twentieth anniversary? He is just the *dearest* man. He took me away on a weekend getaway to the *sweetest* little cabin in the Ozarks and then surprised me with this dress. He sure knows how to dress a woman, doesn't he?" Krista fished so deep for a compliment she had to come up with a whale.

"He does," Ellis replied, the strain evident in his voice, though Krista didn't seem to notice.

"How about we finish up in here? You two lovely ladies can gather all the guests to the dining room," Julia offered to the evening gown-clad women.

Both nodded and Krista started for the door first. Lacey realized Krista's intent and began to race her.

If Julia never again saw two grown women racing in evening gowns that allowed for steps of all of five inches she'd be happy. Once was more than enough for a lifetime.

As her mom and Krista closed the kitchen door behind them, Wendy finally released her pent-up laughter, hands pressed over her mouth to muffle the guffaws.

"*You* are an instigator." Julia pointed a condemning finger at her niece. "I know you had something to do with all this."

"Mom decided to wear the evening gown all on her own. I may have just said she looks prettier than every other woman in the house. Especially a certain someone in a red evening gown," Wendy said, brows raised in mock innocence.

"Get out of here," Julia swatted at Wendy's backside with a towel, her niece giggling all the way out of the kitchen.

"Do you think we'll survive that?" Julia asked as she turned to Ellis. She could have never foreseen a competition between Krista and Lacey. Looking back, she acknowledged that she should have, considering the way Lacey could turn everything into a competition. The Prices liked to win. Julia should probably just be grateful that her brother Jack hadn't come out to Whisling or surely he would have tried to start a competition between himself and Ellis's brothers, or even Ellis himself.

"Of course we will," Ellis said, pulling Julia into his arms and pressing a kiss to her cheek. She instantly regretted putting on a red lip that night. No look was worth having to sacrifice kisses from Ellis.

"I'm just glad you're here with me," Julia said as she plated up the last box of curry.

"Always," Ellis promised with one more kiss before he lifted two platters of sticky rice. "But we should probably get out there sooner rather than later." He showed his first sign of unease, and if Ellis was nervous Julia knew there was something to be concerned about.

She gathered a few platters and followed Ellis into the dining room, where all seemed to be well so far. Lacey and Krista had taken seats next to their husbands, who were thankfully at opposite ends of the table.

In the very middle sat Julia's mom Betty, with Wendy and her boyfriend Leo on one side, and across from them were Ellis's parents Sarah and Dave, along with Oliver. The six were engaged in a conversation that appeared to be pleasant, judging by the smiles and occasional laughter. At the head of the table sat Lacey and her husband Mike, as well as her sons Trip and Ryder. Julia and Ellis had been left two open seats next to Rusty and Krista.

Julia set her platters in the middle of the table, letting out a small sigh of relief. So far, so good.

"Oh let me help with that, love." Sarah stood and followed Julia into the kitchen as she went back for more plates of food. "You are so smart to do a dinner like this." Sarah's words sounded like a genuine compliment so Julia took them as such even if she was a little self-conscious about her lack of cooking that evening.

"I'm sure it's not quite what you hoped for," Julia said as she handed Sarah a platter of drunken noodles and the Pad Thai.

"Nonsense. Thai food is a favorite of mine and the holidays always seem to have such a regimented menu. I've had too many years of some kind of roast meat and potatoes. Noodles and spices are a pleasant change," Sarah said with a smile so much like Ellis' that Julia felt at immediate ease.

She was still nervous around Ellis's parents even though

she'd video called them a number of times and had met them the day before. But Sarah was doing an excellent job of calming Julia's nerves.

"Thank you. I've never been great in the kitchen. I've been trying to learn since retirement and well, because I know Ellis loves food. But a dinner this large seemed like a surefire way for things to go up in smoke. Maybe literally," Julia said with a self-deprecating grin.

Sarah set her platters down and motioned Julia to do the same. Sarah then took Julia's hands in hers.

"Ever since Ellis joined this world you all live in I've been worried about one thing. The kind of woman he would end up with. He's brought home a few and all of them have been, well, nice girls but . . . " Sarah swallowed and Julia could now see what Ellis had said about his mom was true. The woman couldn't say an unkind word about anyone. "Anyway, you are a breath of fresh air. I've seen the world you come from. I know it's far from my own. Yet you've opened your arms to welcome us and that is more than I could have ever wished for. So don't you worry about a thing. You are pleasantness personified. And if you'd like I would be happy to come over and teach you how to cook a few of Ellis's favorites. Not that you need any help in winning over my son. He's a smitten kitten if I've ever seen one," Sarah finished.

Julia couldn't help her giggle. The mental image of Ellis as a kitten was pretty darn amusing. Plus with all of those compliments warming her soul right up, how could she not feel a bit overflowing in the joy department?

"Thank you," Julia said sincerely as Sarah passed her platters back to her and they exited the kitchen together.

Ellis had been held up by his brothers but as Julia left the kitchen he passed her to go in and grab the final parts of the dinner.

"You okay?" he mouthed, probably feeling remorseful for leaving her alone with his mom so soon into their relationship.

"Amazing," Julia mouthed back.

Ellis cocked his head but his eyes brightened in pleasure.

Julia followed Sarah, setting her platters in the center of the table and then taking her seat.

"Could we start with grace?" Julia asked even though it wasn't Price tradition. But she knew the Riders started every meal with a prayer and she wanted Ellis's family to feel comfortable.

Sarah nodded with a smile on her face as Rusty volunteered to give the prayer. Julia couldn't tell why Krista was frowning but she figured it wasn't to do with her so she wouldn't worry about it.

Ellis slid into his seat just as Rusty started and soon the families were digging into the meal.

"This is my favorite takeout on the island. Well, besides Scratch Made by Bess," Wendy said as she loaded her plate with vegetable spring rolls.

"So you got the second best?" Krista asked with a glance at Julia as she carefully dabbed a tiny portion of green curry onto her plate.

"We didn't realize we were going to do this dinner until last minute. Bess' food truck is booked up for catering through the holidays," Ellis explained to his sister-in-law, the warning clear in his tone.

Even Rusty shot a look in his wife's direction.

"But get used to it, Krista. Now that you're almost Julia's family this is the way it goes. She'll throw a fancy gala for her friends but won't even buy the best takeout for her family," Betty said as she spooned a giant portion of not-the-best-take-out-on-the-island into her mouth.

Julia felt her cheeks flame red as Sarah's mouth dropped

open. These were the kind of comments that had been absent the first two days that her family had been here. The reason Julia had dared to hope this meal could be successful. But she should have known her luck would run out. Her mom couldn't help the snide remarks. It was simply in her nature. Julia just wished her mother could have hidden them until at least the second meeting with the Riders.

She felt a warm hand take hers under the table, pulling it to his leg. She met Ellis' eyes, shooting him a look of gratitude as he squeezed her hand in reassurance. He was there. He understood.

"We appreciate that Julia does this for all of us. She doesn't ever ask anyone else to contribute to the meal," Wendy said, trying to smooth over her grandmother's harsh words.

"As she should. We traveled all this way to be here for the holidays. The least my sister can do is provide the meals," Lacey said, shrugging a glittery gold shoulder.

Julia would not say that she'd paid for the tickets and they were staying in her house for free as well. Her family hadn't had to contribute a single cent to being here for the holidays.

She pressed her eyes shut and then opened them, forcing a smile to her lips as she reminded herself that her family *had* taken time off of their jobs and *had* left the comfort of their hometown to join Julia at her home. She should be grateful. She had been grateful. Until Lacey had acted like Julia providing for them was the least she could do.

But she couldn't let this rub her the wrong way. She was going to be calm, to enjoy the evening.

Wendy opened her mouth to speak again but Julia gave a slight shake of her head.

Ellis seemed to be biting his lip hard but he too picked up on Julia's wish and stayed quiet.

"I really think Alabama will take it again this year," Trip said out of nowhere.

Wendy shot her brother a giant grin of approval as Ryder added, "They take it every year. That's like the easiest prediction of all time."

Soon all of the men around the table as well as Wendy had fallen into a conversation about college football and Julia felt she could finally eat her meal in peace.

There had been a few bumps in the road but most of the evening had exceeded her expectations. Especially her private conversation with Sarah.

"If I hear the word 'football' one more time my ears are going to bleed," Krista said and then giggled as if that would offset the words she'd said. "That can't be all we can speak about." Her voice was brighter now, her smile dazzling.

"I'm sure we don't have to," Rusty said supportively and Krista turned her smile to her husband.

"I'd love to hear more about Julia. She's why we're here, after all." Krista motioned to Rusty and their family.

All eyes turned to Julia as she struggled to match Krista's smile. She was the last topic of conversation she'd hoped for but there was no changing things now.

"I'm not sure what you'd like to know?" Julia said with a shrug. "I mean, I'm kind of an open book. Well, at least an open tabloid."

Most of the table laughed.

"They didn't get it all right, though. Those magazines blamed us for our strained relationship with Julia when she was the one who left us," Betty said as she stabbed a noodle with too much force.

Julia's heart dropped. She'd thought they were beyond this. They'd talked through it at length. They'd all been at fault. Or at least that's what they'd agreed at the time.

"We know we weren't in the right, but Julia was in the wrong as well. Of course, no one would ever say that about Hollywood's darling," Betty added.

Okay, that was a bit better. Julia still felt like an anvil pressed on her heart, though. Would her family ever get past their past? It didn't feel like it.

"I had no idea. I'm so sorry." Krista said all the right words but the gleam in her eye scared Julia. "So you all tried to be a supportive family but—well, what happened, Julia?"

Julia felt her blush rise once more.

Ellis opened his mouth but Julia beat him to it. She loved that he wanted to protect her but she could handle this. "Lots of miscommunication. I didn't understand what it was like to be left behind and didn't realize how much I was hurting them. I only saw my own hurt and blamed it on my family."

Julia wanted to be more honest but that would paint her family in a bad light and apparently her mother felt they'd already carried more of the blame than they should. It was the first Julia had heard of it so she was trying to be cognizant of that.

"It's amazing how selfish we can be in our younger years," Krista said with a sympathetic nod as if she understood. There was no way she could understand any of this.

"It wasn't all Aunt Julia's fault," Wendy began when Lacey cut her off.

"She always thought she was too good for our town. Turning her back on us as soon as she could. Unless . . . oh Jules, was it embarrassment that ran you out after you threw up in front of the whole school? You did leave a few weeks later," Lacey said, her words unusually cruel. At least unusual for recent days. Some of the old resentment seemed to be bubbling up. Or at least Julia hoped that was her excuse. Because making Julia relive her one of her most mortifying moments in front of people she hoped would one day be her family was plain mean.

"Wait, she what?" Krista asked, eyes wide.

"Krista," Rusty warned.

"I peed my pants in third grade," Dave spoke up and Julia could have reached across the table to kiss him.

Sarah smiled at her husband, showing Julia the quiet man might have been prompted as Krista cringed in Dave's direction.

"But this wasn't third grade. This was high school. At a prom assembly when Julia wasn't crowned prom queen," Lacey went right back to what the others were trying to avoid.

"No doubt because she couldn't quite live up to her sister's legacy," Betty added easily, probably because she and Lacey spoke about this often. Julia's insufficiencies.

"Enough!" roared Ellis at Lacey, Betty, and Krista before turning his glare to Rusty and then Mike. The table fell silent.

"Julia has graciously invited you all to her home. Yes, you traveled a long way, but she bought you first class tickets to make your travel as comfortable as possible," Ellis said to Lacey and Betty. "She has let you all in." Ellis turned his focus on his sister-in-law. "And then you spend the majority of the evening speaking about her as if she were an enemy. I just don't understand it. I've kept my mouth shut. But you are her family. And until you step up and start acting like it—because family uplifts and loves, they don't degrade and throw our worst moments in our faces—we are leaving," Ellis said as if the words were surprising him as he spoke them.

"Is this okay?" he whispered to Julia.

She nodded even though she wasn't sure where he was going with this, but Ellis was right. The vindictive words were tearing at her, causing searing pain, and she didn't want to spend another moment with her sister, her mom, or Ellis' sister-in-law.

"Now wait a minute," Mike said as he stood.

"This is when you decide to speak up?" Ellis stood as well. "Your wife verbally batters her sister for a quarter of an hour and only now do you decide to say something?" There was an edge to Ellis' tone that caused Mike to drop back into his seat.

"I don't want the woman I love in this home with you all. I know she loves you too much to kick you out so we will leave. And until each of you," Ellis looked from Mike to Lacey to Betty and then to Krista, "apologizes, we won't be coming home."

Betty sputtered. "She's—"

"She has said nothing, Grandma. I tried the whole night to see your side but Aunt Julia sat there and took everything you said—she even took the blame for something a fool could see was all of your faults. She never lashed out. Never even fought back. She did nothing." Trip crossed his arms across his chest, daring his grandmother to contradict him.

"Trip!" Lacey admonished, her eyebrows nearly to her hairline.

"You're no better, Mom. To Aunt Julia's face you say you've forgiven her, but I've heard you and Grandma gossip behind her back. You've kept your anger alive when the wrongs are in the distant past. Ellis is right. Aunt Julia deserves a sincere apology. And a real change," Ryder sat up beside his brother.

Wendy nodded in agreement with her siblings.

Her sister and mom still spoke negatively about her? It shouldn't surprise Julia, who had been worried their truce had been crafted just because they wanted to stay close to Wendy, but to hear the words aloud? Julia tried to swallow back the pain.

"Go ahead and pack a bag, Jules," Ellis spoke softly. "Unless you want me to kick them out? We can even have them stay at my place with my family and I'll come stay here with you," he offered.

Julia shook her head. No matter what her family did, she couldn't kick them out. And if she did, she feared that would put an end to any hope of real reconciliation.

So Julia did as Ellis asked, her feet like lead as she left the dining room and went up the stairs. Maybe she'd hurt her family too much. Maybe there was a statute of limitations on forgiveness and she'd passed hers when it came to her family.

Footsteps sounded behind Julia and she turned, bracing herself for more accusations.

"I'm so sorry," Sarah said quickly as she fell into step beside her. Julia couldn't help smiling at the oddity of the situation—Sarah was one of the few people who shouldn't be apologizing. "Ellis told me a little of your family situation. Don't worry, he'd never betray your confidence, but he shared just enough so I'd be prepared for tonight. But I couldn't have ever really been prepared for what you would go through."

Julia nodded. She didn't blame Sarah for not understanding just how deep her family's resentment for her was. Someone as sweet as she was surely couldn't imagine family that acted like Julia's.

"And as for Krista, she will be hearing it from all of us. Rusty is already speaking his mind and that boy isn't often upset. But I have to apologize for her behavior. She instigated it all. I can't help but think if she weren't here . . . "

"My family would have found a way to air their grievances, trust me. Krista might have sped up the timeline but it's obvious they are still upset with me," Julia sighed, each word paining her.

She arrived at her bedroom and Sarah seemed to sense Julia's need to be alone.

"Again, I am so sorry," Sarah said before she began to turn to leave.

"Please, don't be. If anything, you brought me my one saving grace. Ellis is everything I've ever dreamed of and he's protected me in a way I haven't been able to do for myself. So if anything I should be thanking you," Julia said earnestly.

"Well I guess we'll thank the good Lord for that," Sarah said with a last smile before leaving.

Julia didn't know how to deal with her feelings toward her family so as she threw her clothes into her overnight bag she didn't. She thought about how grateful she was for Sarah and that even though painful things had surfaced this evening, she had also learned how lucky she'd be if she ever got to have Sarah as a mother-in-law. And she was reminded she'd be even luckier if she got to have Ellis in her life as her companion forever.

Ellis joined her a few moments later. "Daniel has already arranged two rooms for us at the B&B for however long this takes. Ollie will pack my bag so that I don't have to leave you and—"

"You don't have to come with me, Ellis," Julia said quickly. The last thing she wanted to do was ruin his family time.

"And stay in a home with Krista after what she did?" Ellis shook his head.

"But your family . . . "

"They all understand. In fact, my mom would probably have my head if I left you on your own after this. We'll meet up with them, spend time with them and your niece and nephews. But they all know my place is with you. It will always be with you, Jules."

Julia had pushed down her emotions for so long but with Ellis's words they seemed to well up at once and she wasn't sure if she was going to cry or laugh or shout. Her body settled for tears filling her eyes.

"I don't know—" Julia began but couldn't finish when her voice began to waver.

"You don't have to know. I love you, Julia."

Julia's tears turned to laughter. Her emotions were taking her on a wild ride today.

"You good?" Ellis asked, relief filling his features at her laughter.

"With you? Always," Julia spoke her truth.

Ellis kissed her head and Julia felt a peace fill her. Outwardly nothing had changed. Nothing with her family was better. But seeing Ellis have her back like this . . . she'd always known he cared for her, but to see it? She realized she really was good. As long as she faced her future, whatever it may be, with Ellis by her side.

CHAPTER TWELVE

"OH MY GOSH. You cannot come out of nowhere like that," Amber reprimanded Josh right after she'd nearly jumped out of her skin.

Josh chuckled as he raised his hands in contrition. "So sorry. I didn't mean to scare you. I just had to make sure you weren't with Elise before . . . "

"You came out of the shadows?" Amber finished for him. "I think you've worked on one too many horror movie sets."

Amber shook off the feeling of unease that had overwhelmed her moments before. It was just Josh.

"I've only done one horror movie," Josh replied, an eyebrow arched in defense.

"See, that's one too many," Amber contended.

Josh chuckled once more.

"Where's Elise?" Josh asked, looking up and down the hall as Amber began to relax. She had been leaving her office when Josh had stepped out from behind a potted plant, and he was a big guy. Well, not fat big. Like Hollywood would ever allow that. But he was broad in the shoulders and tall and just big in the Hollywood way. Amber knew 'Hollywood way' could also be defined as attractive for most but she wasn't ready to go there yet. With any man, but especially a man like Josh. Not that he would want Amber to find him attractive. Well, maybe attractive, but he wouldn't want her to really like him. Nope, men like Josh thrived on being available to all women.

"In the kitchen," Amber said, glancing down the hall toward the large kitchen that created the inn's incredible dishes. A place Amber hadn't been able to set foot in for over a month now. And Elise, the incredible sister that she was, had seemed immediately in tune with Amber's apprehension and had taken over all things kitchen related ever since they'd hired a new chef. Ever since their old chef—Raul, Amber's ex-fiancé—had trampled over her heart.

Amber both despised and missed the man. It didn't make sense but the ways of the heart so often did not.

"So we're safe?" Josh asked, gesturing to the hall they stood in.

Amber pursed her lips. She knew what he was asking. He and Amber were a part of a covert operation to bring Elise and Aiden together and if others overheard their plans? It wouldn't be good. Amber knew what she should do and yet she hesitated.

She hadn't been alone in a room with a man since Raul. She knew planning subterfuge with Josh wasn't significant—and yet it was. Because any first after Raul felt ridiculously important.

She hated Raul for having left her in this way. Once confident and independent, Amber now hated being on her own and worse, she second guessed her every decision.

"Not quite," Amber said, drawing strength from who knew where as she tugged on Josh's arm—his quite well-muscled arm if she was being completely honest—and pulled him into the office she shared with Elise.

She closed the door behind him and had to smile at the

bewildered look on his face. At least she'd now gotten him back for scaring her earlier.

"You never know who'll be roaming the halls. This is the only place I can assure we won't be overheard. Elise might come back but we can tell her we're . . ."

Hm. Amber hadn't quite thought that one through.

"That I came in here to ask you out?" Josh supplied unhelpfully as he took one of the guest chairs at Elise and Amber's desk.

"As if Elise would ever believe that," Amber replied with an eye roll, taking the other guest seat so that their conversation wouldn't feel like a business meeting.

"Oh, I've got it—you came because I'm asking you to do a special musical number at Genevieve's wedding," Amber said as she clapped her hands together.

"Me doing a musical number at Gen's wedding is more likely than me asking you out?" Josh asked, that brow arched one more. But this time Amber could almost hear the skepticism written across his face.

"You used to sing, right?" Amber asked. She acted as if she didn't know but she had followed Josh's musical career quite closely. He'd started on one of those singing competitions, formed a boy band, and when they broke up he landed on his feet in the world of acting.

"A long, long time ago. Heck it was a lifetime before," Josh said as he began shaking his head. "You're not really thinking of having me sing, are you?"

"Not until this moment. But yeah, why not? Genevieve would love it."

Josh nodded. He knew she would.

"And the guests would love it."

Josh nodded once more. There was a point in time when his band had broken records left and right. People had been shocked that he hadn't gone on to build a solo career but had left it all behind for the silver screen.

"But I . . . " Josh met Amber's eyes. "I don't sing anymore," he said with a finality that made Amber curious.

She was about to press when she noticed the way his face had shuttered. Right, Josh didn't want to talk about it. And if anyone understood not wanting to speak about their past, it was Amber. She still wouldn't speak even to Elise about how she felt about Raul.

"Okay, well, we can say I asked and you said no," Amber said.

Josh cocked his head as if he were surprised. "You're not going to ask why, especially when you know I have such a lovely voice?" The way he said the words told Amber it was something Josh had heard many times. "You had my posters on your wall, so you know the kind of talent I had." And that one seemed targeted right at Amber.

Thankfully she hadn't had his poster. Yes, maybe a poster of his group, but Amber had tried not to discriminate back then even if Josh had been a clear favorite for her and every other teenager on the planet.

"I'll admit I know the kind of talent your group had. As to your personal talent . . . " Amber shrugged. "Maybe you were good. It was hard to pick out one voice from another."

Hard, but Amber had done it with ease because she'd been a little bit obsessed.

"But you confess you listened to us," Josh said, that eyebrow raised once more but this time in cockiness rather than confusion. No wonder the guy was an actor if he could make even his eyebrows express just what he wanted. Too bad the cocky look was absolutely adorable.

"I listened to the radio nonstop between the ages of fourteen and eighteen. There was no way to avoid you folks." Amber was again on the verge of a lie but she'd saved herself. She *had* listened to the radio . . . but she'd also owned every one of their CDs. She decided Josh's ego didn't need to know that.

"So you never drew a heart around my face?" Josh asked.

Amber's eyes narrowed at the strangely specific question while her mind spun through possible responses. The reality was that Amber had, and she wasn't sure how to semi-truth around this one.

Amber rolled her eyes once more as if even the thought of drawing a heart around Josh's face was ridiculous. "How many girls did that?" She tried the art of distraction.

"Enough. Were you one of them?" Josh pressed as he leaned forward so far that he was getting into Amber's personal space.

She should mind it. Josh had plenty of his own personal space. But Amber felt the ghost of a smile on her face instead.

"How do you propose we get Aiden and Elise together?" she asked because she was out of ideas. She knew this basically painted her as guilty but better than admitting it out loud. Ever since Raul she'd vowed to never lie when she could tell the truth. Even when it got uncomfortable.

"I'm going to guess you did it more than once." Josh leaned back with a satisfied grin. Now both of his brows were raised in victory. He really was talented.

Guilty, Amber thought but kept it to herself.

"You're wasting our time." Amber tapped at her watch. And it was the truth. Who knew when Elise would be back?

Josh chuckled softly with a shake of his head. "Fine, you win. This time." But the way he spoke let Amber know that he didn't mind losing to her. In fact, it seemed as though he was already anticipating the next time they'd go head to head.

Amber pushed that thought from her mind. There would be none of that. It was too close to flirting and heaven knew the last thing she needed was a flirtation with a guy who'd be leaving the island in the next few days.

Better to focus on Elise and Aiden. The man who'd proved that, even if he didn't live on the island, he was willing to go out of his way for Elise time and time again. He really liked her. Unlike some guys who were big-time flirts.

"I'm thinking a romantic dinner," Josh said. Amber knew she probably wore a look of pure business on her face now. She'd lost herself for a minute there but this had never been about her and Josh—heck, Josh probably would have never spoken to her again were it not for Elise and Aiden.

"A little cliché, don't you think?" she asked skeptically.

"But simple to trick them into attending. I mean, I won't have to trick my boy, but your sister?" Josh replied as he crossed his arms over his chest and leaned back in his seat, all traces of teasing likewise gone from his face.

"True, but I think we can do a little better. There's this room in the back of the inn that we never use. We could put up a white sheet and play a black and white movie for them. Deck the room out with snacks and twinkle lights," Amber spilled her idea.

"Your sister's into old movies?" Josh asked.

"The older the better," Amber replied with a grin. It had been a constant source of contention growing up. Amber always wanted to watch the latest blockbuster, while Elise preferred to rewatch anything from the Hollywood's Golden Age.

"No wonder Aiden's so into her. That's totally his thing too," Josh said with a nod of satisfaction. As if this was just another reason Elise was perfect for Aiden.

"Do you think once Elise gets there and sees it's a set-up she'll leave?" Josh asked.

Amber shook her head. "She'd never be outright rude. If

Aiden asked her out right now she'd let him down easy. But if they were already on the date? She'd give it a chance."

"Cool," Josh said, standing.

Oh, their meeting was done. Yeah, that made sense. So why was Amber feeling a loss? This was stupid.

Josh pulled out his phone, already typing away. Returning texts or emails, surely. It made sense. A guy like him was probably in demand twenty-four-seven.

"Here." He passed his phone to Amber.

She looked down at it, unsure of what he was asking.

"Can you type in your number? I'm thinking we should do this set-up tomorrow night so they'll still have a few days after the date to spend together. You can gather the lights and decorations and the sheet and I'll find a projector, movie, and get a bunch of snacks. But even with a plan in place we should still be in contact."

Really? Amber had been expecting to do all of the heavy lifting. That was the way Raul had been even if they were doing something together. But Josh was happy to do his part. Maybe even more than his part, because he was taking the harder jobs.

Amber took the phone and entered her number.

"I have a video conference call at three tomorrow but I can get off by four. You can text me directions to the room you mentioned so I can meet you there to decorate and stuff. We also still need to come up with a plan on how to trick your sister into getting to the room," Josh continued.

He'd really thought this thing out. Unless . . .

"Wait, have you done this before?" Amber asked, holding Josh's phone hostage just in case he wasn't willing to answer her.

"Tricked a woman into going out with Aiden Christensen? Can't say that I ever have," Josh said, implying how outrageous that would be. But it was what they were doing now. Surely Elise wasn't the first woman to deny Aiden a date even if she really did want to go out with him but was too scared to see it through. And then Amber thought about Aiden, what he had going for him. Yeah, maybe this was the first time.

"But he really likes her. And I'll always have my boy's back." Josh shrugged.

She was trying hard not to note how loyal Josh was. Compared to how disloyal Raul had been.

"And I normally wouldn't ever trick my sister like this. But she likes him too."

"But she's too scared to give him a chance because he lives so far away and he's in a world so unlike hers. Yeah, I get it." Josh nodded as if he'd given this a lot of thought so that he could understand Elise's point of view.

Amber felt her mouth drop open but she quickly closed it. Hopefully before Josh had noticed.

"So I'll see you tomorrow?" Josh asked. Amber appreciated that even though he'd come up with a plan he wanted to make sure Amber was on board before just running with it.

Loyal and considerate.

This was becoming a problem. Amber missed the days when she'd assumed Josh had to be full of himself and flighty. Weren't all famous guys?

"Yeah," Amber managed as Josh grinned one last time and then left her office.

Amber pressed on her chest, annoyed at her thumping heart. So Josh turned out to be a good guy. So what? It wasn't like he was into her. He was only speaking to her because she was the other half of his plan. Once that was over she'd never see him again. As it should be.

Or at least that was what Amber would continue to tell herself.

A KNOCK at the door had Elise and Amber exchanging glances.

It was eight pm, so not late by any means, but Amber hadn't been expecting anyone. By the way Elise shrugged her shoulders she hadn't been either.

For a second Amber wondered if it could be Aiden and Josh but she decided that wasn't likely, considering she'd set up a meeting with Josh for the next day.

Amber put down her fork—she'd gotten home from work only half an hour ago so she was in the middle of eating her simple pasta dinner—and got up to check the peephole.

"Hm," Amber said, surprise filling her voice as she reached for the doorknob.

"Hey Amber," Mack said as Amber opened the door.

"Hey." Amber let in Mama Nora's boyfriend. It was freezing out there and she didn't want to leave them standing out in the cold.

"This is a pleasant surprise," Amber said as Mack walked in and she held the door open a moment longer.

"Oh, it's just me," Mack said as he realized why Amber wasn't closing the door. He was right. Amber had assumed Mama Nora was somewhere out there in the darkness and would be coming up their porch steps momentarily.

Just him? Not exactly strange but definitely not normal either. Amber couldn't remember spending time with just Mack.

"Hi Elise," Mack greeted Amber's sister who stood in the kitchen stir frying up some vegetables for her meal.

"Mack!" Elise greeted him with a conspiratorial smile.

Wait, did Elise know why Mack was here?

"This probably seems weird," Mack began after Amber closed the door and sat back down by her food.

Mack took the dining chair opposite Amber.

"A little," Amber admitted and the three of them laughed.

"Wait, is Mama Nora okay?" Amber asked when she realized what Mack being here alone could mean. Surely, though, if it had been an emergency he would have called. This just didn't make any sense.

"She's fine. At home. I made sure she left painting for the day before I came up here because—" Mack pulled a small black box out of his pocket. A box that could only mean one thing.

Amber gasped.

"You're proposing!" she squealed.

"Finally you get it," Elise laughed as she joined them at the table with a plate of her own dinner.

Amber, now over the shock of seeing Mack and the ring box, realized that she had food in front of her and now Elise did as well.

"Oh shoot. I should have asked before. Do you want anything?" Amber asked Mack, waving to her plate of pasta. She'd been surprised by his visit enough to forget her manners.

"No, I'm good." Mack opened the box and this time Amber and Elise gasped in unison.

In the box lay a diamond-encased gold band in the midst of which sat the biggest emerald Amber had ever seen. It was perfect for her artistic birth mother.

"It's gorgeous," Amber muttered, unable to take her eyes off the ring.

"Enough for her to say yes?" Mack asked, hopefully.

"There is no doubt in my mind she'll say yes, Mack. Even if you got her a fake superstore ring, she'd say yes," Amber replied, finally looking at the man who was going to be her stepdad.

Oh my gosh, Mama Nora was getting married!

"What about you?" Mack asked, meeting Amber's eyes. "I'll speak to Nora's dad soon. I know he's quite traditional but I wanted to ask your blessing first. Of all the people in the world, what you think matters most to Nora."

Amber's heart warmed as immediate tears welled in her eyes. She tried to shake them away. She was sick of crying. But then again, if she had to cry she wanted it to be for this reason. That her birth mom was going to have the very best man in the world.

"I can't think of anything more I'd ever wish for her," Amber said honestly.

"Really?" Mack asked.

"Of course!"

Mack let out a huge breath as he leaned back so far in his seat Amber was surprised when it didn't topple over.

"You were worried she'd say no?" Elise asked, a forkful of stir fry near her mouth.

"I don't know. It's just, you hope you're enough for the woman you love but you see her and you see yourself and you can't imagine anyone being fooled into thinking you are worthy of her. That I'm worthy of Nora," Mack explained as he rubbed a hand over his forehead.

This time a few tears fell down Amber's cheeks. This was all just so sweet.

"Well, you are," she said after pausing to clear her throat. "As long as you take care of her the way you have been? She'll be happy forever."

"I will be too," Mack replied instantly.

"When are you going to do it?" Elise asked around a bite of stir fry. She didn't normally talk with her mouth full but she was apparently too excited to wait.

"I have a few surprises up my sleeve, so I think Christmas morning. She might be expecting it, but you know how she is about Christmas."

Amber nodded. Yes she did. No one loved Christmas more

than Mama Nora. She believed it to be a day full of magic and she'd passed on that tradition to Amber and Elise as well.

Amber got up, as did Mack, and wrapped her arms around her soon-to-be stepdad. They deserved every happiness. Heaven knew both Nora and Mack had waited long enough.

"If Grandpa gives you any grief, send him my way," Amber said gleefully.

She was just so thrilled for Mack and Nora.

"Will do. And Amber, I just want you to know as I take my vows with Nora that you are a part of that. I know that you are grown and you might not feel like you need another father figure, but I am here for you. Always. Getting to go on this journey with Nora, I immediately knew that I wanted to protect you from the moment I met you."

Amber blinked away even more tears. What was Mack doing to her?

But this man wasn't just perfect for Mama Nora, he was the perfect addition to their unconventional family and she couldn't wait for Christmas morning.

Mama Nora didn't know it yet. But she was about to have the very best holiday of her life.

CHAPTER THIRTEEN

"I LOVE THIS SMELL!" Alexis exclaimed to Jared, twining her fingers through his as they entered the Christmas tree lot. Even though they both had artificial trees, Jared had decided that this year he wanted a real tree as well.

Alexis had been on board with the idea immediately. The pine needles really were a pain to clean up, but having that fragrance was worth the work. Especially because the tree was going to be at Jared's house so she'd rarely, if ever, have to clean up after the tree. The holidays seemed to be shaping up quite beautifully, even if things weren't all glittering lights, spectacular scents, and presents.

The wedge between Marsha and Alexis had grown once again after that disastrous dinner. But at least Marsha had apologized. In the form of an insincere text, but Alexis hadn't minded. Since the kids had gone back and forth without any negative impact on them or on her relationship with them, Alexis wasn't too concerned. There would always be drama where Marsha was involved.

But what had changed since that dinner was the way Alexis and Jared communicated. There was something about that night, the way they'd come together instead of dealing with their own hurt separately after Marsha had attacked them, that had Alexis feeling more sure of her relationship with Jared than ever. She'd known she loved him for a long time, would sacrifice anything for his kids, but what she'd learned that night? She would face the fiery inferno that Marsha could be time and time again. Her relationship was worth it. Jared was worth it. Jared was everything to her and he treated her the same way. Alexis had never felt more treasured in her life than this past week. It felt like they'd gone up a level. To where, Alexis wasn't sure. She just knew she liked it.

"I get the final say, right Dad?" Brittany asked as she and Peter piled out of the backseat of Jared's new truck. He'd gotten it as an early Christmas present to himself, just in time to take home their Christmas tree.

"No," Peter countered. "We all have to vote, right Dad?"

Both children looked expectantly at Jared.

"Can we just not fight for, I don't know, fifteen minutes?" Jared asked.

Peter narrowed his gaze as he turned to Brittany and Brittany with her hands on her hips looked at Peter.

"But who gets to choose the tree?" Brittany asked. Her plea was way more important to her than her father's request.

"Alexis does," Jared said, causing all three of them to turn to look at her.

Alexis glared at Jared. Was he really going to put her in the middle of this?

Out of the corner of her eye Alexis saw Brittany drop her hands from her hips. So for a moment Alexis turned her full attention to the teens and saw that Peter had even stopped scowling.

"Okay," he agreed with his dad.

"Can we give you suggestions?" Brittany asked Alexis.

"Uh, sure," Alexis said, blinking at the unexpected turn of events.

"That one's nice," Brittany pointed out a tree to Alexis. "But don't make any decisions until we look at all of the trees."

Alexis nodded as Peter and Brittany walked ahead of them into the lot, arguing but without heat because they knew it didn't matter what they chose. Alexis had the final say.

Alexis turned to Jared once again.

"I overheard Brittany tell Peter you had the best taste in the family. And Peter agreed. When they started fighting about this I knew you were the only solution."

"Brittany said I have good taste?" Alexis actually held a hand over her heart. But she was seriously worried her heart would stop if she didn't keep an eye on it.

"Best in the family," Jared said with a grin. "I mean, you did choose me, after all."

Alexis shook her head, fighting hard against the smile that begged to appear. "That's probably a negative in Brittany's book," she teased.

Jared pulled her into his arms as he frowned dramatically. "But what is it in your book?"

"The best decision I ever made." Alexis couldn't tease about that.

"Good." Jared dropped a kiss on Alexis' lips that she was eager to receive.

"Stop kissing and start searching!" Brittany demanded.

Alexis pulled away immediately.

"You know, we don't have to listen to her," Jared said as he caught Alexis' hand before she could get away completely.

"We do if we want any peace in our lives," Alexis replied.

Jared sighed, knowing she was right.

Hand in hand, Alexis and Jared wandered down the first aisle of trees with Peter and Brittany up ahead, laughing about something Peter had done. The air was brisk but not too chilly. With her white puffer coat over her fleece-lined leggings Alexis was pretty comfortable, and with the scent of pine permeating the air? She was pretty sure this was her version of heaven.

"So what are your plans for Christmas day?" Alexis asked Jared as they swung their hands together.

"To be with you," Jared replied quickly.

Alexis grinned. "Really? Even with your parents in town?" She'd been worried that since Jared's parents were coming in from Portland for the holiday they'd want just family time, with no "outsiders."

"*Especially* with my parents in town. You know they love you," Jared replied.

Alexis had only been able to spend time with Jared's parents a couple of times over the months they'd been dating. A big part of that was because things had been so rocky with Marsha and the kids for a long time, but work schedules played a role as well. Getting time off to go to Portland wasn't easy and Jared's parents only made the trek to the island once a year for Christmas. They didn't do well with boats. Even Thanksgiving hadn't been spent together because his parents had decided to go on a railroad trip of the Canadian Rockies instead of the traditional holiday get-together.

Alexis had wondered if Jared's parents were purposely avoiding her but with this invite to Christmas day and Jared's declaration, Alexis felt those worries dissipate. She'd had no idea they loved her but Jared wouldn't lie to her.

"Really?" Alexis asked, probably fishing for another compliment. But she really did have low confidence when it came to Jared's family.

"Really. How could they not?" Jared said as he pulled Alexis into his arms once more.

"This one is good, right?" Brittany called down the aisle, motioning for Alexis to join her.

"Maybe I should have just told Brittany she could choose the tree," Jared muttered as Alexis pulled out of his arms once more so that she could look at the tree Brittany had chosen.

"Oh, it is nice. But maybe a little too sparse around the very bottom?" Alexis pointed at some scraggly branches.

"You're right," Brittany said the words that almost never came out of her mouth. "We'll keep looking."

She and Peter rounded the next aisle without the adults and Jared tugged on Alexis' hand to hold her back.

"What about this one?" He pointed to the tallest tree of the bunch. It wasn't as full as Alexis would typically choose but there was something charming about it.

"I like it," Alexis said. "But I think Brittany will be a hard sell."

Jared pointed once more. "Even with that in there?"

Alexis followed Jared's finger but couldn't see anything out of the ordinary. It was a tree with branches and needles and . . . Alexis squinted. Was there something blue on the branch?

Jared stood back so Alexis decided it was up to her to get the blue thing out of the tree. Had someone lost their . . . Alexis dug her hand through the branches, the majority of her arm disappearing into the needles. She felt around and paused when her hand felt something firm yet soft. It was a small velvet box.

She pulled the box out and looked from Jared to the box, her breath coming a bit faster. The size of the box was auspicious but she didn't dare get her hopes up. They'd talked about this as something that would happen in their far future—just a few days before, Jared had mentioned how long it would take to save up for the ring he wanted to get Alexis.

But . . . was this one of those pranks? Where a guy gave a pair of earrings instead?

Yes, it had to be a pair of earrings. Not a prank, just a sweet early Christmas present for Alexis because Jared had bought the truck for himself.

"Open it," Jared prompted and Alexis realized her hands were shaking.

She didn't truly think this box held earrings even as her heart begged her to reconsider. She'd be crushed if she opened this box and it held earrings. Because more than anything else she wanted this to be a ring. She wanted to say yes and start her forever with Jared.

She swallowed as she did as Jared had said, opening the blue box little by little.

The gleam of something shiny was the first thing Alexis saw and the instant the box was fully open, the smallest sigh of relief escaped her lips before she flung herself into Jared's arms.

"Yes!" Alexis shouted as Jared laughed.

He set Alexis back on the ground before dropping to a knee.

"Maybe I should ask you before you answer?" He gazed up at Alexis, the love in his eyes unmistakable.

Alexis nodded fervently, unable to open her mouth to speak.

"Alexis," Jared said and then paused, his eyes locked on hers. Alexis somehow felt her love for him growing right in that very moment. "You brought sunshine back into our world when I wasn't sure it was possible. You gave me hope for a brighter future and each day I'm with you I see it. You make me want to be better, you help me strive to be stronger. To stare hardship in the face and win, like you do. You are my support and my favorite best friend. I want nothing more than to be the same for you forever. Even though the days may be filled with craziness and who knows what else, I want nothing more than to come home each night to you. Will you be my forever companion?"

Alexis let out a breath she hadn't realized she'd been holding. Her hands were clenched so tightly she was beginning to feel the nail marks on her palms.

This was happening. Jared had proposed. And even though she'd already shouted the answer she found she didn't quite know what to say. He'd spoken such beautiful words. Alexis wanted to match them with a fervency of her own.

"We approve. Just in case you were wondering," Brittany said. She and Peter had come back from the next aisle, smiles on their faces as they watched.

"Well, in that case," Alexis said, grinning so hard her cheeks hurt from. "You've helped me to learn to love myself in a way I didn't think possible. I'm not perfect, nor will I ever be, but with you in my life I have perfect moments. In fact, this is one right now."

Jared's eyes glistened as he smiled up at Alexis. As if he couldn't believe his luck when it should be the other way around.

"I can't imagine wanting anything more than this. Yes!" Alexis shouted as Jared slipped the gorgeous white gold band housing a stunning oval-cut diamond onto her finger.

Jared then hopped up, his arms immediately encircling Alexis' waist before he twirled her through the air.

"I'll be your bridesmaid, right?" Brittany asked as she joined them. "I'm way too old to be a flower girl."

Alexis chuckled as Peter groaned. "As long as I don't have to be a groomsman."

Jared paid them no heed as he lifted Alexis in his arms, kissing her long and soundly.

Alexis hardly noticed the ews and yucks from Brittany and Peter.

Jared pulled away all too soon for the sake of his kids. But the shine in his eyes told her there would be much more where that came from and Alexis warmed at the thought.

"So I guess we have to choose this tree? Now that it's sentimental and stuff," Brittany complained even as she pulled the tree Jared had hidden the ring in out from the others.

Brittany couldn't fool Alexis. She clearly wanted the tree now because of the sentimentality and stuff. The girl was a lot softer than she'd ever let on.

"Well, yeah. Especially because it has this hanging on it." Jared brought an ornament out from his pocket and hung it on one of the scrawny branches.

Peter and Brittany leaned forward to look, smiles on their faces as they pulled back. Alexis stepped close, reaching a hand to still the little ornament that swayed on the branch.

A tiny clay cartoon family hung from a ribbon. Even from the faces it was easy to see who they all were but each was labeled by name. Brittany and Peter were on the edges, hugging Jared and Alexis in the middle.

"Whatever. But next year I get to choose the tree," Brittany proclaimed as she handed the tree off to Jared.

Jared shot Alexis a grin and Alexis immediately knew why. They were already planning next year. And they could plan the year after that and the year after that because Alexis was now officially a part of their family. Forever.

CHAPTER FOURTEEN

THE FRONT DOOR SLAMMED, the rattle startling Lou. She had four kids. She knew how to withstand door slams. But this was different.

Lou rose from her seat at the dining room table where she'd been helping Cash with his homework as Emma came tearing into the house, tears streaming down her swollen, red cheeks.

"Emma," Lou gasped as her daughter flung herself into Lou's arms.

Lou could feel Cash's curious eyes on them. "Hey Cash. How about you go play with Aiden?" Lou offered.

"But I'm still doing my homework," Cash said in a very un-Cash-like manner. The boy would often come up with the most outlandish excuses to get out of homework. The fact that he was trying to keep doing it was a sign that he really wanted to hear what had happened to his sister.

"It'll keep. You can play that new video game your dad gave you." Those were the magic words and Cash shot up from his seat, dashing to the room he shared with Aiden before Lou could change her mind.

That stupid video game had been a source of contention for

Lou and Harvey for the past few days. He'd gotten it on a whim the last time he had the kids and had thought it would be a great idea to give it to the boys without consulting Lou first. Harvey hadn't seen the big deal—the game had fit the strict parameters Lou put on video games in her home—but Lou didn't want her boys to randomly receive expensive gifts. For a birthday or Christmas? Great. If they worked their little booties off to earn them, that would be fine as well. But as a 'just because' gift, it had been too much. But Harvey had protested that it was wrong to take it back and Lou had conceded. So they had a new video game. And hopefully Harvey now understood her point.

"What happened, Em?" Lou asked after a few minutes of quietly holding her crying daughter, stroking Emma's soft hair. The tears had now somewhat subsided though the ragged breathing that followed a truly heavy cry had taken their place.

"I'm just so mad," Emma choked out as Lou's phone rang.

"Ugh!" Emma cried out as she looked at Lou's phone. "She's already calling to tell on me."

What? Lou was severely confused. She looked at the name on her caller ID and saw that it was Susan. Emma had been hanging out with her daughter Megan that afternoon.

"Did something happen at Megan's house?" Lou asked, her attention still on her daughter.

"Just answer it," Emma said, her voice at odds with the fact that she hugged Lou even tighter.

"Are you sure? Because I'd rather speak with you," Lou said, letting Emma know she was there to support her.

"Yes," Emma said before burying her face in Lou's side.

"Okay," Lou answered, reaching for her phone slowly to give Emma a way out.

But she continued to hold fast to Lou without saying a word.

"Hi Susan." Lou accepted the call just before it went to voicemail.

"Did Emma make it home?" Susan asked, thankfully sounding concerned about Emma. Lou had been sure from Emma's reaction that Susan was about to rail on about something Emma had done. Though that was totally outside of Susan's character so Lou probably shouldn't have thought that about her friend. But seeing her baby so crushed had awakened the roaring mama bear in Lou and she really hadn't been thinking straight.

"She did," Lou said slowly, "and she's crying." She decided she should let Susan know just in case the woman wasn't aware.

Had Megan and Emma had a fight? That seemed unlikely. The two had been friends for years and although they had little disagreements Megan had never made Emma cry before.

"I feel terribly," Susan said and Lou felt her shoulders release some of the tension she'd been holding.

"I didn't realize the girls were eavesdropping and—I guess I should start from the beginning."

"That would be nice," Lou replied as she put the phone on speaker and set it down on the table.

She looked to Emma who nodded, understanding that Lou was inviting her into this conversation if she wanted.

"Just letting you know I put you on speaker. Emma's here with me." Lou felt she should give her friend the heads up.

"Thanks," Susan replied before saying, "I think you know I'm pretty good friends with Amy Hyde?"

"I do," Lou said. She personally didn't know Amy very well although she'd lived on the island all of her life as well. What Lou did know was that Amy had graduated from high school a few years after Lou and then left for college. She'd come back to the island with a husband and a child and then had two more. Oh, and Amy was also a bombshell. People had been sure the woman would go into modeling or acting or something that showcased her pretty face.

"Well, she came over today. She's been having some marital issues and . . . Emma already knows all of this and that's why I feel okay telling you, but I'd appreciate it if Amy's situation wasn't shared with anyone else."

"Of course," Lou replied quickly. She understood the need to keep things of such a personal nature to herself. She just wasn't quite sure what any of this had to do with Emma.

"She's decided to get a divorce. It's been a long time coming and basically she told me that she was ready to get out in the dating world again. Starting with Jax." Lou bit her lip as she tried to ignore the pit that had suddenly developed in her stomach.

Jax was a catch. Of course all of the available women of Whisling would want him. But if he and Lou were meant to be, it would work out. Even if they had obstacles in their way.

"I—maybe I shouldn't have said this, but I've heard through the grapevine that Jax is interested in you. I figured Amy must not know if she had decided to pursue Jax, so I wanted to let her know that she'd be stepping on your toes if she moved forward."

"She called you fat, Mom!" Emma shouted before burrowing her head into Lou's shoulder once more.

"If I'd had any idea the girls were listening—heck, if I'd known what Amy was going to say—I would have seen her out sooner." Susan sounded truly contrite and Lou felt badly for her.

"I understand that you're just the messenger. We don't shoot them around these parts." Lou felt the need to joke.

Susan let out a chuckle that was mostly relief mixed with a little amusement.

"Amy used a few choice words that I'd rather not repeat, basically saying the only reason Jax felt the need to even consider dating you was because he didn't know she was available."

Lou had heard worse. She'd probably continue to hear it, especially if she and Jax ever wound up dating. The words stung slightly but her bigger concern was what had happened to Emma.

"Emma came stomping in and shouted that at least her mom had real breasts. I guess the girls had also overheard the conversation I had with Amy about her augmentation." Susan's voice was filled with mortification, and Lou didn't blame her. The girls really needed to stop listening in on adult conversations.

"And then Amy—she shouldn't have said it. The only excuse I can give is that she really is quite torn up about her divorce. She told Emma—"

"That even if my mom was as pretty as she was, Jax still wouldn't date her because we're all snot-faced brats," Emma completed when Susan couldn't seem to speak the words.

Lou worked hard not to show what she was feeling but it took everything in her not to march on down to Susan's and give that Amy Hyde a piece of her mind. How dare she speak to Emma like that?

"I kicked Amy out of the house—really there is no excuse to speak to a child like that—but when I went to comfort Emma, Megan told me she'd already run home. I am truly so, so sorry," Susan said.

Lou tried to swallow down some of her bubbling fury. Susan really wasn't to blame for this. Lou couldn't be angry with her even if she did think Susan should reconsider some of her friendships.

"I'll speak with Emma and then check in with you," Lou said, knowing she wanted to comfort her daughter before worrying about what Susan was feeling.

"Yes. Please do. Again, I'm so sorry Lou. And I'm even sorrier to you, Em. You are a delightful young lady so please don't let Amy's words get to you. You were brave to speak up for your mom," Susan said to Emma.

Emma pulled away from Lou slightly at Susan's words. "Okay," she managed to whisper before going back to her previous position.

"Thanks Susan," Lou said before hanging up.

She took a few deep breaths trying to rid herself of everything she felt toward Amy. Right now was about Emma and the last thing her little girl needed was any residual anger pointed her way.

Lou took Emma by the shoulders, positioning her so that she could look Emma in the eye.

"You were courageous, sweet girl," Lou said, focusing on the positive. Yes, Emma had done some things wrong but nothing worthy of being chewed out by a grown woman.

"And Susan is right. You are delightful. I haven't met a snot-faced brat in my life, much less raised one. You are good and beautiful and kind and talented." Lou wanted to fill the space that had been taken by Amy's cruel ridicule with words that actually described Emma.

"I'm not as mad about that. I don't care what that stupid lady thinks about me," Emma said, wiping her poor little tear-stained cheeks. "But how could she say those things about you, Mom?"

Lou pulled Emma close once more, her arms encasing her in a hug.

"The same way she could say mean things about you. She isn't thinking straight. Do you remember how I was right after my divorce from your dad?" Lou asked, knowing she was doing the right thing even as she wanted to lash out at Amy. But the woman was hurting, and if anyone understood that pain it was Lou.

"Yes," Emma said softly.

"I did things I wasn't proud of." Lou remembered the many times she'd hidden behind closed doors and eaten her weight in junk food. She'd tried to hide the worst parts from her kids but she knew they'd still seen more than they should.

"I know. But you weren't mean to anyone," Emma replied.

Lou hadn't been. At least not in the way Amy had been.

"I'm not saying what Amy did was okay. She was wrong. Plain and simple. But sometimes when we're hurt we act in ways that we shouldn't. I'm not trying to say that Amy was right, I'm just letting you know why she might have acted the way she did."

Emma nodded, too smart for her eleven years.

"Do you want to go sit on the couch?" Lou offered.

Emma seemed worn out from crying and was leaning heavily on Lou. She nodded once more and Lou led her to the couch, sitting right in the middle of it and pulling her daughter down to the same cushion. Lou slid her arm around Emma.

"I think a good lesson to learn here is that sometimes grownups make mistakes too."

"Big mistakes," Emma added.

Lou grinned, grateful Emma wasn't looking at her face.

"We do. But was there something maybe you could take away from this as well?" Lou felt she still needed to teach her daughter. There would definitely be no punishment involved, but Lou did want Emma to know she could have made a different decision.

"I shouldn't have eavesdropped," Emma said softly. She knew it was something she wasn't supposed to do.

"But Amy always says the craziest things. We don't eavesdrop on Megan's mom and anyone else. Just Amy," Emma said as she scrunched her nose.

Lou bit back a smile because Emma was now looking up at her.

"That's how I knew about her fake you-know-whats," Emma added, making Lou wonder what Emma had really said to Amy and if Susan had supplied the word 'breasts' in her retelling.

She still couldn't believe Emma had said that, but then again Lou had no idea what she would have said to Amy had she been in the heat of the moment with Emma.

"Okay, but even Amy deserves privacy, don't you think?" Lou said. She might not be feeling much warmth toward the woman but this was about Emma. She needed to learn this lesson regardless of whether Amy deserved it or not.

"Yeah," Emma agreed mournfully.

Lou nodded as she stroked Emma's hair. That was enough for today. Emma probably shouldn't have jumped out and spoken up about Amy's augmentation but Lou had a hard time reprimanding her when she was so proud of her for sticking up for her mom.

"Can I ask you a question, Mom?" Emma asked.

"Of course," Lou replied, her attention on a snarl her finger had caught in.

"Are you dating Mr. Jax?" Emma asked.

Lou startled, causing Emma to yelp since Lou had inadvertently tugged on the snarl with her slight jump.

"Oh, I'm so sorry, Em," Lou said as she carefully disentangled her hand from Emma's hair.

"It's fine. It scared me more than hurt," Emma replied, giving Lou a few seconds to compose her mess of thoughts. But when it came down to it, the truth was actually quite simple.

"So are you dating Mr. Jax?" Emma pushed once more.

"I'm not," Lou replied as Emma shifted, kneeling and facing her mom.

"Why did Megan's mom say that a little bird told her you guys were?" Emma asked.

"I don't know if the little bird told her that we were or that we might one day . . . " Lou let her words trail off, wondering who this little bird had been and if they knew what a mess they'd created.

"So you will date Mr. Jax one day?" Emma asked hopefully.

This was a conversation they really shouldn't be having. Lou didn't want it to come out that Emma was the reason she wasn't dating Jax. The girl would feel terrible. But she also knew that Emma really loved taking lessons with Lou. It was complicated and she didn't want her daughter wrestling with adult problems. Lou needed to change the conversation topic—and fast.

"I don't know. Hey, Em. Should we get Chinese takeout for dinner?" Lou offered Emma's favorite kind of food. The girl had a major weakness for some pan-fried noodles.

"Can we invite Mr. Jax over for dinner?" Emma asked, her face full of excitement.

"Em, I just—"

"Because he likes you, Mom. I heard Grandma Margie talking about it and it's true. At lessons he watches you when he thinks you're not looking. But I'm looking," Emma pumped her eyebrows with her last words. The girl shouldn't know how to do that, should she?

"And if you don't date him, he'll end up with someone horrible like Amy and he deserves someone amazing like you," Emma added before Lou could get in a word.

Lou scrubbed a hand over her face, reeling from the various emotions stirred up by her daughter's words. Shock, wistfulness, and above all delight that Emma thought her amazing and deserving of Jax coursed through her. "Em, I can't date Jax," she finally had to say. Emma wasn't going to let this go.

"Why not?" Emma asked.

"Should we get some dumplings with our order?" Lou knew it was an absurd attempt but she needed to distract Emma.

"Mom, we're talking about something important here," Emma's voice took on a level of maturity Lou hadn't ever witnessed as she gave her mom a condescending look.

Lou would have laughed if she weren't so worried. Emma was getting too close to the truth. She wouldn't let her daughter get hurt twice in one day.

"Grown-up things, Em. We can't date because of grown-up things," Lou finally said.

Emma threw her hands in the air. "I'm so sick of grown-up things. That's why you and Dad got divorced. That's why Amy is such a mean person and now that's why you can't date Mr. Jax. Because I know you want to, Mom. You like him the way Brittany likes every boy who skateboards."

Lou let a single laugh escape. Emma's assessment of Brittany had been too spot on.

"Are grown-up things always so terrible? Because it seems like grown-up things hurt you," Emma continued, ignoring Lou's laugh.

Lou stopped, taking in Emma's words and seeing the world through her eyes. She hated it. She didn't want Emma to think there were only bad things to come.

"But grown-up things can be great. I get to be your mom and work at the gym, which I love," Lou said, pointing out the good in her life.

Emma scoffed. "That's not worth it."

Lou pressed her lips together. "Maybe not to you, but being your mom, as well as Aiden's, Cash's, and Hazel's mom, is the best thing that has ever happened to me."

"It's us," Emma suddenly said.

"What?" Lou replied.

"It's our fault you won't date Jax, right? You like him. He likes you. Something is in the way. It's us."

How in the world had Emma figured that out? She was eleven going on therapist evidently.

"It's not . . . " Lou began but couldn't bring herself to outright lie. What if the truth came out one day? Emma would be even more hurt then.

"It's a choice I've made," Lou said honestly.

"But doesn't Jax like us?" Emma asked, her bottom lip quivering.

"He loves you guys," Lou replied quickly. And he really did. That was one of the things that made Jax so attractive.

"Is it Aunt Marsha?" Emma prodded.

Lou had to chuckle. But for once it wasn't her sister who had scared a man away.

"Em, I really can't tell you. But you're right. I like Jax and I think he likes me. I know he thinks you guys are the best. And maybe one day it will work out. But today isn't that day," Lou said, hating how much sadness she'd allowed to creep into her tone.

"Call him," Emma demanded.

"Call Jax?" Lou asked, surprise filling her.

"Yes," Emma said as she pulled out the phone Lou had recently gotten for her kids to share, especially for the nights they went to Harvey's, and dialed Jax's number.

"Emma, you can't—" This wasn't like her daughter at all. Sweet Emma didn't demand things.

Jax answered before Lou could wrestle the phone away from Emma.

"Hi Emma," Jax answered.

"Mom's here too," Emma added as she put her phone on speakerphone.

"Hello, Lou." Jax's warm tone sent tingles up Lou's spine. And this was over the phone, with her daughter watching. The man had too much of an effect on her.

"Have you been practicing for lessons, Em?" Jax asked, completely unaware of what he was walking into.

"Yeah, but that's not why I'm calling," Emma said, a confidence in her tone that Lou had been hoping would come back. After Harvey had left Emma hadn't been quite herself. Now she was herself and then some.

Lou was proud of the growth but also needed to speak up. Emma had pushed the limits and it was time to be done.

"Emma, we should let Jax go," Lou said, prompting her daughter to end the call.

"I don't have anywhere to be. What's up, Emma?"

"See, Mom? He's fine. Mr. Jax, I have a question for you," Emma said.

Lou wanted to yank the phone away and hang it up but this was her eleven-year-old daughter. She wasn't doing anything wrong so she couldn't punish her. She was just doing something Lou would rather not have her do. How was she supposed to deal with this situation? This was why dating with kids should come with its very own, very thick handbook.

"Shoot," Jax said as Lou wracked her brain. There had to be something she could do to stop this. She knew Emma's question and although she was pretty sure she knew Jax's answer, it was beyond embarrassing to have Emma ask him while Lou was here. What if he thought Lou had put her daughter up to this, trying to get Jax to confess his true feelings for her? Her cheeks went warm.

Lou looked around for anything to stop this. She saw the fireplace poker and seriously considered knocking herself out. But then how would that conversation go? *Oh my gosh, Mr. Jax, I have to go. My mom just hit herself over the head with a fireplace poker.*

She needed a better plan. But nothing was coming to mind.

"Why aren't you dating my mom?" Emma asked before Lou could do anything.

"Oh," Jax said and Lou sank down into the couch, pulling a cushion into her lap as if it could protect her from mortification. What would Jax say? Her face flamed red but more important than her embarrassment was that she and Jax hadn't planned this out at all. He didn't know she hadn't prompted Emma to make this call. Maybe Jax thought Lou was too much of a coward to tell Emma the truth so she wanted him to do it instead. He didn't know this call was all Emma's doing.

"What did your mom say?" Jax asked.

Thank heavens. The man was a genius.

"She said it was grown-up stuff," Emma replied before adding, "But if you don't date my mom, will you date Amy?"

Lou brought a palm to her forehead.

Jax chuckled. "Em, I won't date anyone else. I'm going to let you in on a secret. I really like your mom."

"Hallelujah," Emma declared.

Lou couldn't help but laugh at that, especially because Jax's words had caused an unexpected giddiness.

"Are you guys not dating because she's worried we want her to get back together with Dad? Because we all know that won't happen," Emma said.

Lou really shouldn't have let Emma watch the movie about twins who tried to get their parents back together. That had to be the reason she was acting like this. She wasn't usually the matchmaking type.

"I don't think that's the case. Em, I really think this is something you and your mom need to talk about," Jax said, firmly in Lou's corner. Man, she loved him for that.

Wait, she didn't *love* him, love him. It was much too early for that. She loved him like *liked him a lot* loved him. Oh, that made absolutely no sense.

"But she won't tell me why. And I know it's because of us. Her face did that weird eye twitch thing when I asked her if it was," Emma said to Jax.

What weird eye twitch thing?

"You like us, don't you?" Emma asked.

"You all are the best. I wish I could spend more time with you," Jax revealed.

Lou felt her heart warm. The man was perfect. At least for her.

"Then why?" Emma asked. "I'm going to find out," she said to the phone but she looked at Lou. "I'll ask Grandma Margie, Grandpa, Alexis, Uncle Jared, Brittany, Peter, everyone—even Aunt Marsha. I will ask everyone. And if they don't give me an answer I'll figure out another way. Because Mom, I want you to date Mr. Jax. Please," Emma nearly begged.

Emma's words had Lou rethinking everything. Maybe she should let Emma make this decision? But she was eleven. Lou knew better, didn't she? Then again . . . there wasn't time to weigh all the variables right now. It came down to what seemed more important to Emma. And right now Lou dating Jax seemed pretty danged important. Maybe more important than taking lessons with her mom.

"Do you like taking guitar lessons with me?" Lou asked. She needed this answer before she could make a decision on what to say.

"Yeah. Especially because it means you get time with Mr. Jax," Emma replied.

"You asked me to take lessons with you so I'd have time with Jax?" Lou needed clarification.

"Yeah. I saw you watching him at the gym and when you told me he'd give me lessons I asked you to do them too because I knew you liked him," Emma said matter-of-factly.

This was definitely all that movie's fault. Except instead of getting her parents back together, Emma was helping her mom move on.

"Seriously? But I thought you loved doing something with me?" Lou said, not willing to believe that her eleven-year-old had tricked her.

"Yeah, that too. But mostly because of Mr. Jax. Do you think I really like the recording room so much? I go in there so you guys have time alone," Emma said with a lift of one shoulder.

Lou was speechless, but Jax's laughter reverberated through the phone.

Lou felt her cheeks heat once again.

This was too much. Here she was staying away from Jax because of her daughter, when her daughter had been their matchmaker all along?

"I'm not dating Jax because he can't date a student," Lou told Emma even though she was pretty sure she knew what her reaction would be.

"That's it?" Emma asked her eyes wide.

"That's it," Lou replied honestly.

"Do you love guitar lessons?" Emma's eyes suddenly narrowed, Lou could practically see her mind going a million miles a minute.

"No. But I thought you loved taking them with me," Lou said.

"It's fun, but we can do other stuff. Wait, so you can date Mr. Jax right now? Quit lessons and date him!" Emma said, lifting the phone.

"Did you hear that, Mr. Jax?" Emma asked.

Lou shook her head as Jax laughed once more. "I did."

"That's so great!" Emma exclaimed as she handed Lou's phone back to her. "I'm going to give you some privacy."

Lou knew her little girl was growing up but this was too

much. Maybe she shouldn't be spending so much time with Brittany.

Lou watched as Emma raced toward the back of the house. She turned to Lou, pumping her arms in the air before disappearing into her room.

Lou's stomach twisted as she looked at the phone in her hand. Emma smelled victory but Lou wasn't so sure. She didn't want Jax to feel like he had to do anything. She wanted him to ask her out but only if he wanted to. Before it was different because there were reasons they couldn't be together, but now that they were gone . . . would Jax feel differently?

"So I've heard it's been an eventful day over there," Jax said, the unease in Lou's stomach loosening with just the sound of his voice.

"You could say that. Look, Jax, please don't feel any pressure. The last time we had this conversation it was all hypothetical and—"

"Lou," Jax interrupted.

"Hmm?" Lou replied, her thoughts all over the place. What had she been about to say? Did it even matter?

"I was wondering what you're doing on Friday night?" Jax asked.

Lou's heart stopped.

"Seriously?" she asked.

"I've never been more serious. I've been waiting for this moment for months, Lou. For the first time, nothing is in our way. And you'd better believe I'm not fool enough to waste a second. Every day I wake up wondering if this is the day you decide waiting for me isn't worth it."

Jax had thought that?

"Well the only foolish thing you've done is think that I could want to date anyone other than you," Lou replied, self-assurance filling her.

"So you're free?" Jax asked once more.

"So free," Lou replied with a giggle.

Lou didn't giggle, yet with Jax . . . apparently she did. She guessed with Jax anything could happen.

"Good," Jax's voice lowered to that register that made Lou's core warm in anticipation. "See you Friday, Love."

Jax hung up and Lou was pretty sure the smile on her face was perma etched. There was no way it would go anywhere. Her kids were happy and thriving and she was going on a date with the literal man of her dreams.

Lou bit her lip. She guessed the best things in life were worth waiting for. She was just grateful her wait was finally over.

CHAPTER FIFTEEN

"SORRY! I promise I'll be quick," Amber said to Elise as they hurried down one of the inn's halls side by side.

It was seven fifty-five pm. They were supposed to meet Josh and Aiden in the makeshift movie room at eight.

The whole day had been a flurry between work Amber actually had to do and prep for the surprise date but the movie room was officially set—a bedsheet screen graced the wall and twinkle lights filled the space, as well as a few potted plants Amber had borrowed from different parts of the inn. She'd passed Josh a few times as they both worked and she'd seen the projector and movie set up the last time she'd been in the room. She was sure he'd have the snacks set up by now as well.

The hardest part of the whole operation was getting Elise prepared and there. Amber had lied about a girls' night to the Whisling movie theater for Elise, Amber, and Mama Nora. Amber thought about fake inviting more of their friends so that it would seem more official but she realized that getting more people involved could make things messy. So she'd stuck with Mama Nora as her only accomplice besides Josh because her birth mom was as invested in all of this as she was.

Amber bit her lip as she thought about who Mama Nora was actually spending the evening with. Her soon to be fiancé—and Mama Nora had no idea. Amber couldn't wait until the news was out. Every time she spoke to her birth mom she felt as if she could just burst, she was so thrilled for her.

"Are you sure you left it back here?" Elise asked as they got to the last door of the hall. The place where the movie room had been set up. Once that door opened all would be revealed.

Amber really hoped Elise wouldn't run. Because deep down she knew Elise liked Aiden. She was scared, for sure, but part of her hoped it could somehow work out. Amber knew this. Yet Elise was letting her fear win, and Amber couldn't allow that to happen.

So Amber had taken every excuse away from Elise. She'd have no plans because the plans she had were fake. She looked adorable in her cropped chunky sweater and dark-washed wide leg jeans, but the outfit was also comfortable enough to sit in for a few hours while she watched the movie. It was why Amber had used going to a movie as part of her cover story. There would be food in their makeshift theater so Elise couldn't claim she was hungry. Every contingent had been covered. Or so Amber hoped.

"It seems like a weird place to forget your phone," Elise said about the room they almost never used.

"I was back here earlier today. I have a thought I want to run by you: what if we used this space as a room for brides to get ready?" Amber said. The idea had just popped into her head that moment, not earlier that day, but it was actually kind of genius. The room was close to the side door of the inn for outdoor weddings but also close to the backdoor of the ballroom for those held inside. "I must have set my phone down while I was in here."

The truth was that Amber had purposefully left her phone

here the last time she'd come in, setting things up for this very excuse.

"A bridal room! I love it," Elise approved as she walked forward, about to open the door before Amber could.

"Before you make any rash decisions, just give it a chance," Amber urged, causing Elise to pause and give her a bewildered stare.

Male voices sounded down the hall and Elise cocked her head as she looked at her sister, her eyes narrowing in suspicion.

"It's for your own good," Amber said, her voice squeaking at the end. She hadn't allowed herself to think about how mad Elise could be until this very second. She might have backed out if she'd considered it earlier.

Elise threw open the door, her eyes darting from the projector to the screen to the lights and the table laden with food.

"Go Josh," Amber quietly cheered as she took in the spread. The man had gone above and beyond.

"Josh?" Elise asked as the man in question came into view, followed by Aiden.

Elise turned to glare at Amber but at least she hadn't run. Yet.

"You didn't know," were the first words out of Aiden's mouth as he took in Elise's frustrated body language.

"You did?" Elise asked, turning her full, indignant attention to the man who had women literally falling out of their seats for a chance to speak to him.

Aiden nodded. "But I didn't know that you weren't in on it. According to Josh, you were thrilled to be spending the evening with me."

He turned a dark stare on his friend and even in the dimness of the corridor it was easy to see the redness infusing Josh's cheeks.

"Amber lost her phone," Elise explained to Aiden.

Amber felt a blush come over her own face.

They probably shouldn't have been deceitful. But this was for Elise's own good.

"I wouldn't say lost as much as misplaced . . . " Amber cleared her throat uncomfortably.

Elise narrowed her eyes.

"Or placed right here on purpose so we'd have to come back for it," Amber confessed.

"So you and Josh planned this together?" Elise asked, her hands settling on her hips.

Amber was in so much trouble.

"It was more my idea. I pushed it on him," Amber said. At the moment, she couldn't quite remember who had pushed whom, but she'd rather take the blame. Josh had been nothing but helpful.

"No, I came up with the idea. You were just along for the ride," Josh replied without hesitation.

That hadn't been quite how it had gone either.

"Regardless, you two misled us," Aiden said, his frustration focused on his friend. "Did you really think this would trick her into liking me?"

Josh cringed and Amber felt badly for him. It wasn't really his fault. Amber was the one with personal knowledge of her sister, and the one who should have foreseen that this wouldn't go well. She'd just been so focused on getting Elise out of her own way. But this had been the wrong way to go about it.

"Elise, I'm sorry. This isn't Aiden or Josh's fault. You know how I get when I think I have an amazing plan and I get caught up in it. I'm so sorry. I'd be so mad at you if the situation were reversed," Amber said, her heart dropping when she realized it was the truth.

Elise's frown softened as she looked from Amber to the movie room they'd set up.

"You did all of this?" Elise asked instead of acknowledging Amber's apology.

"Josh did most of it," Amber replied.

"Amber did all of the hard work," Josh interjected.

Elise bit her lip as she finally met Aiden's eyes and it was easy to see the unrest in them. He was worried Josh and Amber had blown his last, fragile chance with Elise. He really did like her. Amber just wished Elise could see it.

"Well, it seems a shame for the whole thing go to waste. I'm guessing my sister chose a black and white movie because despite this glaring mistake she really does know me well," Elise said as she finally met Aiden's eyes.

Amber watched as Elise's frown slowly rose, almost as if it were on its way to being a smile.

"It is," Amber promised.

"And the food does look really good," Aiden added hopefully when he saw Elise was no longer solidly against the whole thing.

"It does," Elise admitted, her arms dropping to her side, seeming much less like she was ready to ward off an attack. She was actually angling her shoulders toward the movie room now as she peered inside.

"But I feel like it would be a shame if we didn't share this with our best friends, who worked so hard to put it together," Elise added.

Amber took a step back. Nope, romantic movie room was not the place for her.

"I have a call," Josh said lifting his phone, his eyes on Amber.

"That I'm sure you can make another time." Aiden spoke the words in a slow, deep voice as if they were a threat.

"I haven't eaten dinner," Amber blurted and then realized how stupid of an excuse that was, considering the amount of food on the table.

"Then you *have* to join us," Elise said as she stepped behind her sister and shoved her firmly in the back so that Amber stumbled into the movie room first.

Amber looked back to see Aiden raise his arm as if he were inviting Josh in but the invite was clearly not optional.

Josh followed Amber and then Elise and Aiden entered the room as well.

The good news was that both Aiden and Elise were beaming. The bad news: Amber knew it was at her expense.

But soon, after they'd all filled their plates, they were laughing and enjoying their time together. Josh told a story about a movie he'd done where he'd had to be best friends with a monkey. On screen the monkey had stolen the hearts of America but according to Josh the monkey had an evil streak. He loved stealing little trinkets, including an heirloom ring of Josh's costar, and then planting them in other trailers. No one had figured out it was the monkey until friendships had been destroyed. Josh had all three of them rolling with not only the antics of the monkey but with his storytelling skills. Elise then proceeded to tell an embarrassing story about the time Amber had accidentally asked the wrong boy to prom and that opened the floodgates of tales. By the end of their meal everyone had been sufficiently mortified.

"I really should head to bed," Amber said with a large semi-fake yawn. She and Josh had chaperoned for long enough. It was time to give Aiden and Elise some alone time.

"And miss the movie? Besides, we know you'll fall asleep fifteen minutes in anyway, Sis. Might as well catch a snooze right here instead of going back home," Elise joked but the implication was clear. Amber wasn't going anywhere.

Amber shared an annoyed look with Josh who quickly returned the sentiment. Didn't Aiden and Elise see they were doing this for them? How could they get to know one another better if Josh and Amber never left?

"Plus the setup looks so cozy. I really wouldn't want Josh to miss this. I know how much you love a cozy movie night," Aiden teased his friend but again the implication was unmistakable. *You are staying right here.*

Before anyone else could move, Elise seated herself right in the middle of the pillows and blankets Amber had set up on the ground. The spot had been for two. It couldn't fit four, right?

"Sit here, Amber," Elise said, patting the spot beside her.

"I really think . . . " Amber began as she ran a hand through her hair.

"Sit." This time it was a command.

Amber dropped to the floor. She was already on thin ice.

Amber's stomach knotted as she began to regret everything. The spot she'd chosen for them to watch their movie was in a nook between two walls. It was why they hadn't found good use for this room before. It was weirdly shaped. But the nook opened up to a large wall so the screen sheet had fit in perfectly and there was enough space behind the sitting area for the projector. The cramped space was really just where they'd be seated. Amber had thought it a blessing before, but now? Not so much.

She had plenty of room to sit next to Elise but once she took up the space she saw the remaining issue. Thanks to the way Elise had situated them, there were only two viable spots left. One to Elise's right and the other to Amber's left.

"And I'll sit here," Aiden turned off the lights before he took the spot to Elise's right. As he should have, of course, but that left . . .

"I really should make that call," Josh tried one last time from behind the projector.

"Start the movie and sit down." Aiden wasn't allowing Josh to leave.

Josh did as his friend asked, leaving as much space as he could between himself and Amber as he took the final seat.

The cozy, romantic space for two was now officially occupied by four.

"I'm sorry," Josh leaned over to whisper to Amber as the movie started.

Amber shook her head. It wasn't his fault they were here. If anyone was to blame it was Amber. She knew Elise. She should have seen this coming.

"I love this movie," Elise said happily as the credits began.

"It's one of my favorites too," Aiden added.

See, totally compatible. Why was Elise fighting it?

Amber tried to shift to make herself comfortable. She'd placed a wall of cushions at the back of the seating space so that there would be something to lean against. And that would be fine if Elise weren't totally encroaching in her space, her back where Amber would have liked hers to be.

Josh handed her a pillow that should have been part of his backrest.

"I'm fine," Amber whispered.

Josh simply pushed the pillow behind Amber, fluffing it up right next to him because there was nowhere else for Amber to go, thanks to Elise's strange leaning.

"Thank you," Amber whispered and took the spot. She was stuck here for the duration of the movie. Might as well get comfy.

Amber finally looked back at the screen to see what movie Josh had chosen since, unlike Elise, she hadn't recognized the very beginning credits. The title came on the screen right then and Amber recognized the name of a 1940s horror movie.

"Really?" she mouthed to Josh.

"I thought it would be a good excuse for Aiden to keep close to Elise," Josh whispered back with a smirk.

Little did Josh know that Elise loved horror movies. It was Amber who got freaked out by them.

Amber glanced over to see Elise and Aiden both captivated by the movie, although it did seem like there was now quite a bit of space between Aiden and the wall. Apparently he was slowly sidling up to Elise. Good for him.

Amber would have sent Josh to that open space if it wouldn't have alerted Elise to the fact that Aiden was now very close to her. She even watched Aiden's arm brush Elise. Elise didn't return the gesture but she also didn't move away.

Their plan was working!

Well, kind of. Amber had not foreseen herself and Josh being stuck in the room as well.

Amber angled her body away from Elise and quickly texted Josh.

I think it's working.

Josh immediately looked at his phone, stretching before turning in the direction of Elise and Aiden. He grinned at Amber until he realized his arm was how behind her, grazing her back.

Amber hadn't missed the touch—in fact, her body had thrummed in awareness. She thought about pushing Josh away but that kind of movement might jostle Aiden and Elise and the last thing she wanted was for them to move, to break the spell that seemed to be slowly weaving around them.

She could put up with Josh's arm around her. It wasn't a big deal.

All she had to do was concentrate on the movie.

The movie she already knew she was going to hate.

It started innocuously enough with a man in a carriage smoking a cigarette. She really disliked cigarettes. If she could watch the whole thing in this detached way . . .

Amber felt herself tensing as the movie went on. It's the eighteen hundreds. London. A pretty city. A man who was just—

Amber jumped, causing Josh's arm to tighten around her.

"You okay?" he asked, probably thinking her silly since it hadn't even gotten to a truly scary part of the movie yet.

Amber nodded but felt grateful when Josh didn't move his arm. There was something stabilizing about feeling him right next to her.

Needing a break from the tension onscreen, Amber shot the quickest of glances Elise and Aiden's way. She noticed Aiden had moved even closer, his arm around the cushions that lay behind Elise, her head just barely resting on Aiden's shoulder.

Amber grinned widely at Josh, who seemed to be noticing the same thing. Josh nodded once before mouthing, "Victory."

Amber lifted her eyebrows and she knew even though she wasn't a professional actor Josh would understand that meant she agreed with him.

Before Amber knew it the lights were coming back on. She raised her head, blinking in surprise.

"Rise and shine, sleepyhead. The scary movie I'm sure you loved is over," Elise said with a smirk.

Wait, had Amber fallen asleep?

She glanced to her left to see Josh right next to her. Their bodies were still pressed together; it was obvious she'd used him as a pillow.

"I'm so sorry," she stammered as she rose to her knees, her head a little dizzy from the quick movement. She must have been in a deep sleep. Oh gosh, had she drooled?

"I actually enjoyed it," Josh replied with kind eyes.

No he hadn't. But he was just too nice to say otherwise.

Amber tried to discreetly check the corners of her mouth. Thank heavens, no dampness.

It was then that she realized Josh was trying to direct her attention to Elise and Aiden.

Amber glanced over to see that the two had moved from their original seats but were still standing close to one another, laughing about something.

"I think our work here is done," Josh whispered.

Amber nodded. It looked that way.

A blush stole over Elise's cheeks right after Aiden kissed her forehead, the action so sweet Amber felt her heart of ice that Raul had left behind melt the tiniest bit.

"You promise he's a good guy?" she asked Josh in a low voice, somehow trusting him to answer her honestly even though he was Aiden's best friend.

"The best," Josh promised.

Amber nodded once, thrilled for her sister. Amber was sure Elise would still have some fears to overcome but she'd battled away enough tonight to let Aiden in. It was easy to see Aiden was on cloud nine.

Amber turned back to Josh, about to congratulate him for a job well done, when her own stomach flipped.

Why was it doing that? This was about Aiden and Elise. Her stomach should feel nothing.

But looking into Josh's steel gray eyes that were so unlike Raul's dark brown ones, Amber couldn't deny that she was attracted to the man. Worse, she'd grown to trust him, something she'd promised she would never allow after Raul.

Aiden and Elise left the room hand in hand and Amber popped up, taking a few steps away from Josh.

"Maybe we should go into matchmaking," Amber joked as she took another step back.

"Yeah. I guess we're pretty good at it." Josh's voice was a little quieter, as if the distance between them had changed something.

"Pretty good? We're amazing. Well, thank goodness we don't have to clean up. I asked Jenny to do it since she has the night shift. I thought we'd be long gone by now. We should be long gone," Amber blabbed. Amber never got like this and yet . . .

"So have a good night, buddy," Amber's arm shot out and she leaned forward enough to slug Josh's shoulder.

He looked down at it as if he couldn't quite believe what Amber had done. She wasn't sure she could believe it either.

Turning on her heel, Amber hurried out of the movie room as she berated for herself for her foolishness. *Good night, buddy? Who said that?*

Josh had to think she had lost her mind.

But the problem wasn't with her mind. Her mind wouldn't have betrayed her like this. The real problem was that Amber felt her heart was already halfway in like with this guy, a man who surely didn't want it. A man she barely knew. What was she thinking, already trusting him?

During her mad, cold dash across the yard of the inn to the cottage she shared with Elise, she reminded herself of her past. Of the kind of men she attracted. The kind of men she'd once trusted.

Never again, Amber promised herself.

Yes, Josh was charming. Yes, she'd needed to get close to him for the sake of Elise. But that was all over now. She could step back, make sure she kept her distance. Because after Raul she'd promised herself one thing. She would never, ever give her heart away again.

CHAPTER SIXTEEN

JULIA SET the last of her gifts under Ellis' tree. She had never expected to wake up Christmas Eve morning in Ellis' home but that was how things had gone since the disastrous dinner a few evenings before.

Julia and Ellis had left her home to go the vacation rental Daniel had gotten for them. It was crazy that the man could procure just the right place in so little time. But by the next morning things had changed once more. Rusty had given Krista an ultimatum: apologize to Julia or they were going to leave the island. He'd told his family he wasn't about to kick his own brother out of his home. Krista had refused, claiming she hadn't done anything she needed to be sorry for, so Rusty, to everyone's surprise, actually made Krista leave. Apparently the woman wasn't used to her husband putting his foot down about anything, but this time he had so they were on a plane home to Arkansas the next day, leaving Ellis' house a conflict-free zone once more.

So Julia and Ellis had moved once again and Julia had loved every moment of being able to stay with Ellis and his family. She'd grown closer not only to Ollie, whom she'd seen frequently on the tour but hadn't really had a chance to get to know, but Ellis' parents as well. They were sweet people with big hearts and Julia realized she'd hit the jackpot yet again when it came to Ellis. She just wished things could have gone differently with Krista.

"I don't think you bought quite enough gifts," Ellis teased as he surveyed the enormous pile of wrapped presents heaped under his fifteen-foot tree. Julia hadn't had much of a say in Ellis' home décor—it was his home after all—but she had insisted they have matching giant trees. She was grateful she'd done so, considering she wasn't able to enjoy her own tree this season.

Her heart squeezed painfully as she recalled all of the steps backwards she'd taken with her mom and sister. She'd been sure those days were behind them. They'd hashed out past hurts and then hashed them out again. She couldn't apologize any more. She couldn't change their history but it was almost like her family couldn't forgive her unless she did. She honestly saw no way forward.

"I wanted to make up for past Christmases," Julia said as she gazed at the tree. She'd known she was going overboard. She'd bought eight gifts for each member of her own and Ellis' family. She'd thought about buying one for every year she'd missed with her family but even Julia knew twenty plus presents per person was excessive. Though she doubted any of her family would protest.

"I thought we'd talked about this," Ellis said as he put an arm around Julia's waist.

They had. Time and time again. Ellis had been the one to help Julia to see that she couldn't do anything more about what had already happened. She could only look toward the future.

But with that path so murky, wondering if her mom and

sister would ever apologize, it was easier to think could have, would have, should have.

"We did." Julia leaned her head on Ellis' shoulder with a sigh.

Honestly, she didn't know what she would have done without Ellis and his family. They'd warmed her heart when she'd thought the holiday had been ruined.

She'd left her house crying after the disaster of a dinner party. She still couldn't figure out how it had gone so wrong.

"Am I being stubborn? Holding out for an apology?" Julia asked. She just wanted everything to be mended once more. She hated this tension with her family. She'd lived with it for so long and had thought she was finally past it.

"I don't think so. They shouldn't have said the things they did. But if you want to talk to them without an apology, to go on with Christmas as if that dinner never happened, I support you one hundred percent," Ellis said as he pulled Julia closer to him.

She nodded, grateful for the support but still unsure of what to do. Part of her wanted to let everything go, to pretend nothing had ever happened. But the other part of her knew that if she did she would still resent her mom and sister. Maybe not today, but it would end up being a problem somewhere down the line. If they could just apologize she was sure she could let it go.

"I'm pretty sure I'm doing the right thing," Julia said as she lifted her head. "But the kids deserve a good Christmas regardless." Her niece and nephews were not exactly children anymore but she still wanted to give the best holiday, full of joy and warmth and lots of gifts. "So inviting them for this lunch and letting my sister and mom know they are welcome as soon as they apologize—it's the right thing."

Julia knew she was assuring herself more than Ellis.

But Ellis, sweet man that he was, still nodded.

"It'll all work out," he promised, dropping a kiss on the top of Julia's head.

It would, wouldn't it?

Ellis' doorbell rang and Julia heard his mom greeting Wendy and the boys. Julia strained to hear if there were any other voices involved but it sounded like just the three visitors.

Julia's heart dropped as she tried to tell herself it was just as well. Even if her mom and sister apologized, things would have probably still been tense. Thankfully they would be in town a few days longer so hopefully they could all make amends before they left.

"Merry Christmas," Julia greeted as Sarah, Wendy, Trip, and Ryder joined Ellis and Julia in the living room.

From the kitchen came Ollie and Dave, both bearing trays laden with every meat, cheese, cracker, and fruit known to man.

Julia hugged her niece and nephews tightly, grateful that she at least had them.

"Wow, someone is getting spoiled this Christmas," Wendy said as she deposited the gifts she'd brought under the tree, her eyes on Julia.

"Oh they aren't for her, even though I would have liked to spoil her more. You'll see you folks' names on quite a few of those," Ellis drawled.

Wendy's eyes lit up. "Really?" she squealed as she dropped her presents and began pawing through the mound, divvying up the ones with hers, Trip's, or Ryder's names on them.

"Before we get to that." Trip cleared his throat. "I'm so sorry, Aunt Julia, but we can't stay for very long."

"Oh right, that," Wendy said as she sat back with a present on her lap but looked up at Julia with a frown.

"That's fine," Julia said, trying to let them know it wasn't a big deal. She figured if her mom and sister weren't here they'd do something like schedule a meal in an hour so that her niece and nephews wouldn't have much time for Julia. It was the way the Prices worked.

"I told Mom she was being silly, leaving before Christmas day," Wendy said with a shake of her head.

"Wait, they're leaving. You all are leaving?" Julia turned to her nephews. Before Christmas? This didn't make sense.

Trip and Ryder nodded in unison as Ellis' family discreetly stepped back. They fell into quiet conversation with one another to give Julia some privacy. They really were heaven sent.

"Mom kind of got riled up after the whole invite here contingent on the apology," Ryder said, his eyes dropping to his feet as he spoke. These poor kids shouldn't have to be in the middle of this mess.

"I knew that was a possibility," Julia said quietly. She had. She'd just hoped the Christmas spirit might bite her sister in the butt so she'd get over herself and apologize. Julia guessed she'd put too much stock in holiday magic.

"She started looking for tickets home right away and saw that if we fly out today we get nearly a thousand dollars back per ticket." Trip spoke up this time.

Of course they did. Because Julia had sprung for refundable first class tickets. But she doubted she'd see a cent of that money back even though she'd been the one to pay for the tickets in full. Not that any of that mattered. She just thought she had more time.

Her throat felt thick but Julia tried to swallow it down, pasting a smile on her face. This was Christmas.

"I'm sorry they're leaving before Christmas Day," Julia said to Wendy, realizing she was being left behind as well.

"Leo's family has a big thing all day that I'm more than welcome to attend. I'll be fine. But I know you were hopeful," Wendy said, setting aside her gift to stand and give her aunt a hug. "I'm sorry we came from the most stubborn stock in the Midwest."

Julia laughed, grateful for the humor Wendy was infusing into the situation.

"Are you boys okay with the change?" Julia asked, hoping she was the only one her mom and sister would be hurting.

Ryder shrugged as Trip nodded. "We wanted a chance to spend the holiday with our favorite aunt. We kind of got that so we're good."

Julia warmed at Trip's words, knowing he was probably buttering her up with the favorite aunt comment but she didn't care.

"Well then I guess we'd better stop wasting time. Let's get to presents," Julia said as she watched Wendy, Trip, and Ryder gleefully turn back to the tree. It didn't matter your age, there really was something magical about a pile of gifts under the tree.

Julia laughed as she watched them shove one another aside to get to their gifts first—Wendy was the most brutal—and then turned to smile at Ellis and his family, who seemed to be enjoying the show as well.

Julia didn't know what she'd do without their support.

Ellis' arm was once again around Julia, tugging her against his side.

"You okay?" he whispered as Wendy called Ryder a nickel noggin for hiding one of her presents behind him.

Julia shrugged. "Not really. But this helps," she said, nodding toward her sister's kids.

"Good," Ellis said into her hair before placing another kiss on her head.

Julia knew the pain of all of this would hit hard later, but for now she was going to enjoy this moment where she had some of her family with her, sharing in her favorite time of the year.

"KNOCK, KNOCK," Sarah said from the open doorway of Julia's room. Ellis had four guest rooms, three of which were now being occupied—his parents in one, Ollie in another, and Julia in the third. The last had been taken by Rusty and Krista before they'd left.

Julia had just finished getting ready for Christmas Eve dinner. She wore a red wrap dress with long, sheer sleeves. She'd added her favorite diamond solitaire necklace as well as diamond hoops to complete the ensemble. Since the dinner was just downstairs in Ellis' dining room, Julia wouldn't even fuss with shoes.

"Come on in, Sarah," Julia said as she fastened her second earring.

"You look beautiful," Sarah exclaimed as she entered Julia's room and sat on the edge of her bed.

Julia stood in front of the full length mirror near the door to the ensuite bathroom.

"So do you." Julia could see in the reflection that Sarah was all dolled up as well. Her simple black sheath dress was accompanied by a silver duster that made the woman appear positively regal.

Apparently Christmas Eve was a formal occasion in the Rider home. Christmas Day was spent in pajamas but they all dressed up for the feast Sarah made every Christmas Eve. Julia couldn't wait to dig into the special recipe fried chicken Ellis had raved about ever since he'd met Julia as well as the yams. Julia was a sucker for a good yam.

"I'm sorry about how today turned out," Sarah said as Julia spritzed on some perfume. Julia set the tiny crystal bottle down and turned to face Ellis' mother.

"I am too. At least in some ways. Things are always a little more tense with my family around and the day was quite relaxing without them." Julia started with the positive. "But it was hard to hear that they aren't interested in trying to mend fences. I probably asked too much of them by demanding an apology. But I worried that if I didn't this would happen time and time again and I'd grow to resent them until we built an irreparable gap. I just want things to be good between us all, you know?" Julia sighed, crossing the room to sit next to Sarah.

"Oh, don't I," Sarah said with a soft smile. "Has Ellis told you about his grandparents? Dave's parents?"

"He told me they were interesting people." Julia tried to recall if that was all Ellis had said. It was all she could remember.

"That's the understatement of the year. Ellis is great about trying to remember his grandparents in the best light and I usually join him in that but today we're going to dredge up some things I'm sure they wouldn't like," Sarah said as she clasped her hands in her lap. "Dave's parents never liked me. But I didn't take it personally because Dave's parents didn't like most people."

Julia chuckled. If that didn't describe her mother to a T.

"For the first several years of our marriage I avoided them. They'd made their dislike of me clear and I didn't like going to places I felt unwanted. Ellis, Oliver, and Rusty were all born during that time so Dave would go over with the boys about once a month, but considering they lived only fifteen minutes away, they really didn't see them much."

Julia nodded. She'd had a similar relationship with some of her cousins while growing up. She was pretty sure it was because Betty had said something offensive to one of their moms. Maybe all of them.

"When Rusty was about five, maybe six, I was sick of it. I hated that I had this whole part of my family I hardly knew. I'd always just said well, they're Dave's family, but once you have kids you realize just how intertwined you all become."

Julia nodded once more, understanding completely even if she had no kids. It was easy to imagine.

"Dave's parents were unhappy with me even after I tried to mend our relationship. Not only had they disliked me from the start, but I'd then taken years away from them where they could have been ridiculing me to my face. I knew that even in our time apart they did plenty of complaining about me to anyone and everyone who would listen, but they would have much rather spoken their disparaging words right at me." Sarah tried to keep her tone light but Julia could see that it hurt her.

"Dave was always quick to come to my defense but it would have been so much better if he hadn't had to."

That resonated with Julia as well.

"That time was really rough. Lots of giant fights, both sides saying things we shouldn't have. Me crying in Dave's arms after nearly every family get-together. But I was determined to stick it out. So I went in with kindness, sure that would kill their desire to dislike me. And maybe it did, a bit. We eventually got to the point where we could go to a family gathering and I didn't leave crying. Sometimes." Sarah paused, sighing, before she went on. "I wish this story had a happy ending but basically the next thirty years was spent with me trying to not get offended or too upset and them managing to stay on their best behavior for a few months at a time. But then we'd have a big blow up, I'd stay away for a bit, and the cycle would start all over again."

Julia frowned. That sounded terrible.

"I can see by your frown that you don't like the way our story ended. I don't particularly like it either. But for years I tried to figure out what I'd done wrong, what I was doing wrong, how I could fix this. It dawned on me about twenty years into my marriage what I could change to make things right with my in-laws."

Julia cocked her head, eager to hear about the magic key to difficult relationships.

"Nothing."

Julia's eyes rounded in shock. Not the answer she'd been expecting.

"I could play nice until I was blue in the face but his parents didn't want to. I learned that I could only control my own actions. And if his parents wanted to keep being rude to me I had two choices. I could take it and hate them for it. Or I could stand up for myself, get them angry and have to cycle through all of our emotions once more. I typically went for the second. Because that was real. That was life." Sarah clasped her hands together. "That's the thing with family. We often can't choose them, and we can't choose how they act, but we can choose what we want our lives to look like. I tried living life with them cut out and didn't like that. I tried living life with their ridicule and sucking it up. I didn't like that either. So I found the place I could survive. Did I like that that was my relationship my in-laws? Heavens no. But it was what it was. They were and always will be my family. But family is for better or worse. With my in-laws much of the time it was worse, but it was the way we were."

Julia felt tears falling down her cheeks. This was exactly where she was. She was so sick of the cycle but Sarah's words helped to free her of her guilt. Julia really was trying her best. She'd made mistakes but she was trying. And what she was doing was enough. Even if things weren't perfect in her family. It was surprisingly freeing to realize that there was nothing more she could do.

"Thank you," Julia managed as she gave Sarah a hug.

"But between it all I had the best relationship with my own

parents. They loved me and accepted me for who I was. They were there for me whenever I needed them. I want you to know that's who we want to be for you. We've only gotten this short time with you, Julia, but we've seen what you've done for Ellis. Our boy is lit up brighter than that Christmas tree downstairs whenever you're around. He absolutely loves you. So we do too. It's that simple with us. It might be complicated for you on one side, but know you've got this side too."

Julia held onto Sarah tighter. She hadn't known how much she'd needed to hear those words until Sarah had spoken them. To be accepted for who she was without any judgment? Julia let out a sob as Sarah stroked her hair.

"I don't think I can say how . . . " Julia managed that much but couldn't say anything more. Not if she didn't want to break down once more.

"I get it," Sarah said as she finally pulled away from Julia. Julia noticed Sarah's cheeks were marred by mascara tracks as well.

"Thank you," Julia managed once more.

"Thank *you*," Sarah shot right back as if Julia was doing something for her. Maybe she was. Julia guessed that was how family worked sometimes. Julia had also accepted Sarah, Dave, and Ellis' family without question. But for it to happen to her? She'd thought something about her had made it so that she could never be enough for a family. Turns out she just hadn't been trying with the right family.

"I guess I'd better go fix this," Sarah drew a circle around her face with a finger in the air, "and then I'll meet you down there. Dave should be finished frying up the chicken by now."

Julia nodded.

"You are loved," Sarah said, gently touching Julia's shoulder before leaving the room.

Julia was loved. Her family had a strange way of showing it

and Julia often felt like she had to work for their love, but it was there. And her friends on the island had been the first to prove to her that she could be loved for who she was, not what she could give. And now Ellis' family had taken her in and shown her the strength of their love. Somehow this was the sweetest love of all. Ellis had chosen her first but now they had accepted her into their family as well. Julia was loveable. She was enough.

Even though she'd probably always struggle with her sister and her mom, she'd never give up because they were worth it. But to have another family, one where relationships came so much easier? That kind of peace sounded like just the kind of bliss Julia needed. And she would forever be grateful for that.

CHAPTER SEVENTEEN

"CAN I TAKE THIS OFF YET?" Nora asked, touching the blindfold Mack had tied over her eyes before they'd left her apartment that morning.

The moment he'd arrived at her house, saying her gift wouldn't fit under the Christmas tree, Nora had known this was the day. Christmas Day might seem a little cliché of a time to get engaged for many but this had always been Nora's dream. The magic of the holidays was the only time to take this next step in life, at least according to Nora.

"Almost," Mack promised, his fingers intertwined with Nora's as he drove.

He'd only let go of her for a moment while he'd run around the car to get to his own seat after putting Nora in hers. He knew blindfolds made Nora nervous but he'd promised this one would be worth it and since she did love surprises she'd gone with it.

Although it really wouldn't be much of a surprise. She'd been hoping that this would be the day for months now. And now it was here.

Nora's legs bounced with excitement.

How should she answer when Mack asked her the big question? She'd heard *a thousand times yes*. That was sweet but a little overdone. A giant gush of a yes was probably the most common reaction. Is that what Nora should do? Would she cry? Would she laugh? Nora thought she'd be pretty put together—she was older than most blushing brides, after all—but who knew?

Oh, could Mack just get there already?

Nora felt Mack take a turn and then circle around in what felt like a cul-de-sac. Was Mack proposing to her in a neighborhood? She'd assumed they were going up one of the hills on the island or maybe stopping at one of the beaches, but at a random house?

Wait, what if Mack wasn't proposing?

Sure, they'd talked about marriage as some distant thing but it hadn't been a part of their recent conversations. They'd both been so busy that most of what they spoke about was necessary. Talk of hopes and dreams had been shelved, its place taken by everyday life.

Nora's heart dropped.

It was okay if Mack didn't propose today, she encouraged herself, working hard to bolster her flagging spirits. She'd be fine. There were other days. She didn't have to get engaged on Christmas Day. It wasn't a big deal.

But her poor heart never lifted.

If they were at a house Nora wondered if her present was the table she'd said she hoped to one day get. There was a woodworker here on the island who made custom furniture that Nora adored. She'd hinted at wanting that table more recently than a ring.

Oh man. This was all her fault. And she needed to be happy with this table. She'd asked for it, after all.

"We're here," Mack said as she heard him put the car in park.

"But don't take that off yet," he hurried to add when Nora's hands went to the blindfold. "I'll be right there."

Nora heard Mack's car door open and close and then her own open. The crisp mid-morning air hit her face as Mack took both of her hands and led her from the car.

Immediately the scent of fresh-cut wood hit Nora's nose. It was a table. Oh dang. Why had she gotten herself so worked up?

She loosened the muscles of her mouth, preparing to smile even though every part of her wanted to frown. She was getting her dream table. Only a brat would be unhappy about that.

Apparently she was a brat.

Nora's feet fumbled over uneven ground, but Mack held her steady, guiding her across the ground and up two steps before stopping her.

"You can take it off," he said, a smile obvious in his voice. He was so excited about this. She should be too.

Nora grinned hard as she took off her blindfold and glanced around, confused as to what she was supposed to look at.

They were on the front porch of a home. A yellow swing hung to her right and the bright blue door in front of her was perfection against the stark white of the home. The house was beautiful, but Nora was just so perplexed.

"Should we go in?" Mack asked.

Nora shrugged. Should they?

Mack laughed as he opened the door.

"Don't we need to knock?" Nora asked as she tentatively followed Mack inside. Did the woodworker have an open door policy where people could just walk into his home? That sounded strange but weirder things had happened.

Mack shook his head so Nora guessed the woodworker did have an open door policy.

"So what do you think?" Mack asked as Nora took in the spacious entry.

Above the front door was a large window that let in tons of light and from the high ceiling hung a beautiful chandelier. The walls were a bright white, gleaming in contrast to all of the dark wood finishes. To their left was a set of double doors leading to what looked like a study and to the right was an open room.

"They don't have any furniture," Nora said, still quite confused as Mack led her further into the home. "We really should let the homeowners know we're here, right?"

"Oh, they know," Mack said off-handedly as if breaking and entering wasn't a big deal.

They walked past a set of stairs into the main part of the home, a kitchen to the left and a massive family room to the right. The kitchen cabinets were the same bright blue as the door, Nora's favorite color, and the countertops were gray and white swirled marble, absolutely flawless.

Nora looked to the family room and froze.

"That's one of mine." She pointed to the wall where a painting depicting the Whisling ferry station hung. "I gave that to you."

She turned to Mack, whose giant smile had somehow grown. He was watching her with the most intent expression she'd ever seen on his face.

"Do you like it?" Mack asked.

"The painting?" Nora asked, her bewilderment rising. Why would Mack ask her about her own work?

"The house," Mack clarified.

"It's stunning," Nora said as she shook her head back and forth. What did it matter what she thought of the house?

"Good. Because it's ours," Mack said as he dangled a set of keys in front of him, his eyes sparkling brighter than the shiny new keys.

Nora's mouth fell open, her mind working to catch up. Theirs. Mack had bought a house?

Suddenly Mack was on one knee and Nora couldn't breathe as tears immediately sprang to her eyes.

"Nora, I used to think that this day would never come, because why choose one woman when you could date them by the dozen?"

Nora snorted, both annoyed and amused.

"But then one day this woman came along and it was like my world woke up. I went from black and white to color when I hadn't even realized I'd been stuck in black and white. And I knew from that moment, that woman, you, were all I ever wanted and needed. That younger, foolish Mack couldn't even argue with me. I knew you were it. And you weren't sure about me at all."

Nora laughed through her tears.

"But I kept at it or you wore down. I'm not sure which is the case but I thank my lucky stars either way. Because this past year has been the best year of my life. I wouldn't trade a minute with you for an eternity elsewhere. I love you with my entire being. Will you marry me, Nora?" Mack asked, his eyes full of hope.

And after all of her worries Nora couldn't even remember how she responded, just that she was soon in Mack's arms, spinning through the air. So she must have said yes. And she was so glad that she had.

"This is your house?" Nora asked, still reeling from all of the news. She was an engaged woman.

Wait, she'd forgotten to look at the ring. As soon as Mack set her down Nora glanced down at the beauty of a ring on her finger. The giant green stone nearly swallowed her finger and Nora couldn't have imagined a better choice.

"Our house. I built it. Well, not like with my own two

hands, but I hired a guy and his guys built it according to my wishes," Mack explained.

"You built a house? And I didn't know about it?" Nora pushed away from Mack so that she could see his face and then realized that was too much distance so she pulled him into her arms once more.

"It's part of why I've been so busy lately. And thankfully you were so busy too that you didn't even notice," Mack replied.

Nora put a hand over her face. She honestly couldn't believe it.

"I knew I wanted it to be a surprise. I knew I wanted to have this be our first moment here. The start of our life together."

Nora blinked back the tears that threatened. She was too happy to cry again.

"I'm still . . . I don't get it," Nora said, shaking her head.

"It's pretty simple, actually. I met you and then began planning our future together."

And it was then that Mack finally kissed her. Nora knew something had been missing but as soon as their lips met she felt whole. This was happening. She didn't think her heart could handle any more.

She could have kept kissing Mack forever but her curiosity overcame her. She was still so confused.

"So we're getting married?" Nora knew it wasn't a question. Mack had proposed, and supposedly she'd said yes.

She wasn't sure what had happened to keeping herself put together but it had flown out the window long ago.

"Thank the heavens," Mack replied as he tugged at her waist so that she was pressed up against him as he pursued her lips once more.

And even through their kiss Nora smiled. Her cheeks absolutely ached but she didn't care. She would probably smile for the rest of her days. She was marrying the man she loved. And he'd proposed on Christmas Day.

CHAPTER EIGHTEEN

LOU WOULD HAVE NEVER GUESSED that her first date with Jax would be in front of half of the island, but here she was.

Okay, 'half of the island' was an exaggeration, but Nora and Mack's engagement party was overflowing with well-wishers.

She and Jax had tried to meet up before this party on New Year's Eve but nothing else had quite worked out. Lou had been busy with her family over the holidays, of course, and Jax had gone to spend Christmas Day with a brother who lived in LA. He'd come home soon after but either he'd had work or Lou couldn't get a babysitter or Cash had been sick or . . . there had been so many circumstances physically keeping them apart although, thankfully, they had been able to speak on the phone nearly every night.

But here they finally were. In the flesh. Margie and her dad had practically shoved her out the door after Jax had suggested that they attend this party together.

And Lou really was thrilled to be spending the last day of the year with Jax, ringing in the New Year side by side. Her heart sped up whenever she thought of that midnight kiss. It wasn't really a big deal . . . except that it was. Lou hadn't kissed anyone besides Harvey for two decades and honestly, when was the last time during their marriage they'd remembered to share a New Year's kiss? She'd often fallen asleep before the ball dropped and Harvey had gone out with friends the last few years they'd been married. Why was she even wasting thought on Harvey tonight? That was the last thing she wanted to do when she was with Jax.

Because she was nervous about that kiss. But if it happened, it happened. It would be natural, right?

Lou snorted out loud, grateful that Jax had gone to grab a plate of hors d'oeuvres to share and couldn't hear the completely ungraceful sound that escaped her lips. Lou couldn't imagine being calm and cool enough for a kiss between them to be natural. Memorable? Yes, because she'd surely do something foolish, but definitely not natural.

"I got us a little of everything," Jax said as he came back with a heaping plate of food.

"You are the perfect man," Lou cooed in a way that sounded like a joke but really she meant it. She just didn't want to sound as besotted as she felt.

Jax chuckled before passing the plate to Lou and letting her have first pick.

See, perfect man.

"Hi, Lou," said Deb, Nora's sister and Lou's friend, as she and Luke walked up to them, right after Lou had shoved an entire bacon-wrapped shrimp into her mouth.

Lou motioned at her full mouth and Deb laughed.

"I've always had great timing," she joked as she waited for Lou to chew and swallow.

"Hello," Lou replied, belatedly giving her friend a hug.

When Deb pulled back she raised her eyebrows slyly and Lou knew exactly what she was thinking. Deb had helped Lou through a really hard time in her life when Lou had been at her lowest. She'd felt she'd failed her children by her failed marriage and she'd also been sure she was the reason Harvey was leaving. No one could love her. Deb had helped Lou to start seeing her own self-worth once more and taught her how to let go of her rage at her ex, channeling it into being there for her children instead. Lou would always be grateful to Deb for that day.

But Lou knew the eyebrows weren't about that day but about today. Being with Jax. Like the rest of the island, Deb was curious. But thankfully, unlike a pretty loud contingent, Deb was happy for Lou instead of jealous.

Lou was just glad those jealous folks didn't seem in attendance this evening.

"I'm so happy for Nora," Lou said to Deb because she wasn't about to talk about Jax in front of him.

Deb seemed to catch her hint when she answered, "I am too. She deserves the world. And I know that's exactly what Mack wants to give her."

"I heard he proposed in a new house he built for her without her knowledge?" Lou asked, eyes wide. That was quite the proposal. The whole island was abuzz with the news.

Deb nodded enthusiastically. "Can you imagine being able to keep a secret like that on this island?"

Lou couldn't. She could barely keep her breakfast a secret since she often wore part of it as she ran her kids to school.

"And the girls got this party together since Christmas Day?" Lou asked.

Deb grinned. "They might have had a little heads up on the proposal happening. I guess soon after Mack told them he wanted to propose they shifted gears on the New Year's Eve party they'd already been planning to make it all about Nora and Mack."

"They are so sweet," Lou said, smiling toward Amber and

Elise, who stood across the room, not far from Mack and Nora. She didn't know them well but hoped she'd one day get a chance to know them better.

"They really are. They would do anything for Nora and now that they see Mack feels the same, he's being welcomed with open arms," Deb said as she looked toward the sisters mingling with partygoers, each with an extremely handsome actor hovering close by.

"And what's going on there?" Lou wanted to know as she waved a finger between Amber and Josh and Elise and Aiden.

"That's the burning question of the evening," Deb replied as Bess and Dax joined the four of them.

Lou gave both a hug before introducing them to Jax.

"We actually go way back," Dax said, motioning to Jax.

"We do," Jax replied with a smile. "Dax is a big reason why I chose to retire on Whisling."

"You can't call it retiring, man, when you're still under the age of thirty," Dax joked.

The group laughed and Lou could see in their eyes that they all admired what Jax had done. Being in a position to live on the island of his dreams at his age was pretty incredible.

"So I have you to thank for bringing Jax here?" Lou said to Dax.

"You can pay me later," Dax replied. "I really enjoy brownies and chocolate cookies of any variety."

Lou laughed once more.

"We didn't mean to interrupt, though," Bess said in her kind way.

"Oh, we were just speculating about Nora's girls and their new men," Deb replied with a wink.

"My favorite kind of conversation. What do we think?" Bess asked.

The men took a step back and fell into their own conversation about a bowl game that would be taking place the next day. Lou loved seeing how easily Jax interacted with her friends' husbands. Honestly, she might have to take back her earlier thoughts and admit that this could be the greatest idea for a first date ever. She'd had very minimal nerves because she was amongst friends and seeing how Jax interacted with those she loved really was just making her like the guy all the more. Not that she needed any help in that department.

"So according to an inside source," Deb said just loudly enough to be heard over the band that was playing on the other side of the room, "both men are head over heels. Elise seems to finally be opening up to the idea of dating Aiden even though he's leaving early next week to start filming a movie. But Amber isn't even giving Josh a chance. She keeps insisting they're just friends."

"If a friend ever looked at me like that, Dax would have a few choice words for him," Bess remarked as both women observed the way Josh gazed down at Amber. "But she really did have a number done on her poor heart by the man we will never name again."

Deb nodded. "I wish he'd stuck around long enough for me to give him a piece of my mind."

Lou loved seeing how protective Deb was of her niece.

"This looks like the place to be," Julia said, smiling as she joined the women.

Lou glanced over to see that Ellis had already entered the circle of men.

"We thought so too," Piper said, her arm linked with Seren's as she came to stand by Lou. "Especially because we were curious how the tour went," Piper continued after introducing Seren to the women who hadn't met her yet. Lou had had the opportunity a few months before when Seren had begun working out at Lou's gym.

"Yes, I'd love a tour update too," Lou said as she took in a glowing Julia.

"It was actually wonderful. Seeing Ellis on stage is a marvel I could watch time and time again. But I actually won't be going back." Julia proceeded to tell them about the movie role she'd taken and the news that she would have to leave Ellis to go film.

"I really am sorry about that," Bess said, since Dax was the reason Julia had the role.

Julia laughed. "Your husband was just doing his job. And doing it well, may I add. I'm just a little melancholy thinking about time away from Ellis but I'm sure it will be good for us. Absence makes the heart grow fonder, right?"

"Exactly," Deb confirmed as Bess put an arm around Julia's shoulders and gave her friend a squeeze.

"But enough about me. I've heard you two have big news." Julia turned to Seren and Piper expectantly.

"Because this one works wonders," Piper said, facing Seren.

Seren shook her head. "I've been at this for years. It never became easy until I had Piper join my team."

Piper blushed and the women smiled. It really was remarkable what they were doing for the hospital. Especially after the losses they'd endured. Lou couldn't imagine the pain of losing a child, but these women had lived it and were now channeling that pain to give back to others. Lou couldn't put into words her admiration for them.

"I think this is our song," Dax said as he squeezed in between Bess and Deb.

"I think you're right." Bess grinned at her husband and allowed herself to be led to the dance floor.

Seren was the next to pull away, saying she needed to speak with someone across the room, and then Deb and Luke and Piper and Carter followed Bess and Dax. Lou saw that they'd joined Gen and Lily, who were already busy cutting a rug with their own husbands.

"I feel like that might be a married couple thing," Julia said as she nodded toward the dance floor.

Sure enough, all of the couples Lou recognized on the dance floor were indeed married.

"We could totally join them," Ellis replied but Julia shook her head. "Honestly, I think I'd rather stuff my face with that bacon-wrapped shrimp instead."

Julia nodded to the plate that Lou had nearly forgotten about.

"Don't have to ask me twice when food is involved," Ellis said as the two made their way toward the table laden with appetizers.

"And then there were two once more," Jax whispered into Lou's ear. She hadn't realized how close he'd moved to her. And she had to say she was quite pleased with the turn of events.

"Do you want to dance?" Jax offered, extending an inviting hand.

Lou looked down at the hors d'oeuvres that were getting cold on her plate. Eat those or spend the next few dances in Jax's arms? The decision wasn't hard. "I thought you'd never ask."

Jax took Lou's hand—thankfully she wasn't sweating, although now that she was thinking about her hand being slick she worried she'd begin to start sweating—and pulled her into his arms when they were still at the edge of the group of dancing couples.

"So how's your first date with the hot new guitar instructor going?" Jax asked with a smirk.

Lou burst into laughter.

"Not the person I expected to get this question from," Lou replied as she continued to giggle.

"But I'd still appreciate an answer. Kind of like a mid-lesson report," Jax said.

"You can take the guitar instructor out of the studio . . . " Lou let her words trail off because she knew Jax wouldn't let her get away with not answering his question. But how did she do so without gushing that it was her best first date ever?

"On a scale of one to ten," Lou teased but decided it was the right way to go when she noticed a twinkle in Jax's eyes. "I'll give the new guitar instructor—"

"*Hot* new guitar instructor," Jax amended.

Lou giggled once more. "Right, *hot* new guitar instructor. I'll give him an eight."

Jax stopped dancing but kept Lou close. Thankfully they were far enough from other couples that no one bumped into them.

"An eight?" Jax asked, clearly unimpressed by his score.

"Okay, eight and a half." Lou loved teasing the man.

Jax brushed his fingers up Lou's side, causing her to jump away. "I told you that in confidence. And you use it against me?" she joked.

She'd revealed to Jax that she was highly ticklish and had regretted it immediately after. Now she knew that regret had been well founded.

"You gave me a subpar answer," Jax shot back.

Lou grinned. "Well then how do *you* think the date is going?" she asked, turning the tables.

Jax bit his lower lip, looking like he was pondering hard, but Lou was pretty sure she was about to get a taste of her own medicine.

"One to ten?" Jax clarified.

Lou nodded, ready for anything. Even if he said a one he'd just be teasing . . . right?

"Off the charts and hands down the best date I've ever been

on," Jax said sincerely as he pulled Lou back into his arms and they began swaying to the music once more.

Lou swallowed. That had been the only answer she hadn't been anticipating. And it had thrown her for a loop of the best kind.

"Okay," Lou conceded. "You get a ten."

Jax chuckled as he brushed his lips over Lou's forehead.

"And now you've bumped yourself up to a twelve," Lou graded once more, a grin taking over her face.

"So you're going to keep this up all night?" Jax asked.

Lou nodded.

"I've created a monster."

They both laughed as Lou relished Jax's words, replaying them in her mind and storing them up to savor later. She hoped she'd have enough confidence before the night ended to tell Jax that she felt the exact same way.

Jax suddenly released Lou's waist, taking her hand instead with a gentle tug.

Why were they leaving the dancefloor?

It was then that Lou saw who'd just entered the room and was headed straight for Nora and Mack.

Lou loved that Jax knew how important it would be for Lou to greet Alexis immediately. They were both still on cloud nine because of Alexis' engagement and even though Lou had seen her multiple times since then, Jax seemed to understand that Lou would want to run up to Alexis and squeal with her once more.

The man was a gem.

Lou met Alexis' eyes and Alexis took a quick detour, walking quickly in Lou's direction.

"You're engaged," Lou squeaked.

Alexis nodded. It didn't matter that they'd played this out a dozen times before. Lou was still just so thrilled for her best friend.

The two hugged and Lou ignored the look Jared sent Jax. It was a look that said *I don't understand it but I still love them.*

Lou grabbed Alexis' hand to look at her ring once more. It was still just as gorgeous.

"Why are you guys so late?" Lou asked as they started in Nora and Mack's direction once more. Lou had already congratulated the couple but she'd be happy to speak to them again. Especially because Jax held her hand wherever they went. That was big, right? Lou was still a novice at this adult dating world but she loved that she was venturing into it with Jax. Honestly, Lou hoped her only foray into it was with Jax. It was a bit too soon to be having thoughts like that but Lou couldn't help it. It just felt right and she had no desire to try dating anyone else . . . ever.

"Marsha didn't show even though she begged to have the kids tonight. After waiting for hours we ended up dropping them off at your place," Alexis said with a sigh, but then smiled.

Lou knew her sister was a pain in Alexis' rear but Alexis didn't mind it too much because if she didn't have to deal with Marsha it would mean she wouldn't have Jared, Brittany, and Peter in her life, and for Alexis all of the pains in the rear were worth it when it came to those three.

"Your parents are saints," Jared said to Alexis and Lou.

The women nodded. They really were.

They joined Mack and Nora moments later, Alexis and Lou both gushing over Nora's ring. Mack couldn't have chosen better for their artistic friend. Nora relayed the story about the proposal and declared it the perfect Christmas Day, which caused Mack to beam. They'd spoken for a while more when Jax tugged on Lou's hand.

"Want to get out of here?" he mouthed when no one else was paying attention.

Lou grinned her affirmation. She loved her friends but she really did want to get out of there. Alone time with Jax was exactly what she'd been craving.

They slipped away from the conversation, barely noticed. Alexis did raise her eyebrows in Lou's direction as they backed away but didn't say a word as Lou simply grinned at her.

As soon as they were on the outskirts of the party they turned and dashed away.

Jax led the way, seeming to know exactly where he was going. They hurried through the hall that took them from the ballroom to the inn's lobby, grabbing their coats from reception on their way out the front doors.

Jax held Lou's out, helping her to slip into it before putting on his own.

He took Lou's hand once more and began to walk with purpose across the lawn. She soon saw their destination.

A beautiful white gazebo that often held weddings during the spring and summer waited ahead. Lou wondered how long they'd be able to stay out there in this cold, but she was up for trying if it meant getting Jax all to herself.

They stepped up into the gazebo and Lou was surrounded by warmth. She then noticed heat lamps lit up around the gazebo, high enough so they wouldn't burn anything but low enough so they were nearly concealed, not detracting from the vintage beauty of the place.

"How did you know about this spot?" she marveled. It was the perfect getaway.

"Mack said something about wishing he could slip away to the gazebo with Nora and I remembered seeing it on our way in. I realized I *could* slip away to the gazebo with my girl."

Lou's heart flipped at the words.

She and Jax were barely dating. He wasn't declaring . . . they weren't . . . no, it was too soon.

"I had no idea about the heat lamps though. This is a pleasant surprise," he said as he took off his jacket. Lou wasn't quite that warm but was comfortable with her coat on.

Jax set his jacket on the wood planks and motioned for Lou to sit on it.

"Can't get that beautiful dress dirty," he said as his eyes swept over Lou's form.

It had taken her a full fifteen minutes to get into the shapewear under the gold sequined bodycon dress she wore, and she'd almost cried during the task. But seeing the way Jax looked at her now? All of the sweat and near tears were worth it.

"Did I tell you you're gorgeous?" Jax murmured as Lou sat and he wrapped his arm around her shoulders.

"Once or twice," she answered lightly, even though she knew the exact number of times Jax had complimented her tonight. Once when he'd picked her up, once when he'd helped her into his car, once when she'd taken off her coat at the inn, and now again for the fourth time. Lou's cheeks flushed even though she loved each compliment. She just wasn't used to getting them.

They sat quietly together, Lou more content than she'd felt in months. Maybe years.

"How do you think your kids are doing?" Jax asked.

Lou loved that the man cared about her children so much. She hadn't even been thinking about them, yet he had.

"Probably eating way too many sweets and pouring apple cider like it's champagne," Lou replied quickly.

She knew she'd be dealing with tummy aches tomorrow.

Jax laughed. "I don't know how you do it."

"What?" Lou turned up to look at Jax.

"Supermom. Superbusinesswoman. Superdaughter. Superfriend," Jax replied.

Lou grinned. Again with the compliments. She realized her only way of accepting them was to say nothing. At least for now. She figured if she hung around Jax enough she'd get used to them—surely she'd never take them for granted, but maybe she'd be able to accept them without feeling embarrassed.

"Hardly," Lou muttered as she looked at her lap.

See, she couldn't do it.

But she'd keep trying. Thankfully Jax gave her plenty of opportunities.

"I'm serious. You are incredible, Lou. And as much as I hate to add to your list of roles, I was hoping you wouldn't mind adding one more?" Jax asked as his arm pulled Lou in a little closer.

Lou glanced up once more.

"Supergirlfriend?" Jax asked.

Lou felt her eyes go wide.

"I know it might be too much too soon but—"

Lou shook her head, cutting Jax off.

"Nope, not at all. I love new roles," she exclaimed dorkily but she didn't care.

Jax laughed.

"So you'll be my supergirlfriend?" he asked.

"I can't promise the super part, but yes. I'd love to," Lou replied, a smile on her face so big that she felt her eyes squeezing shut.

"Yes!" Jax cheered, showing he could be as big of a dork as Lou.

This time Lou laughed as Jax showed her his watch.

"Impeccable timing, wouldn't you say?" he asked as his watch ticked down the seconds to midnight.

Lou bit her lip. This was it. She was starting the new year as

Jax's girlfriend. As his girlfriend she could be calm and cool, right? A natural kiss of Jax's dreams coming up.

"Five, four," Jax began counting.

"Three, two, one," Lou joined him and then closed her eyes as she waited for Jax's lips on hers.

A soft brush against her lips sent shivers that had nothing to do with the cold all over her body.

It was sweet but Lou needed more.

She wrapped her arms around Jax's neck and used him as leverage to rise to her knees. Jax took the opportunity to slant his mouth over Lou's, and this time fire consumed her.

Riiiip. Lou heard the noise but it barely registered. She just wanted more of Jax but realized he was pulling away.

"Was that your dress?" he asked as the kiss-fogginess in her brain began to evaporate.

That rip. She'd moved a lot and her dress was so tight.

She'd torn her dress.

Lou couldn't help the laughter that bubbled out from her. She just didn't have it in her to have a normal romantic moment.

She felt a chill near her rear and knew exactly where the tear was. She touched the back of her dress and sure enough, right along the middle hem was a rip that went from her upper thigh to right under her butt.

Thankfully her coat was long enough to cover it. Most of it, anyway.

"Are you okay?" Jax asked, probably thinking Lou had lost her mind.

Maybe she had. Jax had not just stolen her heart but possibly her mind as well. No, she still had her mind because she was thinking just fine now, but she was just so giddy. And embarrassed. But she'd known this was coming. Or at least something like it. She was who she was.

"I'm fine. But just a word of caution: moments like this are the norm for me." Lou was half joking but felt she should give Jax fair warning.

"You mean moments where you make my body thrum and then entertain me with how adorable you are? Yeah, I think I can handle that."

How was he so precisely made for her?

He stood and reached a hand down to help Lou up, offering his jacket.

"You could tie this around your waist?" he suggested.

He and Lou burst into laughter as they imagined Lou walking back into the fancy party they'd just left with Jax's jacket tied around the waist of her formal gown.

"I'm sorry to ruin the moment," Lou apologized as her laughter died down.

"You ruined nothing," Jax replied before pulling Lou into his arms, gazing into her eyes before picking up right where they'd left off.

Nora had said there was something magical about the holidays and Lou had to agree. They'd all gotten their magical Christmases, and judging by this moment it looked like Lou's new year was going to be enchanting as well.

JULIA CLEMENS

Julia Clemens always dreamed of putting stories to paper and now she gets to live that dream with her two adorable boys and one handsome hubby. From the sandy shores of Maui to the Rocky Mountains and then back to another island in the Pacific, serene Japan, Julia has lived around the world and found that even though all of these places are majestic with their natural beauty, the thing that makes every place so special...are the people. So she writes about those people and loves every minute of it.

Julia loves to hear from her readers so please reach out to her @ AuthorJuliaClemens@yandex.com

9 798362 015060